17

MAR - 4 2013

KEYHOLE FACTORY

WILLIAM GILLESPIE

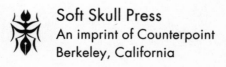

Soft Skull Press
An imprint of Counterpoint
Berkeley, California

Copyright © William Gillespie 2010

All rights reserved under International and Pan-American
Copyright Conventions. No part of this book may be used
or reproduced in any manner whatsoever without written
permission from the publisher, except in the case of brief
quotations embodied in critical articles and reviews.

Library of Congress Cataloging-in-Publication Data is available.
ISBN: 978-1-59376-446-3

Cover design by Quemadura
Interior design by William Gillespie

Soft Skull Press
An imprint of Counterpoint
1919 Fifth Street
Berkeley, CA 94710
www.softskull.com

Distributed by Publishers Group West
Printed in the United States of America

10 9 8 7 6 5 4 3 2 1

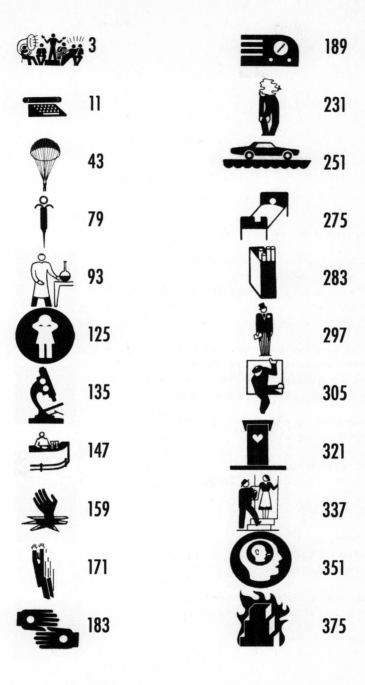

Not how you live, not how your friends live, but there it is. TV puts it right on top of you, too close to home. Standing in church, you infuse the worn hymn with new vitality; other voices attempt to follow the passion you inspire.

Afterward everything is quiet. No crickets in the park. Tranquility or is it shock? You can't read the weather anymore. The cold winds that happened yesterday, changing direction so abruptly, were unlike anything you had felt. Was the world falling over the edge of something? Was there something we needed to be doing? The sound of a dog nosing a trashcan lid in a brick alley raises a scrape in the night.

The next morning there is a parade. Sleepily you scratch by your window peering into the sun. Is it a protest, a march, or do they want us to bring out our dead? Children with pom-poms and decorated bicycles lead a triumphant crowd clad in costumes, parkas, colorful hats and scarves, waving flags and bedsheets, delivering no apparent message.

In bathrobe and slippers you walk out on the lawn. The flag that used to hang by your front door is missing. Some of the celebrants grab your elbows and escort you into the procession. You are too groggy to resist, trying not to spill your coffee. Popping noises you thought were firecrackers turn out to be a noisemaking contraption designed by a child out of a plastic two-liter bottle. The people who grabbed you are wearing strange makeup, but you recognize them as neighbors from down the street. Someone has a tray of pot stickers with soy sauce to dip them in. And your priest hands you a handful of one-dollar bills. He doesn't explain, but you presume the church has closed and collections are to be disbursed back to the congregation.

That night the strangest noise you ever heard rends the sky. A sawing almost, it seems as though some oscillation is taking place between east and west horizons. Is it supersonic aircraft? Missiles? Is it a wind that passes overhead without disturbing the air below? As you sleep it sounds like the sky is caving in above you. You dream of a collision of two winds, each bringing its own weather.

In the morning there is new red gravel scattered about. You go about your day, but seem to have no job to go to. The place is deserted. Chained up, locked, the parking lot empty, blinds drawn. Altogether foreboding. A small part of you can embrace the idea of not working that day, but you can't just not show up. Wanting to be sure, you climb down into the window well's detritus and find an unlocked window. In an empty building where you used to work, not even the furniture is left.

That afternoon the circus arrives in town in a colorful, painted wooden train.

In the evening everyone drifts over to the park. The carousel groans and a calliope blows. But there is a blackout. As you come over the top of the Ferris wheel it jerks to a stop, making your seat swing unpleasantly, and the strings of lights all through the stands and games and rides and stages and pavilions and the radio towers on the horizon go dark. Then silence, save for the creaking of your swinging seat, the wheezing of an incessant accordion, and one kid crying. The carny at the duck shoot stand has a radio and he turns the volume up, yelling *the moon, the moon*. People laugh. But look up at the clouds.

Somebody uses the word *comet* and it spreads through the crowd until everybody is using it. They mean *meteor*, you think. You want off the Ferris wheel.

A clown sends cotton candy up to you on the end of an extensible pole. You take it but do not eat it. A few shirtless men work to make the Ferris wheel turn so people can get off. They need only to release the engine and the weight of riders causes the wheel to rotate. They brake it chair by chair, helping each rider off. You are afraid it will come loose from its axle and roll forward, crushing you. As you descend in jerks you stare at the light passing through a gap in the clouds, black veins in white glass.

The calliope is in a different key from the tattooed lady singing "Fly Me to the Moon" but for a moment it sounds like one new music. Only then are you frightened, but it passes.

The next night as the sun sets, you and your neighbors stand on your lawns and turn your backs on it, awaiting moonrise, joking a little, to reassure yourselves that it had been an atmospheric effect. Soon there will be radio stations again, you say. And there is its red arc coming over the horizon.

The young poet Blake Stone had had a fight with his best friend Jasper Pierce and then they weren't friends anymore. The fight was about bad poetry.

Blake had only spoken, he felt, the truth: that most of the poetry being published was bad. His friend had said there was no bad poetry. The ferocity of his friend's defense had taken him aback, and had shown him his friend's hand. It was perhaps not irrelevant that Blake was a better poet than his friend: Blake wrote very good poetry and was a very good hard serious writer. The friend in question, after all, was a poet, and, to be fair, some of his poems were somewhat good, but the majority were in fact bad. Obviously his friend had trouble facing that fact. But this did not need to be a personal issue, so neither pressed it, and, in fact, they never spoke again. At poetry readings, they simply got into the practice of leaving the room when one another read. Blake didn't want to hear his friend's bad poetry and his friend presumably had trouble with good poetry, though it was not clear whether this was due to jealousy, or to a simple inability to grasp the complexity, the meticulous interweaving of elements, the daring play of line breaks, the metaphoric architecture and anomalous structural consistency of a truly good poem.

So it went. Poetry was more important than their friendship, and at least they could agree on that. How long his friend would go on living in denial was uncertain, and a pity. He might learn something if he just shut up with his bad poetry and listened to some good poetry once in awhile. There was even a slight chance that admitting that good poetry was good might make him write better poetry. It was by no means certain, but it was possible.

And also (and this was a point actually of considerable irritation) good poets didn't get the respect they deserved. Given that the good poets were ignored by the marketplace, it was not unreasonable to expect that they should at least be appreciated by other poets. Certainly an appreciation of good poetry should be a prerequisite for anyone who adopted the title "poet." Good poetry was not only good, but a blissful relief from the problem of bad poetry.

Blake went to visit his advisor Claude Reagan, a poet friend of his, an older and widely published poet and anthologist who did Blake the honor of receiving his visits at his house, where they could take coffee in the kitchen which Claude might occasionally leave in search of some volume relevant to their discussion. Claude was a tenured professor at PU and the editor of *Fairweather Review*.

Talking to Claude, Blake approached the subject of his disagreement with his friend Jasper with all due tact because, as he explained, it was an argument about the Edson Fellowship, which Claude would soon award to one of the first-year MFA students (a group of people that included Jasper and even Blake himself) and Blake did not wish to make Claude uncomfortable by bringing it up, but brought it up only because his disagreement with Jasper had touched on larger issues regarding the differences between good and bad poetry.

Claude seemed disinterested in Blake's story about his friend, which had ended with a scathing remark about what Blake wished bad poets would do. The famous poet looked at Blake emptily. Blake shrugged reasonably, smiling.

Looking away, Claude sipped his cappuccino and told Blake about his friend Max Winchester, whose poetry Claude had previously tried to convince Blake to read. "Max used to have an admirable callousness with regard to bad poets. He was known to shout pointed comments at me at readings. I despised him for that. Max was not a good poet then, but productive."

"Too much emphasis is placed on quantity, such a crude industrial standard to apply. It's a way poets capitulate to capitalism, and Protestantism," Blake exclaimed, then inhaled cappuccino.

"Max conducted experiments on language. Some were successful, others not so successful. But it was research we could all benefit from by reusing his better techniques in our own writing. And generally, we were dishonest about this. He would explain his compositional techniques with unusual clarity, but the rest of us claimed to write following pure intuition. He had enough ideas to share."

"I've heard of Max Winchester. He used to be part of the Brickwall Circle along with you. Is it true that he lives here in town?"

"Yes, it's true. When I met him, he was very different. Now he's a bit of a recluse. He was thinner then, of course. I made friends with him because I was envious of a project of his: a book-length poem called *Sphere*. It had some stellar passages. He's still working on it, as far as I know. I was always hoping he'd finish that one. But our experiences at the university—things were more conservative then, you understand—seemed to repel him. I guess he wondered what language could do besides, ah, being polished and served up on a sheet of paper. He was a voracious reader, and he seemed to consider academic poetry sort of like filet mignon. It tasted wonderful but couldn't satisfy his appetite. He also sneered at cappuccino for many years."

"Did he ever come to appreciate your poetry, and retract his heckles?"

"Well, we're still friends. I don't know whether he ever developed a fondness for my work. I think he thinks it's ego poetry."

"Well," Blake snorted. "Strong words from a man with no credentials."

"I wouldn't go that far. I've published Max a couple of times, and I've arranged for him to give a presentation next week at the Gertrude Stein conference on his work as a performance poet."

"Oh great, so he's a mouth poet."

"No. Max was working out of a different tradition. He used to draw large crowds, but he lost interest in performing, became more absorbed in writing and teaching."

"What universities has he taught at?"

"No universities. High school three days a week, prison on Thursdays."

"Oh, I thought you meant he was a professor. And he's got problems with *your* writing? You're one of the founders of RealPoetry, the David Whitewater Chair of Poetics, editor of *Fairweather Review*, and a two-time Danto recipient."

"Max has been a very important influence on me. His mechanical approach to the art helped me think outside the voice, showed me alternatives I would never have considered articulable. He wouldn't believe the text was fixed. His dissertation was about typos in canonical works."

"What do you call people like that, who think they can be poets without appreciating good poetry?"

"I call them *poets*. But any poet would be wise to focus on the ends of variant means. Listening to other people is one way to do that."

Blake was a trifle undone by this remark. Was Claude implying that Blake should respect the opinion of Jasper? That didn't make sense.

It was really quite simple: Blake's poetry was good. He knew that because Claude Reagan had said so in class. Jasper was there and heard. Anyone who couldn't appreciate good poetry didn't understand poetry: they were bad poets. It was unassailable. They didn't see the seriousness of it, the importance. They thought they could fake it.

Most of the grad students studied at Exquisite Corpse, but Jasper preferred the cafe whose hand-painted sign read *The Waste Land* because it was the least pretentious cafe in the city. In fact it was a genuinely dirty and uncomfortable place, and the coffee was often bad. Jasper, the bad poet, liked to drink bad coffee. It usually hurt him, but it seemed necessary. He would drink until he was too wired to read anything but white space. Higher and higher, all the way up. Because then he would get ideas, and become capable of deconstructing any artifice, no matter how tangible. The arrangement of tables and chairs was no less poetry than the furniture on the page. There were nine letters in "Waste Land" and nine utensils in the silverware rack beside the cream pitcher. And the clatter of saucers and demitasses was no less music than the Charles Ives that issued from the battered radio behind the counter. The air shimmered like a signifier giving up its transparence. On the bathroom wall, Jasper wrote the letter X, and nodded in satisfaction: his truest work. In the cracked bathroom mirror the bald poet looked at his reflection and behind it his poem was still readable. When he returned to his book, the letters seemed shriveled on the page, spindly glyphs dangling from a dead tree.

It was in such a mood that Jasper had gotten into the argument about bad poetry. Jasper had had to prove to a résumé poet, Blake, that, unlike Blake's, Jasper's writing practice was not geared toward the Poetry Machine, as Jasper called it, but part of a living vital practice directly engaged with the social, and to prove his point, he had taken the poem he had been working on during the argument and put it in a crumpled blank envelope he had tucked in a spiral notebook. Carried away with the validity of his point, but in fact unsure who he would mail a poem to, he marched outside, and, leaning on the mailbox, triumphantly wrote his own address, affixed a stamp, and mailed the unfinished poem to himself.

Standing next to the mailbox, a bedraggled man with an artificial leg asked Jasper if he would like to buy a poem. The man clutched a sheaf of homemade broadsides. Surprised and charmed, Jasper gave the man a dollar in exchange for one of the poems. Determined that the poetry of a homeless man should merit the degree of scholarship normally reserved for Homer, that evening he cleaned off the tiny table that blocked off one side of his kitchenette, sharpened a pencil, lit the lamp, and sat down to read the poem. That the poem employed a number of unconventional spellings, was the first thing he noticed. He decided he would not make the mistake of overlooking this disruption of the hegemony of proper academic spelling by dismissing the variants as unintentional "mis" spellings. Similarly, the slant rhyme, he reasoned, should not be taken at face value. Several minutes later he put down the pencil. This poem is—well, it's not bad, that would be an easy dismissal of it, he mulled.

Later, at work, Jasper wrote a poem about the poem:

Did society make the homeless person into a
poet? Or did society make the poet
into a homeless person?

He changed "person" to "guy," then he changed it back. He liked that "guy" had a decidedly unlyrical quality, and through the artifice of colloquial discourse hoped to challenge the barrier between the myth of the poet and the construct of reader. But he couldn't decide. He considered showing both versions to one of the other MFA students, but the thought of exposing his creative process made him uneasy. His technique, if laid bare, might be appropriated, and he was loath to give any of his colleagues the opportunity.

He wanted somehow to express that this was a poet marked by homelessness, as opposed to Claude Reagan, a poet marked by a ranch in the suburbs. It was just like Blake, Jasper thought angrily, to suck up to Claude Reagan. They were good sportsmen, playing poetry by the rules. Me, Jasper thought, I'll play golf with a whiffle bat. But I'm not keeping score.

But none of that needed to bother him, because he would outdo Blake. After work, Jasper would be following up on an important clue. He was going to visit Max Winchester.

Jasper had seen Max Winchester perform only once, and it had been an inspiration. This performance had taken place in *The Waste Land* after hours. Jasper had arranged the event by inviting Winchester, posting a flyer in the cafe, and hoping management didn't object. Since only three audience members attended, Jasper wasn't sure the barista even noticed the performance in their space. Winchester had read directly from his journal a series of observations he wrote according to a systematic procedure. Taking the bus to his job to teach at a local prison, every week when the bus approached a particular corner, Max would write a description of the corner, always starting his observation with a word or phrase taken from the headline of the day's newspaper. If the newspaper was not at hand, he would look for another dated piece of printed material (using in one stanza words taken from his own personal mail: "Final Notice Prior to Disconnect"), or he would use a street sign or an advertisement on the bus.

Jasper was taken aback by the mountainous Max with the spectacles and white beard, and his studied but somehow casual disregard for notions of good poetry. No professor manicuring Shakespearean syntax in the most antiseptic of ivory towers, Max Winchester cut his poetry from the fabric of life.

After Max's performance, Jasper went up to thank the man and to ask if he had any books in print. Max had nothing in print, but gave Jasper his phone number and invited him to drop by his house.

Jasper dismounted his skateboard in front of Max's cottage. The yard was an assemblage of meticulous clutter. A string anchored by stakes fashioned from broken plastic forks and bits of shattered ballpoint pens wound around the perimeter of small herb gardens, ornamented with scraps of brick. An ancient scooter was parked beside the house, an absurd number of rear-view mirrors mounted to the handlebars like an array of solar panels.

The doorbell chimed a monophonic approximation of Wagner's "Ride of the Valkyries" and a dog inside the house went crazy barking.

Max let Jasper in and had him sit at the small kitchen table, which was almost covered by crags of stacked books of all sorts.

As he fixed coffee, Max chuckled: "My dad was a logger. Tough guy. Once killed a bear with a pistol, and got fired for it, went to jail. He was conceived during the Seattle General Strike. 1919. Heh. So not all work was stopped after all. If it wasn't for the Wobblies, I would never have been born. He's still trying to take down Seattle. I had to tell him to stop coming by. The police were always looking for him. He's got a cabin somewhere in New Mexico, waiting for civilization to collapse. When I was twenty, I told him I was a poet. He said, 'So you're a faggot after all.'"

And they talked about poetry.

When the Valkyries next rode, Max announced that his next guest had arrived and Jasper reluctantly understood it would be polite to offer to leave. He was surprised to see that the guest was Claude Reagan, which reminded him again of his fight with Blake and a hot pencil passed though his stomach. But it reaffirmed his suspicion that Max Winchester was the source of all poetry, a wellspring of pure language that would trickle down to fill the cups of bartenders, who would sip it themselves while pouring their clientele tankards of wretched, watered ale.

Claude always had tea with Max on Thursday afternoons. It was one of the nicest parts of his week's activities. They almost always started by talking about the poet in space. The poet in space was a scholar-astronaut alone on a flight to the nearby star Alpha Centauri. While his writing was not always taken seriously in academic circles, he was easily the most well-known American poet, and was rumored to be in line to be Poet Laureate—in absentia.

Claude had respect for the man, who, he believed, was so committed to scholarship that he had arranged perfect silence in which to read: no earthly distractions, just the naked cosmos bearing its secrets. Even an email would take years to arrive. There was some jealousy there (Claude would admit), so Claude got some satisfaction (he would not admit) out of Winchester's contempt for the Biblionaut.

"He is the worst poet in my opinion, and he will outlive both of us."

"But you must have some respect for him. He is, after all, an enduring figure in American letters."

"No respect. He's an enduring figure, but that doesn't make him talented. Before he got shot up in that thing, his career was stillborn. Now he's as famous as Elvis."

"Well, he didn't start out as a poet, remember. He was a whiz kid, went to some government math and science high school. He could have gone to any university in the world on the strength of his math, but what did he do? He decided to become a poet. And it was difficult. He was getting laughed out of workshops, while, in his spare time, winning chess tournaments and calculus contests. And he persevered, getting a Ph.D. in poetry at the age of, I think, 21, almost landing a professorship, and then he lost the chair and became an astronaut. And I can't help but wonder what career path I would fall back on if I lost my position. Or how I would get published if I were starting out today. A man sometimes does more than one thing."

"That's exactly it: he doesn't have to do more than one thing. The man does nothing but write. It's not like he's hanging onto a steering wheel, squinting to watch out for meteors: he just sits there in his little electronic library in space. Does he have to deal with the pressures you and I have to deal with? Does he have broken water heaters, obsessive ex-con former students calling to leave the apocalypse on his machine, a lawn that needs mowing, and the like? Does he have to fuss with giving readings at universities and chairing panels?"

"No, I guess not. He probably has to fuss with solar panels, but that's different."

"Exactly. And the pay that man's getting is incredible. What does he need that money for, if he even makes it back to earth to spend it?"

"He's been incommunicado for a few days. I think mission control is getting worried."

"I believe he never existed, and that all his work has been computer-generated."

"Max. I don't believe that. It doesn't feel computer-generated."

"Well what's the difference between a computer and a man in a can a million miles away from the world? Can a man in a can see, feel, taste, or smell? Can a man in a can experience sex or failure? He's described as a brave pioneer, but his adventurousness stops with fastening his seatbelt. He's an autopilot on a mission he didn't even make up."

"But Max, your poetry is not about the smells of lust. It's about words. The poet in space has nothing but words to work with, and he has computers that can perform at light speed some of the same kinds of systematic operations that you do by hand. He has even written a longer palindrome than you. Perhaps you're jealous."

"Claude, I'm not jealous. The man's in space! He's got some real problems! Anyway, you're the one who should be jealous. You know you were on the laureate shortlist. Anyway, we'll probably still get to have more sex in our lifetimes than him, unbelievably enough. I just wish that the money invested in this mission had instead been distributed among all American poets. I'm jealous of his cake."

"Unfortunately, the purpose of the mission is astronomical, not aesthetic. If only the National Endowment for the Arts had the budget of the National Aeronautic and Space Administration."

"Yeah but the poet in space has made the mission into his own literary career. He's got an international audience, and nothing really to report: 'It's full of stars!' In a few years, he'll be able to clarify the chemical composition of the next star, how many dead rocks are circling it. All this information will be extracted by scientists working on earth, he'll just put a poetic spin on it. Until then, our favorite national news item can get his doggerel on the front page of every paper every few months when he finishes a star poem."

"I wouldn't hold it against him that he revises his work, Max."

"Too much emphasis is placed on quality, such a bourgeois notion."

"You're really not being fair. He's traveling at about half light speed, he's aging more slowly than us. For every piece of manicured doggerel he churns out, you can fill a notebook with random words filtered from your bus rides through the text-polluted world."

"Never random. I do not use aleatoric methods and I haven't since 1980. Please don't accuse me of throwing dice with my poems."

"What do you have against quality?"

"Language is a living process, a flawed and, yes, polluted beast that staggers through our mouths mutating in constant, unexpected ways. There is no perfect English. Not Milton, not Shakespeare, not Lenny Bruce. These are all baby pictures."

"A beast that leaves a few exquisite footprints, which should be preserved."

"History is now, the world is an everchanging chaos."

"There's the world, but then there's poetry."

"That's where you and I disagree."

"Actually, I'm working on a book of nature poetry. Sonnets. *Natural Selection*."

"Sounds artificial, Claude. You don't like nature."

"I happen to like sonnets."

"Trying to capture nature on a page is a worse fiction than trying to capture a beautiful person in a photograph. Beauty is dynamic, not static. The canon is porn."

"What do you have against porn?"

"Nothing! But that's not my point."

They laughed.

The bad poet wanted to see his friend Hunter Thurston. When Jasper went to the payphone to call Hunter, and opened up the phone book, all he could do was stare. Six-point type, he thought, brilliant. Look at how...*big* this thing is. He returned to the table with the phone book, put his anthology away, opened the phone book to the very beginning, and began reading. Then he decided to flip through the front matter and begin at the beginning proper.

Aaronson, Ella. 2400 Stratford. 384-6494

Hunter was a musician, but he had a good job, so Jasper suspected he wasn't a real musician. Hunter was coding. His eyes, obscured by dreadlocks and thick-framed glasses, fixated on the tiny glyphs on the monitor. He hunched before his machine and tried to correct the imperfections in a database application. Perl/MYSQL/CGI, Web-based, some JavaScript. His computer table was a surfboard laid atop more computers. An oscilloscope transcribed Segovia into morphing emerald waveforms. Hunter said: "I wanted to show you this crazy website called *newspoetry.com*, but the internet was shut down yesterday. For 48 hours. The president said it's to stop terrorists. The idiot."

The bad poet leaned in toward the screen, his reflection floating behind the code. A look of delight: "It looks like poetry!"

"It *is* poetry, man. The real thing: with this kind of poetry, you can tell whether it works. Because otherwise it crashes. Actually, though, the semicolons are the line breaks. I just put the line breaks in to make it easier for other programmers—poets—to read."

"Wow." The bad poet's paradigm, a compost pile of rotting printed canonical verse, had just been overturned, and, like insects, a million worthwhile ideas streamed away from the exposed decaying core of tradition. "And the stanza breaks?"

"Oh you mean like here? Yeah, those are for people. The curly brackets here are more like stanza breaks. When the machine reads it. But the machine doesn't read it straight through. It starts at the beginning each time, but it will jump from stanza to stanza depending on what the, er, images, ah, mean."

"Oh man that is so brilliant. I can't believe I'm about to get a degree in Gutenberg-era poetics. And here you are writing this. So, does it read every stanza each time, or..?"

"No, it jumps around, and repeats stanzas. And it's recursive, so the stanzas are nested."

"Nested stanzas? There's a dissertation right there. Wow, look at that punctuation. There are lines that don't even have words, they're just punctuation! All along my work has suffered from being word poetry. I gotta go write!"

The programmer finally looked away from the screen. "But you just got here."

"You've saved my life."

"Well, why did you come over?"

"Destiny."

"Oh."

"See you."

Jasper wrote newspoetry. He took a story from the stack of newspapers under his bed and substituted line breaks for all its one- or two-syllable words, leaving only polysyllabic words of three syllables or more. As a title, he kept the headline: UNITED STATES DECLARES WAR ON CHINA.

The Gertrude Stein Symposium was held at a local hotel and conference center. Sunlight flooded the lobby in which excited poets lined up for nametags, sang greetings to old acquaintances, and looked for opportunities to introduce themselves to poets they recognized. Men shook hands and women embraced stiffly. Vest-clad desk clerks checked well-known poets in, betraying no recognition of famous names.

Blake anxiously leafed through his copy of the conference schedule. After hearing that Max Winchester thought that Claude Reagan wrote "ego poetry," he decided he did not want to go to Max Winchester's reading, an engagement that, after all, Claude himself had arranged for Winchester, the ungrateful beatnik has-been. But he was torn, because Claude himself had told him he should go hear Winchester. Finally he decided to go with a mission: somehow to avenge Claude.

This conference session comprised a reading by Amethyst Quinn, followed by Max Winchester. Blake entered late, in the middle of a poem by Amethyst Quinn called "Keyhole Theory."

Keyhole Theory

   you shape one elastic future
   you remember one fixed past

you step backward through snow
blindly choosing a best path
watching your footprints recede into where you were

the snake swims upriver
writhing against the current without going forward
the snake knows no curves   no shore
the snake thinks it is an arrow in flight

   you were to remember your future
   you were to make decisions that affect your past

you were to walk through snow
stepping into footprints already there
erasing them

   you were to explore futures
   you were to explore pasts

you were to move as a smooth human blur
from origin to destination
never arriving
photographic film with endless exposure time

every moment of your life   at once

a flame passes through a candle
without consuming its wick
strands of seaweed unfurl in the river

a river were to change course but never arrive
a river were to move not with its current   but perpendicular to it
a river were to flow slowly, erratically sideways   not rapidly downstream
a river were older than the water in it
            dammed   damned   it would always find new courses

slither sideways across time
fork
alter every second of your elastic life
simultaneously   constantly   eternally

Blake, with barely concealed horror, was impaled by this. Was this what people were writing nowadays? He repressed a shudder. A blind female poet, a poet who cannot read proper books, identity politics standing in for scholarship, the victim gimmick. A poet who pandered to sight guilt. Was it time to claim his identity as one who has been misunderstood, considered inauthentic, and denied opportunity because of his own heritage, his vast inheritance?

At the front of the carpeted conference room, Max Winchester opened with a grainy videotape of himself giving a performance in a huge concert hall. In front of a row of Marshall stacks, a leather-jacketed Winchester bellowed into a microphone. Screaming people reached up from the edge of the gigantic stage. He handed the crowd his notebook and told them to write poetry in it. Then Winchester read a poem. Then he read the same poem backwards. At the end of the reading, he took his notebook back from the crowd and read the poetry the audience had written. He left the stage by falling into the hands of the crowd, who carried him away, cheering, and throwing books. An announcer said, "And now, ladies and gentlemen, The Who!"

Max turned the videotape off. As he talked about why he stopped touring with rock bands, he passed around a photo album.

"I like a tough crowd, but when I was opening for the Sex Pistols in England, it got too rough for me," he chuckled. "Like my friend Robyn Hitchcock put it," Max said, "'if they like you they spit on you, if they don't like you they throw cans. If they really like you, they do both.'"

Claude was leafing through the photo album. Blake looked over his shoulder and saw pictures. Winchester with Janis Joplin. Winchester writing on the shoulder of a shirtless Lou Reed. Winchester in leather on the set of *Quadrophenia*. Scrawny Winchester standing before a wall of Underwoods—the caption read, "My collection of famous typewriters circa 1972." There was a psychedelic poster advertising Max Winchester opening for Howlin' Wolf and Captain Beefheart at the Fillmore East. Winchester had no books in print, but he had had a single put out by Atlantic Records, and a full-length stereo LP that was just the sound of him typing, with occasional muttering and incidental noises.

As Max began to read his poem, Blake sighed loudly. It was obviously prose. He stood up and walked out.

Rock Star Particle Theory

The universe is composed of tiny particles called rock bands. These bands are generally conglomerations of a few smaller particles known as rock stars. Rock stars are usually magnetic, but sometimes magnetic particles repel each other, and they have generally unstable relations, so the life span of a rock band can be anywhere from a few minutes to a couple of decades, as the stars accumulate mutual repulsion. They are dynamic clusters and rock stars will be passed from rock band to rock band when rock bands collide. Some rock stars are bright and have short life spans, some are dim and tend to live longer. Sometimes a rock star will change into some other type of particle, although this is uncommon. It can be proven that this same principle is recursive and describes the universe on larger and smaller scales, and evidence of the rock band model can be seen in the plant and animal kingdoms, and even in the formation of crystals and clouds. The hub of our galaxy (the Milky Way) can be thought of as a gigantic rotating mirrored ball. The large-scale movements in the atmosphere responsible for weather produce larger variations of the same patterns seen in the dispersal of dry ice vapor from a smoke machine. A flock of geese will tend to have a drummer, a bassist, one primary vocalist, and a multitude of guitarists and percussionists in the manner of a very large rock band of the sort performing a reunion or large-scale benefit concert. This is why people drink and smoke: they are composed of sub-microscopic rock stars.

Jasper was late for the Gertrude Stein conference because he had to work at his new dishwashing job. He arrived after Max's reading had ended. He was pissed. He had left work carrying a teetering large coffee and wore his wet and dirty apron to the conference to serve as an ugly reminder to the other poets that, as tenured poets, they were of a privileged class. They did not have to confront the Man, and suffer the indignity of corporate oppression as he did. Well, it was a family-owned business, but still. Jasper entered the conference room after the panel had begun, strode to the front row, the wet conference agenda tucked into the pocket in his apron, and sat down.

"Did Gertrude Stein have a job?" he scrawled brazenly on the program, and showed the note to the woman (Hello my name is Amethyst Quinn) seated next to him. She took no notice, so he tapped her on the shoulder. Her dark glasses swiveled to him, she hissed something inaudible, and turned her attention back to the critic reading the paper at the podium.

Having thus succeeded in politicizing the proceedings, Jasper took out the battered pad with which he wrote at work, and composed a poem. Practice, he thought, is everything. He was a man of action and not to be lulled into inactivity during this precious moment of free time. The critic took a couple of questions, the microphone fed back and then cut out abruptly, leaving her unamplified. She finished answering the last question, attempting to project her voice, and then there was some applause giving way to the murmur of poets exiting the conference room and moving out to the foyer, mingling over coffee, eyeing nametags and university affiliations, shaking hands, exchanging cards, ignoring rivals.

Soon Jasper was all alone, writing his poem in the empty room. Rebelliously, he worked a double dactyl (the knowing words "higglety pigglety") into what was essentially a free verse stanza, to display his irreverent and anti-elitist approach to formal matters. Then he leapt up, realizing that he was missing free pastries.

Jasper accidentally elbowed Claude Reagan while reaching for the last bear claw. The famous poet shot him a glance but made no comment, as if Jasper was not worth wasting his honeyed words on. A swarm of biting adjectives descended on Jasper, who stuck the bear claw in his mouth and, leaning over the refreshment table, began to write a poem on a napkin about the incident that had just happened in which he had elbowed the famous poet. Other poets reached around him to take the last of the jelly donuts, but were careful not to look at what he was writing, as if they sensed correctly that the words on the napkin would implicate them all.

Halfway through the poem, Jasper already knew that he would send it to *Fairweather Review*, napkin and all, showing his rakish disregard for the stifling protocol of the poetry establishment.

Deconstructing Mambo played a tight set. Conference goers in nice clothes smiled and moved back and forth to and from the small bar in a corner of the dim conference center ballroom. A few knew how to dance, others believed they did or were drunk. An older male scholar still wearing his conference nametag was leveraging his passable skills at ballroom dancing, approaching female poet after female poet in turn to ask for a dance. They reacted variously, considered implications, clustered, eyed other clusters over glasses, lipstick curled into sneers as they looked down upon the other poets at their level and their absurd attempts to party. This was the conference that had gained some notoriety in the past: scandals had occurred, marriages had been betrayed and destroyed, publishers had discovered new talent in hotel beds, and from hotel bars alcohol rivered through conference center hallways and in waterfalls down elevator shafts. The tension, the ambition, the introversion, the repression, and the competition all fused into one red-hot liquid moment lent art by a virtuoso Mambo quartet who stifled yawns as they wrought from their instruments a throbbing lively excited music largely misunderstood or ignored or received with an anthropologist's dry enthusiasm by the inhibited crowd. Everyone wanted to meet Claude Reagan, and numerous newly bought copies of *Black Attitude* (featuring his well-received poem "The Sky Was as Blue as Sky-Blue Paint") were offered to him to sign by sycophants and enemies alike. Max Winchester, having no instincts for this sort of situation, and an irreversible resentment for a poetry world that had passed him by, was at a corner table, hunched and rotund in overalls from which he extracted cans of cold beer, a denim sphere, frown undetectable behind white beard, eyes obscured behind dark polarized lenses. His only friend here, Claude Reagan, seemed to refuse to approach him.

Max Winchester had once slept in a room that Samuel Beckett had slept in. He had won the American Poetry Board's Younger Poet Prize when he was younger, and had discovered that the oppositional stance he had fashioned in the sixties had left him opposite everything, including poetry. He had performed in a controversial multimedia piece by Himmler Linz Kestral Kraktow written especially for him. He had taught prophets and astronauts to write palindromes.

Wherefore meat, he mused. How many of these conversations pertain to poetry, that layer of gas between the abstract cosmos sketched by the endless constellations of twenty-six stars, and the rocky floor it describes. Poetry, the lexisphere our brains die immersed in, having never known an absence of language.

The bad poet was also drinking uncatered beer—Pabst Blue Ribbon in the can, most of a sixpack slung in his apron pocket. He sat down by Winchester.

"Max! Let's play a writing game."

"There's no writing allowed here."

Darren O'Dell, publisher of Head Trip Press, several hours late for his panel, having tried to drive in from Brooklyn in one night, had had a few too many. He weaved toward their table. A burning cigarette bobbed in his right hand, conducting an unseen orchestra. Jasper's fingers curled around his beer. Here was the man whose hamstrung press had broken the talented Greta Peacock Rachenbach, lingering scandal about the contest judge's being Greta's thesis advisor and lover notwithstanding. But Head Trip either stood behind its author or was too disorganized and strapped for cash to issue a statement. Head Trip had gained some notoriety in the beginning through widespread failure to fulfill book orders. It was said that they sent out their catalogs postage due.

Darren reached for Winchester's hand. "Mr. Winchester. I recognized you from your photo in the liner notes of the Kraktow CD. I've read parts of your unfinished epic poem *Sphere*. It's really an honor to meet you. Here's my card. Keep Head Trip in mind if you're shopping that manuscript around."

"Well. And your name is?"

"Darren."

"Darren, I think you're the best motherfucker at this conference. The whole motherfucking thing."

"Thanks. You're the best poet to come out of the Brickwall Circle." And, gesticulating for emphasis, his eyes perhaps seeking Claude, Darren O'Dell poked Jasper in the forehead with his lit cigarette. Darren apologized profusely and introduced himself, and, as Darren led him away to administer medicinal Irish whiskey, Jasper smiled. He had just made an important contact.

The conference long over, the hotel bar closing, Blake finally approached Amethyst Quinn to get her to sign his copy of her book. She was to be the judge of this year's *Silt River Poetry Review* Prize. She acted as though they had met before. He tried to introduce himself but she seemed too drunk to absorb the information. She asked him for his name three times until he excused himself. Don't get my girlfriend drunk, he heard her say.

The language was cloudy. The last conference shuttle had departed. He decided to walk home.

Night. Strange streets strewn with savage broken bottleglass. A shout and a slammed door, a car squealing away. A man slumped in the darkness, against an alley wall between trashcans. Is he on the nod or dead? Do I dare check? And if I don't am I complicit? And if I do am I daft? Next time I'll check. A manged and halfbald three-legged cat hisses at you from above its prone mangled rat. Strung between lost buildings, wires slash a dirty night.

It shone on the sidewalk in a pool of shadow. The light from the flames dancing at the mouth of an untenanted oil drum articulated its curves. Blake crouched on the pavement to look closer. It was a silver handgun. Surprised, he picked it up and discovered that it had a convincing weight. He stared at it but could determine nothing except that he stood there holding a gun. It was silver, it had ornate engravings, a barrel and trigger. He had never held a gun. He tried to remember something about guns, manufacturers, calibers. This one seemed somehow antique. *Revolver*. Trying to consider his responsibility just then, he had undertaken trying to prove it was unloaded, but those shining dots, he reasoned, were indeed bullets, and he didn't know how safely to remove them, and perhaps he ought not to be pointing it at his forehead to better see the bullets. A prick of dread bled a hole through his stomach. He looked around, and saw nobody, nothing but dark, boarded-up buildings, a string of refuse along the gutter, a fire hydrant spraying a drizzle of water. Blocks away a dog barked.

Now what? Because he could not stand the thought of it, he decided to get it off the street. He zipped it into his backpack next to *April Syntax* by Quinn and walked stiffly on, mind racing, eyes clawing streetsigns for orientation. Bad neighborhood; he had no idea. What if someone saw him, could he be killed for taking a gun? An elevated train rattled overhead a block away sending a shower of sparks down over cinderblocks and coiled razorwire. Shadows in shadows in windows stared back. As fast as one could walk without visibly running. A gutted car with missing tires and windshield, a peeling billboard, and then black space, the opposite of poetry, without electricity, where the night he walked through had closure.

"Hey," the voice said to him. He walked on as though he hadn't heard, the pretense laughably artificial in this silence. "Hey slow up slow up," it coaxed. The voice had feet and was following him down a street that now ended in a cul-de-sac with houses preventing passage. Blake slowed up. Tense as a ballerina, he turned, mouth smiling. A face melted out of the night, speaking softly. "Excuse me sir can you help me? My car broke down up the street. Do you have a phone so I can call a towtruck? Or money for a payphone?"

Blake was a single nerve ending. Somewhere off to his left a scream pierced the night followed by a tinkle of crashing glass. Opening his wallet would be like opening his heart to this stranger. The gears in his head seemed to lock. The ground tilted.

"You need to make a call? I can let you use my phone."

"Yeah?"

"Sure." Blake moved his backpack to one shoulder and unzipped it. When his fingers touched the heavy gunmetal his heart vomited something warm into his chest cavity. He pulled out the phone, opened it, and handed it to the man.

The man called someone who, after a brief negotiation, agreed to pick him up.

The man handed back the phone.

The man thanked Blake.

Blake asked how to get to the university.

The man pointed.

Blake floated away.

A few blocks on he paused amid drifting newspaper to slide the gun between the bars of a sewer grate where it went clanking down into some subterranean oblivion. AIR TRAFFIC SHUT DOWN, a headline said. Crouching there, from the corner of his eye, he saw a shadow approaching.

Blake stood to help the next friend.

Momentum compresses the distance between knuckle and teeth. Impossible to react, blink, as the impact reverberates through tear ducts. No instinct to hit back. Blink, cling to the composure being torn from you. Just don't cry. Your alienation is a brick wall that hits back, a door slamming between you and people. Lying in the street in the fetal position, Blake felt his backpack pulled from his shoulders and his pockets cut off.

Jasper was seeing double when he made it back to his apartment building. He sensed the rejection letter the moment his fingertips touched the mailbox. Sure enough, it was addressed in his own handwriting. He noticed his hand was bloody and thought at once that Amethyst Quinn would never know what it meant to be steeled by continuous rejection, and to struggle forward, enduring with one's vital oppositional poetics, in the face of relentless exclusion from the mainstream whose borders were carefully patrolled by obedient and unimaginative editors, who curried prestige among the big names while ensuring that they and their readership would remain unchallenged by the new, the young, the revolutionary.

Jasper realized he would put the whole self-addressed, stamped envelope, rejection letter and all, into another envelope and send it out like that, maybe with a cover letter stating, "Please consider the enclosed rejected poem for publication." That would throw those pinheads for a loop. To submit a poem along with its rejection letter from another publication would be to ask for its rejection, which would show that he had anticipated his own rejection before they could even think of it, and, by rejecting his already-rejected poem, they would be following his lead. By exposing the whole nature of the game through his refusal to play it, he would show them up for what they really were. True art, he reasoned, takes place on a higher plane than this shallow and earthly competition for the cheap satisfaction of recognition.

Walking up the stairs to his apartment he slapped his knee at the brilliance of it. He didn't even have to open the envelope to know that the poem had been rejected. By not opening it he would show that he had never succumbed to the base hope of recognition and acceptance in the first place. Rejection was his art. It was as brilliant as Andy Warhol, John Cage, Marcel Duchamp.

But wait, he realized, pausing outside his door, what if the envelope didn't contain a rejection at all? He stared at it, tried to hold it up to the light cast by the dingy bare bulb in the narrow hallway, shook it. An acceptance letter would taint this project, fouling the purity of his rejection, by co-opting him into the system, which he was sure was a risk, because what better way was there for the system to defy his oppositional poetics than by trying to appropriate them, to, essentially, buy his silence? What if the poem had been accepted?

What if they were paying him?

He stared at the envelope. It had been mailed recently.

Upset by the uncertainty, by the schizophrenia induced by being simultaneously inside and outside the system, he entered his apartment and threw the envelope away unopened. Schroedinger's, he thought, cat, and that's that. He stared at the self-addressed, stamped envelope in the garbage can lying atop the coffee grounds, the banana peel, and the plastic wrapper from the Ramen noodles. The stench was revolting. He would decide in the morning whether to open the rejection, when his head was clearer and he was better able to assess the possibility that the poem had been accepted. It was, after all, he felt, actually a good poem, though it was unlikely, of course, but not inconceivable, that it would be recognized as such. They couldn't all be idiots at poetry journals. Surely an intelligent person must slip through the cracks now and again, and make it into a position of editorial influence. He decided to leave the letter on the table and deal with it in the morning. As he bent to pick it up, unexpectedly he threw up. And again. Wait, there's more. The letter was soaked and unopenable.

As he fell asleep, he saw stanzas behind his eyelids. He dreamed he was ink and the universe white space.

The bad poet came awake in the middle of the night remembering he had left some mean cocktail napkin haiku at the Gertrude Stein conference, and that there was more to remember. He suffered a sharp conviction that somebody would find the napkin and show it to Claude Reagan, and that Reagan would take it personally. But, he reasoned, in all the chaos it was unlikely that anybody would find it. Or, if they found it, it was unlikely they would read it. Or, if they read it, it was unlikely they would understand it. Or identify who had written it. And it wasn't that insulting, though one supposed it could be taken that way. Probably nobody would read it though. And maybe he had actually kept it and hadn't left it there.

And which did he fear more as a poet, being punished or being ignored?

And if everybody were dying, what would these arguments mean?

A list of things I always took for granted: Batteries, knives, flashlights, canned food, water, boots, blankets, aspirin, bandages, candles, matches, waterproof containers, paper, typewriter ribbons. Can I think of anything else? What sort of mental gymnastics are necessary for me to figure out what is required for pure survival, to weed out the superfluous nonsense that saturates my life?

Will I help others? Will I be brutalized, unable to think on my feet, unable to defend myself? If I throw a single punch, will I mutilate my hand?

The next time Jasper woke up, throbbing, painfully insistent decibels of daylight crowded the small apartment and Claude Reagan was leaving him an answering machine message explaining that the bad poet had been awarded, based on his promise as a writer, the need-based Edson Fellowship. Although, Reagan explained, things were temporarily confused, because the president had declared all university activity indefinitely suspended to stop the terrorists. Hopefully everything would be back to normal next week. Although Claude might be accepting a government position and leaving the university.

The coffee stung the lip. In the cafe bathroom mirror Blake's changed face stared back through its distortion. He had not cried though the temptation remained. The scab was an amber crust of pus above the swollen, distended lip, a splotch of purple skin underneath.

It was a rough conference, he thought, it's a rough MFA program.

Blake, wounded, left the Corpse.

On the street he saw the homeless poet, from whom he had bought the same broadside every week. The homeless poet did not recognize Blake, and offered to sell him a poem, possibly the same poem. Having lost the Edson Fellowship meant that Blake would have to pay for his MFA out of his savings, or maybe he would be forced to teach remedial English to freshmen. Down and out, Blake made an effort to see the homeless poet as an equal. Thus he would not condescend to paying him. "I'm broke, bro'," Blake said, with a tone of voice he felt the man would understand, "but I'll trade you one of my poems for one of yours."

The man shook his head no.

Somewhat insulted by this, Blake walked away.

He was to be the poet, he realized, who would make it without a helping hand, who persevered, howsoever slighted, overlooked, ignored.

But everywhere bad poetry screamed at him. From the depths of every greeting card aisle, every bumper sticker, left-wing news magazines. In the city center, activists stood around a statue chanting bad poetry. In the elevator, bad poetry crooned to him through a tinny speaker. Even the president spoke it.

He wanted to know what it was made of. He ate a Hallmark card, straining to taste the bad poetry. He wrote angry letters to officials demanding that a board be set up to look into bad poetry. He proposed a branch of the federal government be established to address the problem of bad poetry and to serve as a watchdog for the NEA as well as art agencies offering grants to poets at state and local levels. He studied the headlines of newspapers. MARCH ON WHITE HOUSE, DOZENS EXECUTED.

And the edges of his stomach turned to ice. His poem, the one poem he had been working on for a year, *Remission*, was possibly bad.

i've just awoken from another dream of dark cities
silent neighborhoods
family homes full of corpses

there's nothing on the radio but you

won't you tell me my dream was
just a dream?

i have been monitoring your transmission on this frequency
my name is rock
i am an american astronaut and poet
returning to earth
i have been away for fifteen of your years
and eight of mine
estimated splashdown in fourteen of your days
i have not spoken in years
i may not sound human
but i am human
or was

i have lost contact

alone out here i have dreamed through the web of my lives
though bound by this capsule
i came unstuck taught myself to fly
soared above a timescape divided by a line of fire
a horizon with no light on the other side
a moment nobody lives through

a fire nobody could see approaching
no matter how the smoke encroached

this event horizon the only line that might be
said to sever past from future

in these dreams i lived pre-lived re-lived my life

every new card i drew made another house collapse
every domino i tipped caused a different
chain of consequence and catastrophe

i know these dreams are real
but only you can prove it

my communications satellite detects no radio activity
frequency sweeps show only a tiny spike
on this frequency in the middle of north america

the earth has a ring instead of a moon

its orbit is different

how can i know whether i have returned
to the same history i left
or whether it is possible to return
when one has traveled as far as i have

it appears my mission was successful
but earth has malfunctioned

i have made strange discoveries i must report
in case i do not survive re-entry
the speed of thought is a constant

time changes its course over time

let me explain

those who sent me may not
have expected me to return

i cannot discount the possibility that i have gone insane

but during training they found i have an extraordinary memory
i am able to hold entire books in my mind
they tested my accuracy precision and capacity with numbers
strength dexterity vision
and my knowledge of astronomy
they put me in 20g
in a sensory deprivation tank
and into freefall
they starved me suffocated me
irradiated me with glasses of
metallic-tasting liquid isotopes

but at no point was i asked to read anything
more difficult than eye charts

one test never happened
they kept me locked in an empty waiting room all day
an honest mistake they said
i think that was the test

the waiting room didn't even have a magazine
i could have screamed but i wanted this mission

at no point was i asked to write anything
the subject of my poetry never came up

yet i have to assume there was more to the mission than i was told
of the four finalists in training all were poets

white wrote mostly verse
he was a private pilot employed by the government
he was not at liberty to disclose the details

smith had been on space missions before
he staged the first zero gravity performance of hamlet
his hearing was extraordinary and he could stand on one hand

hawkins was working on a poem he didn't expect to finish for five years
when i saw him hold his breath underwater for more than nine minutes
i knew he would finish his epic

when i was chosen they got me drunk
i spent the next day in a centrifuge covered with my own vomit

finally my handlers isolated me
from even my wife
and told me my mission

i would travel to alpha centauri
to test a weapon capable of destroying a planet

i was happy to be sent into deep space
to experience pure isolation
and pursue my writing in perfect solitude

i would take all of history with me
an electronic library
i would begin reading with the ancient greeks
and be caught up with the present by the time i returned

i thought

was scholarship part of the mission?
the voyager space probe left
the solar system with the music of bach
and blind willie johnson
did they want an astronaut to curate human thought

as an ambassador?

as a specimen?

my computer displays two clocks
my ship clock shows time as i experience it: now 2011
my earth clock shows time from a signal sent from earth: now 2018
when i began the voyage the clocks were in sync
accelerating toward the edge of the solar system
approaching a velocity of 85 percent light speed
the earth clock decelerated
each electronic newspaper came later
though i sent earth a poem every week
critics said i had become less prolific

they were cruel they lost interest

after i crossed the orbit of pluto
communication with earth became increasingly
asynchronous
it took days then months
for a message to cross the gulf

i saw a review of claude reagan's new book of poetry: natural selection
i requested an electronic copy
by the time that request reached earth
the book had already been unfavorably reviewed
by the time the copy reached me
the book had been remaindered forgotten

my handlers threw me a party
to celebrate my birthday
the video reached me two years into my voyage
grainy and incomprehensibly sinister
the song slowed to a morbid pitch

the gap widened

the political situation was terrible
but there was no way to respond
my news was your history
i signed an electronic petition protesting plans to put
a nuclear reactor on the moon
but it was already too late

my wife and i were both scientists
we knew we were each aging more slowly than the other
though we understood the math
i don't think we got used to how it felt

i sent her anniversary poem months early
having calculated when it might arrive
the next day i received a message sent much earlier
saying she was divorcing me
immediately i sent a plea
a response from her
would have taken years to get to me
her silence spoke truth
passion was impossible to sustain

did i love her as i said?
which of us had left the other?

my poetry suffered

when uprooted from earth
words died
dried drained of meaning
pressed flowers
no force driving them

nothing makes sense in space

the sun became a speck

i slept longer and longer
i had a recurring dream about an accident
that happened when i was four
my father backed the truck out of the driveway
collided with a station wagon
killed a married couple
leaving behind an eight year old girl
i saw her taken away in an ambulance
covered with her parents' blood
i wanted to know where she went

i caught chills
my marrow was cold mercury
no adjustment of the cabin temperature
could alleviate the icy feeling

during a long sleep
i had a beautiful dream
i had landed on a forest planet
with a red-haired woman
i raised children in the forest
among the buildings of a vanished culture
we fished in the shallows of a lake in the summer sun
when i awoke
computers indicated my bodily temperature had risen
i thought there was a malfunction
i could not tell whether the earth clock or
my clock was moving at the correct speed

rereading plato i found mistakes
whose i could not determine

in the latest old newspaper
headlines announced
united states declares war on china

i slept for weeks

in my dream i tried to
prevent my father
from getting in his truck
i ran away through the snow
and hid until the station wagon had passed safely

i dreamed my ex-wife was in a lab
she held the spark that would burn
a wall of fire across the river of time
in a hypodermic needle

above the woman with red hair
and the girl from the accident

my wife wanted to kill them both

i tried to scream
but i was not there

i made no sound
but my wife heard

she hesitated
the woman with red hair
kicked the needle from her hand
and attacked the guards

one of them went down
the other lowered a machine pistol

i landed in the lake and my capsule
floated to shore beneath the skyscrapers
but i was alone

all alone

except

when i howled
i discovered the ruins
were full of savage dogs

i opened my eyes
but could not decide i was awake
dogs howled in the airlock
the ship shook
the earth clock
was ticking at one second per second
while my clock spun

i remembered the son my wife and i
as teenagers had given up for adoption

in a poem by claude reagan
tintinnabulation of brood x
he wrote he wanted to see his own lost son
in a park against the kiss of sprinklers
the glitter of fireflies
the drone of cicadas

natural selection was no longer in my library
i saw another poetry book i did not know existed
sphere by max winchester

i went back to the newspaper where i had read the reagan review
its headline announced
united states declares war on columbia

plato's republic was not in my library
the closest thing i could find was called pluto's republic

it was unlikely my particular computer would make mistakes
if so my life was in danger

i knew i could not be dreaming errors into the text
i can't read in my dreams
letters are ciphers swimming on the page
text will not stay fixed

in a quantum universe
is the instability of dreams more of a fantasy
than the constancy of consciousness?

i was getting to where i didn't know the difference

if the text can change
scholarship is doomed

if the text changes and memory with it
scholarship is perpendicular to history

do ideas roam the universe like radiation or matter
independent of language or mind?

if the laws of math are immutable
existing whether or not people discover them
is language also a constant?
are poems not written but discovered?

if so
is the text then fixed
but human efforts to discover it unstable
and error-prone?

the flyby of alpha centauri brought me around
the computer injected me with stimulants

alpha centauri was a three star system
becoming less blue as i decelerated

i wished i had a window
but my ship was shielded against all radiation

my equipment counted ten major rocks in orbit
either barren or too dense with gases
for their surfaces to be observed

the weapon was presumably deployed
but the results of the test were not revealed to me

my clock decelerated as i went into braking orbit
three stars passed between me and earth
i was exposed to more g forces than i had been
and cut off from radio contact

i could not move a finger

i pried one eye open long enough to see my clock frozen
the clock for earth time should have spun like a fan
instead it ticked
one second per second

i could hear the cicadas at dusk

now i dreamed of my son

he was a poet apparently of some importance
he met with claude reagan

walking at night he was attacked
by the son of the red-haired woman
i put my hand in my son's fist
and punched the attacker
my son won a poetry fellowship

he became a celebrity
at a posh casino he saw the red-haired woman
he notified security
her body was dumped in the desert

i was surrounded by canines
gleaming in the smear of weird light
in the night sky
shed by the ring crossing the night sky
of the forest planet

i waited a year to resume radio contact
but it never came about
i should have been flooded with communications
rocketing toward the sun at 85 percent light speed
in a head-on collision with earth transmissions

something was broken

in my library were books i did not know
the capitalist manifesto
communism and freedom

my own book mood landing was gone
the only book by me was called natural selection
identical to the book of claude's
i had written the poem about my own lost son
i went back to find the book review

united states declares war on canada
the headline read

on the return
i became manic

my banjo playing was extraordinary

playing chess against the computer
i began to win
i would contemplate a move
and see the consequences unfold

i could read pages faster than i could turn them

i couldn't sleep but took frequent dreams
i remembered books i hadn't opened in decades
discovered things about my childhood i never knew

i got in the truck willingly
i turned my son's back on his attacker
i ignored evil in the world
i trained hard for the mission

i went back to the lake
and found my children there

i became a master of my sleeping mind
and retired from nightmares
now i dream of water the sun
floating eyes closed in a canoe
one hand trailing in the cool water
seaweed unfurling downriver
through the shadows of tall empty buildings
shallows over watersmooth sand
children playing nearby
i dream of a lake
where i have floated to shore beneath
towers covered with leaves

i left the earth
on a precipice so precarious
no human touch was gentle or deft
enough to pull it back from the tipping point

the computer has finished the calculations
to match this earth's changed orbit
to bring me through the ring

i am going to splash down in lake michigan
meet me at the chicago public library
near plato's republic

repeat

i've just awoken from another dream of dark cities
silent neighborhoods
family homes full of corpses

there's nothing on the radio but you

won't you tell me my dream was
just a dream?

i have been monitoring your transmission on this frequency
my name is rock
i am an american astronaut and poet
returning to earth
i have been away for fifteen of your years
and eight of mine
estimated splashdown in fourteen of your days
i have not spoken in years
i may not sound human
but i am human
or was

i have lost contact

* *During the incubation period, the infected organism may appear healthy, even vital. Meanwhile, the pathogen is reproducing, altering its host's systems such that some cells are damaged by asphyxiation and others by superfluous nourishment, allowing the bad idea to thrive.*

The bad idea has an incubation period of two to four centuries.

The bad idea is not known to infect any species other than humans, among whom it is communicable through language and violence.

It is purely parasitic, and it is believed it cannot exist without people to perpetuate its life cycle.

The bad idea depends on camouflage. It must attach itself to and hide behind good ideas. The host appears healthy as it feeds voraciously to satisfy the hunger of its parasite. Peering out through a screen of reasonable foliage, the bad idea looks like the stray weed in the bouquet. But it is a support column. History is a sleight-of-hand, a distraction scripted by the bad idea to defend its consolidation. In a cloud of newspaper ink the bad idea's tentacles accumulate all within reach.

The bad idea's growths, lesions, scars have transformed my face and will take centuries to heal.

I have seen its effects on the infected, possessed by the bad idea, who in private meetings decide which life will be crushed quickly and which slowly, which will be incarcerated, which eradicated, which harvested, and which harnessed. People are not evil or powerful, but there is evil power loose in human thought. When a bad idea has a grip on a mind, ideas kill people to overrule other ideas. The philosophere is out of balance. The bad idea will affix a number to every star, subordinate all thoughts, or render them impossible within its systems.

There is no cure to the epidemic. The bad idea cannot be eradicated, so its host must be burned. In the wallets scattered among their melting bones, the bad idea will go extinct. The dead leaves will blow away, the bad idea that infuses them with force having evaporated back into the ether of thought.

One outbreak to stop another. Ring containment: the biosphere.

The forest fire is nature's cleansing ritual. Dead wood is cleared for new growth.

So with epidemic: virus an ember, people timber.

My wildfire spreads fastest in hot, dry, overcast weather.

My fire starts in the mind of a weapons designer. The bad idea teems in the rich growth medium of its vanity. It thinks it has accomplished things no other person could have. But all it has done is uphold my destiny with the utmost efficiency. It thinks it is not a person. It will be disappointed.

A virus destroys its host to survive. Power wields people. War as well as peace, bad and good ideas, pathogens and antibodies, swarm in this man. He thinks he created the idea, but he was merely a carrier.

Burning embers too small to see or feel will float on air, borne on small winds, follow human wakes, infiltrate ventilating systems, stream through fans, vents, doors, air conditioners.

Subways will plunge through tunnels, hypodermic needles injecting fire deep into the skin of the city. The fire starts in the lungs and quickly spreads throughout the body, but it takes a few days before you feel the heat. Smoldering people spread sparks with every exhalation, igniting family, secret lovers, elevator strangers, cute babies, cashiers, other people in line, on the bus, in public toilets, first class seats, salad bars, rental cars, revolving doors. Those human kindling will burn down hospitals before their fires are diagnosed as inextinguishable. Following railways and highways, my vectors radiate. Smoldering airplanes trace threads of smoke across oceans, burning missiles spinning webs across the globe, San Diego to Tierra del Fuego to Johannesburg to Sydney to Hong Kong. Flames sail across oceans, eat human fuel, smoking ships drift into untenanted harbors. In the cities, it will whip up firestorms to cut through every building, people toppling.

Fire only destroys. When it is not consuming it cannot be said to exist.

So it was with the bad idea. So it will be with my virus, my antibody.

I am the good idea. The meeting of one need leads to the meeting of the next. Hierarchy leads to its own collapse. Symbiosis made durable through constant, gradual structural adjustment. I've got you. You thought you could pile enough currency on your side of the scale to outweigh me, but your currency is given value only by my own gold. I escaped. I am light and slippery and tinier than light. I needed you. For a time. Your crumbling structures and porous landfills will provide a diversity of new habitats. The good idea crawled out of the primordial soup, stoked by lightning. Above the Halloween Masquerade fireworks blossom. Above their pops my thunderhead rakes the sky, provoking gasps from the costumed astonished. Millennia of fireworks can't top this.

I had started thinking perpendicularly. I had become absorbed by and obsessed with my routine. Maintaining routine meant continuously pruning alternatives. What would happen if I did something I would never think of doing? Every intersection and offramp I passed on my way to and from the lab where I worked, for example, was a perpendicularity to explore. The streets that looked the most interesting were the most plausible, but what about the streets I didn't notice? And so my mental exercise while driving, or engaged in some routine and tedious dissection, became to try to identify precisely the last thing I would think of doing. This heuristic, a means to better science—new discoveries—was hard to approach in any kind of scientific, systematic fashion. The last thing I would do might be an untried direction of research. Surprisingly, the last thing I would do didn't turn out to be the worst thing I could do. For example, while performing an autopsy, puncturing my rubber glove with a syringe of infected monkey blood was the worst thing I could do, but by no means the furthest from my mind. Survival in the lab meant constantly identifying and scrupulously avoiding the worst thing you could do, a simple accident that could kill you. When you break a test tube, you have to find all the pieces, because if you step on a piece of glass it could cut through the biosuit's boot straight to the foot, exposing your bloodstream to whatever had been in the tube, whatever was in the air, on the floor. When a simple accident could kill you, you learned to foresee incidents, to remember the futures to avoid. So, spending fifty hours a week in the lab or more, my life penciled itself in somewhere between the worst thing I could do, and the things I always do. And the last thing I would do, I finally discovered, was to quit my job. But the last thing I would think of doing was quitting science. To abandon my research into the mystery of life in favor of life.

At the moment I discovered this about myself, I was squinting through the visor of my biosuit through the electron microscope into a tangle of imperceptibly minute, inconceivably destructive viruses. My mind was wondering, wondering whether a virus was creature or machine. I saw a flash of movement reflected in my helmetglass. I looked up, and blinked to bring the room back into focus. I saw nothing moving except Jacob in his suit, oxygen hose trailing from above, maneuvering carefully toward the door to the autopsy room. I wondered whether I had imagined the movement, and, since I was not imaginative, wondered whether it would be more disconcerting if I had or hadn't. It was then that I heard my breathing inside my helmet lurch as my eyes fell upon an open cage door.

The lab was a level four biocontainment core in which we tested deadly diseases on monkeys. There was one very solid door and no windows. The room was depressurized so that, if there were a broken seal, air would enter and not escape. To leave, you had to pass through a sterile airlock and bleach shower into a grey area, dropping your suit and gloves into a laundry chute leading to the incinerator. The lab had two rows of cages on opposite walls of the small sealed space. In one row were monkeys infected with our latest variant, in the cages opposite were uninfected monkeys. We hoped to see whether the agent was airborne. A plexiglass partition eliminated the possibility that the disease could be transmitted through flung excrement. The open cage door was on the infected side. Somehow, an infected monkey, one we had given the name William Patrick, had escaped.

I shouted to Jacob and that noise startled William Patrick such that he leapt on top of the electron microscope and bared his fangs at me, emitting a fierce guttural trill I had never heard before. Before I could stumble backward, he was two more places, then began jumping up and down on the row of infected cages instigating a monkey riot. Even the monkeys in the final stages of death gurgled their support, twitching their dissolving musculature. Their shrieks drowned out whatever Jacob and I tried to say to each other. He was proposing we evacuate. Instead I reached for the net, hoping to protect the experiments in progress. It was the wrong decision. You have never seen a more talented monkey. As I approached William Patrick with the net, cooing sweet lies, he clambered headfirst down the side of the cages and darted between my legs. Jacob had the tranquilizer pistol and barked at me to stay back, leveling it at the desk where William Patrick now poised as if studying my papers. The first dart bounced off the wall. William Patrick retrieved it, and threw it directly at me, it bounced off my faceplate and my net swept air. The next moment, William Patrick had wrapped his tail around Jacob's neck, yanked his air hose out, and knocked him to the floor along with a tray of pox-smeared microscope slides. With his strength, claws, and teeth, William Patrick could have done much worse damage to Jacob, but he hopped off, chattering, and ran back across the lab. He wasn't trying to injure us, he was just trying to let us know how it was in the jungle. Even in the throes of his shrieking tantrum, his eyes, already pink from the onset of the virus, showed only disappointment. To demonstrate his powers, William Patrick, as I swung the net down, leapt over my head and sailed across the entire room so quickly I could not tell whether he found handholds on the ceiling or simply flew. The other monkeys bounced, turned in circles, and covered their eyes.

When it was all over, William Patrick sedated and back in the cage where he would die, our biocontainment suits were covered with rips and infected or uninfected human or monkey blood. The damage to the lab was impossible to survey. The monkeys would be destroyed, along with all the remaining samples in the lab, which would have to be sterilized top to bottom before testing could resume. Jacob and I were both scrubbed, irradiated, sterilized, quarantined, and debriefed through glass. Then I saw nobody for two weeks except the nurse. I lay in isolation, deriving new ways to outlast the clock as I waited to see whether death would punch me out. I was bored enough to think about my ex-husband, how space travel must also feel like solitary confinement on death row, your only contact with technicians who regard you as a specimen, as you wait to see whether the odds will commute your sentence. Although no human had ever contracted the disease I might have—it was in fact brand new, our team had engineered it—I had some idea of what it would do to me. If I became infected, I would have wanted euthanasia to spare myself the agony of the symptoms, but that would have been a betrayal of the project. Instead it would be my duty as a scientist to allow the disease to take its course so that its dreadful effects could be studied in a human. But more than that, I thought that if I decided for euthanasia, the others would believe it was because I was a woman— too emotionally weak to be a scientist. I'm glad I didn't have to make that decision. I'm glad I didn't die that way. Was I glad to go on living this way?

So lying in the tank, to excite myself with the possibility of living, I thought about other jobs I could have. They brought me my journals and other books I requested. I had heard of a team that was investigating the neurological basis of memory, hoping to isolate neural inhibitors preventing prememory. Given what was known about the physics of time—there being, in Einstein's universe, neither an absolute present nor a consistent rate of time—their theory was that it made no sense that our minds would allow us memory of our past but not our future. Their leading paper postulated that this inability to remember the future was an evolutionary adaptation, because organisms with memory of their own deaths would not be motivated to flourish or reproduce. I read an intriguing article about surgically-altered mice who knowingly avoided the place where they would be killed. The government had shown no interest in sponsoring this research, though it had provided at least one test subject—a prisoner—who "reproducibly made improbably perspicacious estimations of her immediate future." My quarantine room had windows of wire-reinforced glass and in the grid of wire I mapped an invisible timeline, the steps I would need to take to remove myself from Project Pandora without endangering the project. Finally I had to chart two futures, because my leaving the project was contingent on Jacob's being able to continue, as he held most of the knowledge I did.

Our fifth day in the "slammer" it was reported to me that Jacob showed traces of the agent in his blood, though no symptoms were visible, but that I had apparently escaped infection.

A strange feeling I could not name changed the focus of things. It had the flavor of relief but was not that exactly. I had never felt anything like it: I wanted to quit my job. The thought was dangerously addictive. I worked twice as hard to find a solution to the puzzle we had been assigned, lost sleep. And so it was that I found myself making wrong turns. Our secret complex built mostly underneath the city of San Diego was sprawling and I had seen only a fraction of it. The quarantine wing where I visited Jacob as he died in isolation was enough off my normal route that I found myself wandering tiny catwalks and cement labyrinths under the city. The game was to walk until faced with a forking path, then to choose a direction without thinking. Not thinking was a state I was able to achieve only fleetingly. At these times I thought about the memory research. According to some of these scientists, it would be only through not thinking—relaxing inhibitions—that we could make sound decisions with complete foreknowledge of their outcomes.

The facility was built in concentric rings to contain the level four core, where I worked. My clearance allowed me access to almost every corridor in the center. Doors opened for me when I held my badge to their electric eyes. I became familiar with most of the building except the area directly beneath where I worked, the bottom of the core, which was off limits to everybody. The facility was a city without sky, and somewhere above its cool silent overhead fluorescent panels was the noisy gridlocked glare of California. Corridors unfolded into cantinas, boutiques, and a lounge (with smoking), interspersed with sealed doors bearing red biohazard flowers. A post office, apartments, a library. And a veritable zoo of laboratory animals: mice, guinea pigs, ferrets, rabbits, birds, and of course apes. Most of the animals seemed happy. Some seemed asleep or dead, and a few were clearly in the throes of diseases they had contracted naturally while waiting to be infected with an experimental disease. The facility had everything I could think of except windows or plants.

There was a part of the center that extended above ground, presenting an impressive front for official visitors. It had dizzying Star Trek-esque catwalks with exposed cable and ductwork running beneath them. Glass cases depicted various projects ostensibly sponsored here: agribusiness miracles, new cures for deadly diseases (partly true), and the like, most of it perhaps factual if misleading. Broad steps ascended through vertigo-inspiring emptiness to the upper catwalk where suicide could be considered. Colored banners bearing the SP logo hung two stories down to the tiles traversed by only the handful of us who had security clearance. Complex arrays of arched beams held in place a metal roof. Walking the catwalk I looked across the void into third-floor laboratory windows where innocuous research was conducted for the benefit of the press. The complex was built around an older scientific building, which had been kept in place, wrapped in a metal superstructure, and balanced above a hidden underground labyrinth. The clash between the old brick building I was staring at, in which the official research was conducted, and the new metal building, where the real work was done, revealed how in secretive government bureaucracies things are layered on top of things in an accumulation of scientific advances and foreign policy imperatives, while tearing down and rebuilding was blocked by ensconced interests who feared the velocity of advancement might overturn their power. And so millennial research was built on a foundation of Cold War paranoia. The Pandora virus, the disease that was now killing its lead architect Jacob, wasn't a curiosity to show schoolchildren, like some rare specimen of parrot or tropical fish. Neither was it mustard gas to be sprayed on a twentieth century battlefield. It was a monster. It made nuclear bombs look like shiny pistols. It was a tiny keyhole through which, if one squinted with an electron microscope, one could glimpse a future without people. It was dubious to bring it out of theory and into the world at all, even if our primary purpose in engineering samples was to find a vaccine. Or was it?

Two bland combed-over white technocratic misfits walked past, beslacked, beclipboarded, windbreakers whispering. I ignored them, feigning absorption in a colorful computer graphic-laden wall display promoting incomprehensible research involving mousepox. A photo of a smiling child attested to the wholesomeness of these advances. Behind it, a locked closet's sign read DATA. I turned my attention to a few abstract paintings hung in shadowed corners as an afterthought, then went back down into the labyrinth to see Jacob.

Jacob was somewhat chipper until his mind started to go from the hemorrhaging. He had tried to cheer *me* up, strangely, claiming that I needed to observe him because when would we get another human subject? He seemed excited to be the lab rat but how could he be? He described his suffering with an attempt at clinical precision but enough subjectivity that it was clear it was a ploy for company, tight and desperate, which I responded to, though I found it almost impossible to take notes on the progress of the disease. My enthusiasm faltered. His family had been told that he had already died, and had been given an urn they were told was filled with his ashes. Though Jacob and I weren't exactly friends, and I would rather not have known what our virus would do to a human subject, I had to sit across the glass from him, listening to him rasp through the speaker. I was the only one who could offer company. I had security clearance. But I had seen enough monkeys crash and bleed out that I was still able to look him in the eyes even after they were swollen and pulpy with the onset of symptoms it would have been impolite of him to discuss with anyone but me. "We built it," he said, "and now I'm trying it out. And I have to say that we did a fine job, because this sucks. Write down that it turned out to be slightly more devastating in a human than a monkey because the psychological effects, as parts of the brain short out one by one, are more pronounced." He seemed surly and delusional. He showed symptoms of classic senility. He would go away into his memory and come back, and passed through different times in his life, mistaking me for various people. "I have mnemonia," he moaned, "My dreams are a mirror of the future because I can't tell," he started to cough, "when I am. Or whether I'm awake. Because if I had different futures, I must have different presents."

We never figured out how the monkey escaped. The locks on the monkey cages were electronic. Did the monkey resolder something, Jacob joked, choking on his own detaching throat, as he in vain replayed the events leading to his death. Could an electrical failure have unlatched the door? A surge, spike, or momentary outage? And what would such a malfunction mean in the case of a sustained blackout? Jacob had been my favorite coworker because of his open contempt for our employers—the military, and "Mr. White Man," as he often referred to Adam White, our boss. "You just know those fuckers would go to all the trouble of building a state-of-the-art level four biocontainment zone, and fuck up on the monkey cages. Those cages are every bit as important as the airlock. Did they pick those computerized locks with the blinking lights to impress the generals? A padlock doesn't malfunction."

"William Patrick could have opened any lock," I joked, and some of Jacob's mouth tried to smile. "We should have named him Harry Houdini."

I had made visiting Jacob a regular morning and afternoon ritual—really the first breaks from labwork I had allowed myself since beginning work there—and I continued to take the breaks long after Jacob had dissolved, leaving only a deadly, hot, contagious stain in a mattress destined for testing and incineration. In the back of my mind I was trying to complete a proof but was unable to concentrate as well as I had before. I developed a mild narcolepsy, and would prop myself on hallway benches for brief dreams in which I looked for exits.

And so I came awake discovering I had wandered perpendicular into the security hub and struck up a conversation with a large and amiable guard named Mac, who addressed me as "Ma'am." He was standing over me, having awakened me to make sure I was okay. A reassuringly solid African

American, Mac would have made a good bartender or priest. He personally apologized for the escape of the monkey and wanted to know how security could respond to future monkey escapes. I searched his eyes for irony and found none. Studying his nametag more closely I saw that he was security director, not a guard. And he obviously knew who I was.

"Funny you should ask, Mac, because I had a lot of time in quarantine to write up my recommendations. I'll print out a copy for you. I'm disappointed you never received one. But please, don't call me 'ma'am,' it sounds so formal. Just call me Doctor. Doctor Adorno."

"Okay Doctor, I look forward to reading that. There's usually lots of time to read." He smiled, and I decided to visit him again. What could be more perpendicular than to try to befriend someone not a scientist? Someone whose world was visible to the naked eye, the world I never saw.

I considered social intercourse a generally trivial level of the natural order, though I had to admit its trivialities were endlessly vexing. Mac had charisma. Charisma was social, but was clearly an adaptation that would lead to proliferation of its gene, if it were genetic. But being stimulating, likable, genuine, persuasive, was a good idea, and a good idea could perpetuate itself through generations, or even emerge simultaneously in disconnected social clusters, without any Lamarckian genetic encoding. But bad ideas also had a staying power. Why didn't bad ideas die out? To be fair, many bad ideas had, like smallpox, been contained and eliminated forever from the language. *Slavery* had become pure metaphor. But what about, say, *war*, that uniquely human social cancer. The word thrived. Why hadn't war died out like slavery? That that bad idea was bad was well documented. In few cases was war fought and won for survival, so how could it perpetuate itself? Rethinking this, if ideas were species, they were certainly parasites, as they were dependent on human minds for survival. It is not always the most beneficial parasites with the holding power. So perhaps war was somehow beneficial for the survival of the human species, or perhaps again predatory parasites had an edge over beneficial ones. Suicide, for example, was an idea that could not effectively perpetuate itself, it seemed. But then an idea like that wouldn't be concerned with survival. So why did it survive?

Security had been concerned that the young man with the jeans and white V-neck T-shirt and gold crucifix was a bomber of some kind. I watched Mac's men interrogate the young priest on a video monitor. Mac had called me over to see whether I recognized the man, and because, respectfully, he sought my opinion. Security had picked him up spray-painting our building. LIVES EVIL, he had begun. That anybody noticed our building had never to our knowledge happened: streets around the complex were reportedly filled with plainclothes security posing as city workers of various sorts, and of course the building had no address or entrance save the underground parking tunnel that one entered through a guard post half a mile away. Not even those of us who worked in the building would recognize it from outside. They told us it was in a dangerous neighborhood. And of course it had no markings or features of any kind. Its outer layer was weathered brick, to fit the neighborhood and disguise the bombproof concrete shell. All this security for a laboratory facility, we had been told, was to foil animal rights extremists. It was surrounded by a razor-wire-crowned chain-link fence which the interlocutor had clipped with wire-cutters and stepped through.

He said he was a priest, that his name was Joe, and claimed there was evil in the building. The interrogators could get nothing more out of him, though the priest story wasn't believable. When the interrogator asked him whether there was a church who would vouch for his identity, he claimed to be an unaffiliated, freelance priest.

What put the interrogators on shaky ground, to my mind, was first that they had intercepted him at all. Second was that this youth with the neatly trimmed beard and no credible story was correct: there *was* evil in the building. How could one plausibly deny it? First of all, for security reasons none of us really knew everything in the building. The things I knew were pretty frightening. If there existed a Satan, some of our virus samples would belong in the same category. How else would you categorize a fragment of nucleic acids smaller than a nucleus, too simple to be considered a life form, that could possess a person and reduce them to jelly, in the process feeding off their flesh, reproducing itself, and spreading its violence to everyone who tried to help its victim, until there was nobody left to touch, with a 100% fatality rate, infection requiring as little as a single airborne viral particle, communicative through symptoms resembling those of cold or influenza, with a four-week incubation period during which the subject was infectious but not yet visibly ill? A weapon whose only imperfection was that it was indiscriminate and had a potentially infinite blast radius. Viruses were not malevolent, they were mechanical—as unconcerned as a rock—but were as close to evil as I would want to get. I was fascinated by the freelance priest. How vexing this social intercourse, fathomless, and yet somehow funny. This guy just had no access to appropriate behavior, was oblivious to intimidation, but came perilously close to speaking the truth.

They left him alone, with a pack of cigarettes on the table (which he didn't touch), and I studied him through the screen as they returned to the office, conferring quietly. This lone zealot had somehow defeated the most elaborately contrived security system in southern California simply by calling its bluff. By dragging him into the debriefing room they had essentially confirmed his suspicion that something was going on. Whether he was delusional, a lone man bent on seeking out and eradicating bad things, or a spy either for China, or, as he claimed, God, I was intrigued. He stared through the wall in the general direction of the core. If he was a spy, I was the one he wanted: I may not have known the most terrible secrets, but, what secrets I knew, I was the only one with the technical knowledge to explain. If he could see evil, as he reasoned, then I wondered how he would react to me.

I asked Mac to let me talk to him. Mac was reluctant and picked up the phone to contact Adam White to request permission, but did not restrain me as I walked down the corridor the guards had entered from, found the room, let myself in, and sat down across from the priest. A guard entered behind me and positioned himself in a corner. Sharp blue eyes looked into my eyes. His gaze was direct as only the gaze of an animal, child, or psychopath can be. Like the sun, one could not stare back into it.

"Mr. Priest, I was wondering if you could answer a few questions."

"And your name is?"

"Doctor. Mr. Priest, I am concerned that you think there is evil here. If this turns out to be true then we will certainly have to take whatever steps are necessary to clean it up. I'm sure there are theological waste disposal teams who specialize in that sort of thing. But if your story is true then why aren't there other men of the cloth surrounding the complex?"

"Most priests," he said, leaning forward, "don't see evil. They set their sights high, heavenward, hyperopic. To be God's agent, you have to take your eyes off Him."

"What do you mean by evil?" I asked.

"Rational murder. I see shimmering rifts, borders between futures. One of these futures has people, the other is the end. These rifts intersect here. Soon it will be too late to choose."

Behind me I could hear the security man clear his throat to deflate the creepy silence, because I had felt a click. Something I wanted to talk about, or was this his charisma? I longed for privacy in which to talk to this man. Security would never allow it.

ⓣ MBTA COMMUTER RAIL

SOUTH SERVICE		NORTH SERVICE	
GROUP FARE		**ROUNDTRIP**	
MONTHLY PASS PRESENTED			
OUT		**IN**	

PASSENGER'S RECEIPT
Valid for round trip and group fare only on date punched. Otherwise, not good for passage

FORM A	SERIES 8		BOSTON		
	SR. CITIZEN		ZONE 1A		
	ADA		ZONE 1		
	STUDENT		ZONE 2		
17	1	JAN	ZONE 3		
18	2	FEB	ZONE 4		
19	3				
20	4	MAR	ZONE 5		
21	5	APR	ZONE 6		
22	6	MAY	ZONE 7		
23	7	JUN	ZONE 8		
24	8				
25	9	JUL	ZONE 9		
26	10	AUG	ZONE 10		
27	11	SEPT	SPECIAL		
28	12	OCT	BOOK No.		
29	13	NOV	**38217**	SHOW FARE COLL- ECTED
30	14		CHECK No.	
31	15	DEC	**061**	▼
	16			

$Tens	1	2	3	4	5	6	7	8	9
Dollars	1	2	3	4	5	6		8	9
¢Tens	1	2	3	4		6	7	8	9
Cents			0				5		

That night I left through the tunnel and the sunset did indeed look like a shimmering rift where two futures met. Those making the decisions in the research program ought to have perfect foresight or common sense but there was no evidence of either. I, on the other hand, an isolated workaholic who devoted more thought to smaller topics than all but a handful of schizophrenics and molecular physicists, agreed with a lunatic re: "evil."

And, Priest or no Priest, this is what it boiled down to, exiting the expressway beneath the sky of colliding futures, and being waved through my subdivision gates by a new guard I did not recognize: my life was my results, and my home was an avalanche of data, to be spread out over any domicile I might rent or be assigned. At night I would arrange the piles, by day my kitten Ebola Reston would rearrange them.

Was this his charisma I felt? Evil in dialectical struggle with good? Or mutual loneliness? How would I find this young man? Well, if there was evil in me, I supposed he would find me.

And what about quitting? I had no exit strategy. One did not simply retire from well-paying, high-level, top secret military research. If I quit, it could kill the project. Whoever's project this was wouldn't like that. This is something I should have brought up during the hiring process.

Somewhere underneath a gigantic windowless casino, in front of rows of tiny monitors, I conduct an orchestra of surveillance cameras. On an empty staircase used mostly for access to conduits, I see a monkey. But when I zoom in I am startled to see it is a dead woman descending the stairs.

I woke up scared. Something about working in that place, perhaps. There was much kept inside. And I didn't much like living and sleeping alone, not like this, not when I also worked alone and ate alone. During the few months of marriage when my husband and I lived together, I enjoyed sleeping with him more than I would admit, bodies locked, fused in a heat so primal as to seem solar. But I was never into having a long-distance relationship with anybody—not even a writer, not even my husband—and especially not the longest-distance relationship in history. So when he left Earth and broke that osmotic warmth that infused the marriage certificate with life, it died like a leaf in winter. Ebola Reston could be depended upon to sleep with me inasmuch as a kitten could be considered dependable, but now it was the feline crazy hour when the hallucinations must be routed from every room.

I was not at liberty to discuss my work with anybody, and so I talked about it with my cat, which was still probably illegal. I was perhaps the leading virologist in the world but perfectly isolated from the larger genetics community. In fact I had signed forms promising never to publish. In my sealed employment contract, I was technically an immunologist, identifying vaccines for potential viruses, focusing on viruses that were most lethal. But I didn't really know. I was alone in the lab these days, but I didn't know what happened to my research after I handed it off to Adam White. It was not clear who we were working for. Though my paychecks came through Monsanto, we entertained occasional visitors from the federal government. And my boss was always flying to the University of Washington where the main computer—Bertha—was housed.

Beginning with known viruses such as smallpox, Marburg, and Ebola, we used the computer to develop permutations of their DNA. Bertha crunched these variations and made predictions of the epidemiological vectors of these new diseases such as how many particles of virus were necessary for infection, how quickly and by which means the disease was communicated, and how quickly the infected people would die. The disease model was then subjected to a calculus, which would randomly generate factors such as weather, wind drift, and human movements, to simulate how any given virus might spread through a human population.

Using this calculus, which we understood was constantly being doctored by programmer-researchers we never met, we were able to find out how many particles of any given virus would erase how many millions of people. We were looking for agents that fit a matrix. Numbers in that matrix included fatality rate, contagiousness, and incubation time. We sought to determine whether, in epidemiological terms, an agent with a longer incubation period might prove more devastating, because infected people would come into contact with and infect more people before the onset of symptoms might alert the presence of the agent. HIV, for example, might never have broken out of Central Africa if it killed more quickly or dramatically. Because the disease is so slow in its onset, by the time an epidemic became visible, it had spread too far to contain (despite being relatively easy to block transmission of compared to an airborne agent such as influenza or smallpox). AIDS is the persistent smoldering rather than the raging forest fire that consumes all available fuel and dies.

When the simulation consistently reported global catastrophe, comprehensive depopulation, it was a cause for celebration. And then the real work began, as we understood it: finding vaccines for these devastating, nonexistent diseases. These vaccines were then tested on various animal models at different secure labs. Ours was the monkey house, one of the more important sites for translational research. The goal, we knew, was to create stockpiles of vaccines and, in some cases, cures for the deadliest diseases yet unknown to humankind.

Of course, to conduct these tests, it was necessary to synthesize these diseases, bringing into existence fragments of nucleic acid: unthinking, unfeeling, remorseless, microscopic killers, capable of erasing people from the world. The creation of new diseases, we believed, was a necessary sacrifice for the important public health work we were engaged in. Of course, if any of these creations were to escape the lab, the consequences would be historic in proportion.

And so I found Mr. Priest's talk of evil somewhat refreshing. I did not believe in evil, *per se*, but it was somewhat satisfying that someone had noticed and taken an interest in our unmarked building, because what went on there was truly of interest.

I was invited to an elite club by my boss Adam White. I assumed it was for a professional meeting, though I did not know how I would respond if it was meant to be a dinner date. As my car window descended, a valet leaned down, and I half-expected him to tell me that my brown Oldsmobile could not be allowed in the lot due to the exclusive establishment's dress and vehicle code, but instead I was looking into the eyes of Joe Priest, wearing a vest and nametag that read Joe Flist. His eyes met mine though they showed no signs of recognition. Flustered, I got out and handed him the keys to my car. As he drove off, too late I remembered my briefcase in the trunk. I tried to think what papers were in it and considered retrieving it. Just then Adam pulled up in an obnoxious red Porsche. He unfolded himself from it, popped the trunk, tossed a tennis racket in, and handed off his keys without looking at the valet, coming to shake my hand with both of his, beaming.

Adam White: amateur pilot, tyrosemiophile, vecturist, labeorphile, cigrinophile, iconophile, record collector, entrepreneur, epidemiologist. I wanted to ask him to take the sunglasses off his head while we ate. They seemed affected, a token to prove he was always a man of leisure, accessories at the ready. But I knew full well that leisure was out of the question for the man who daily mediated between scientists and unknown underwriters, and who was probably entrusted with more secrets than I could understand. But he seemed the perfect bachelor with his red car, white hair, business casual, and, I wondered, glancing around, bodyguards. While he regarded his immediate surroundings with childish excitement, as though he might at any point jump up to go hang gliding or scuba diving, I was sure his skis and crampons were getting no more action than a regular dusting by a hired housekeeper in a home he seldom saw.

A waiter hovered and I asked for any red wine. The waiter nodded, and did not try to overwhelm me with a luxury of alternatives. Adam White ordered an appetizer and water for himself.

As if sensing my thoughts, Adam admitted: "I have a lot of interests but I regret I'm not a colorful conversationalist. My dad had dozens of stories. He worked for Pinkertons. He killed a bear with a pistol, he claimed. But I didn't inherit his gift for hyperbole. I'm afraid I brought you here to talk about work."

After the waiter reappeared with wine and water, took our dinner orders, and disappeared, Adam White cut to the chase. I felt briefly foolish for suspecting this man of wanting to date me, and felt begrudging respect.

"I have an offer to make you. We are looking for scientists involved in the project—especially women—to promote to the next level. The next level of, of course, salary, as well as security clearance. You are one of our best candidates and I wanted to take this opportunity to interact with you socially and get a sense of your ambitions."

I squirmed at his use of the word *socially*, but any suggestion that the two of us might enjoy one another's company was over quickly enough. *My ambitions?* This was the time to discuss quitting, then.

He seized and buttered a hunk of bread, continuing.

"What it boils down to is that in the event of an outbreak, immunizations will be in short supply. There will have to be ring containment, of course, through quarantine, but should that fail, the question of who gets vaccinated will be...nontrivial. Are you following me?"

"An outbreak of what?"

"Pandora, for example."

"Are you telling me that you anticipate an outbreak of a virus that we synthesized this year, in total secrecy?"

"The point of our work is to be prepared for a worst-case scenario."

"How could there be an outbreak unless we sponsored it?"

"It's unlikely, very unlikely, which is all the more reason for secrecy. And for keeping you on the team."

"Those agents are serious. You know that. We've seen Ebola eat equatorial villages, but what we're working on is worse. I don't even feel comfortable *talking* about an outbreak. That would be a crisis of unprecedented proportions, unimaginable."

"Unimaginable," he smiled, "but calculable."

My attempt to introduce my discontent was stumbling. "If something went wrong in the world, like an epidemic of a deadly genetically-engineered virus, I suppose I'd be one of the last to hear about it. To be more isolated than I am in the lab, you'd have to work in that reactor on the moon."

"Yes, but, on the positive side, in order to be more well protected from an outbreak than you are in the facility, you would indeed have to be on the moon."

The shrimp scampi appetizer arrived. Pink chromosomes swam in oily yellow cytoplasm. The promotions were happening to me quickly enough to inspire a certain cynicism. I realized that, if I were to negotiate a new contract, I might also reopen the issue of my retirement.

"So to return to my proposal, in such a worst-case scenario, inoculations will have to be rationed and *distributed rationally* to preserve the infrastructure of government and commerce." Two shrimp on my plate seemed engaged in meiosis as I stared down at them. Infrastructure? "We won't be inoculating, for example, murderers on death row." He smiled at this seemingly rehearsed reasoning.

"Not at first," I offered.

He paused, his nostrils testing the odor of my comment.

"But of course," I continued, "preserving all human life will be a priority for us all. In this worst case scenario."

"Of course. A priority. But strictly infeasible. But by agreeing to be part of this team, you will of course ensure that you are among those to be inoculated." He chuckled and peeled a shrimp. "Believe me, some of the men, military men, involved in planning worst case scenarios were not interested in choosing women based on their talents as scientists."

I stared at him.

"Oh, you know how some men are," he smiled. "But in any event, doctor, there is human survival to consider. You are young and your medical records indicate perfect reproductive health. This is something we are looking at with the men too. Jacob, incidentally, would have been wrong for this next phase of things."

I wonder if my mouth hung open as I stared. Professional mind meanwhile wondered how to broach the subject of retirement in the light of this more urgent matter of the invasion of my privacy, and all the implications of what he was telling me, all with regard to a project that was framed as, essentially, being one of those whose lives were spared. Infrastructure. In a worst-case scenario, retirement means death. Another question regarding professional poise had begun to gnaw at me: When is it appropriate to throw burgundy in your boss's face? When is it imperative? Would I be immediately taken down by Secret Service? And: How perpendicular is that?

"The Olds. You don't need to get it for me, I can drive."

Joe handed me my keys and walked with me to my car. I watched him out of the corner of my eye. He caught my eye and unexpectedly smiled. They're all crazy, really. Would he attack me? Did he recognize me?

"Is this your day job? Or is there evil here?" I ask.

"Your building. I can see it from here."

I looked off into the lattice of cloud beyond. Serrations of mountains stamped the indigo sky. We were thirty miles from the complex.

"I see a shining plume," he said, "of glowing smoke. It's bright enough to read by. But I suppose you don't see it."

Was it possible he could see the smoke from the bioincinerator, where used monkeys were destroyed? Were there people who could see infra-red? But even so, there must be hotter smokestacks than ours in the city's industrial sprawl. I looked at him. He was looking at me. He had striking blue eyes. A recessive gene. Is a genetic code, I thought, a destiny? Truly the way things will go, things that matter, life?

I did not remember a lover so affectionate. Obviously a spy, professionally trained. Did he get up while I was asleep to photograph my scribbled genetics with a camera concealed in his eyelid? Did brave, lazy Ebola Reston defeat him by knocking the papers behind the desk earlier, rolling on his back during a catnap, dreaming that an outbreak of Australian mousepox had left the apartment scattered with tasty morsels? Were foreign spymasters listening to my snores, needles scrawling my beta waves onto printouts? When would he kill me? Would he do so respectfully, mercifully, quickly? And would he kill me to obtain military secrets or to destroy them? In order to build a bomb or to defuse one? Certainly a submicroscopic speck capable of replicating itself in a human host at dizzying exponential speed and radiating through the entire species was a credible deterrent. Because if you're willing to destroy yourself to defend yourself then one ought to take you seriously—right?—this shows that you are a serious person. Or was he a spy for God, copying our DNA? This is why I needed to publish, because God subscribed to the *Journal of Genetic Research* and *Virology Annual*. God probably stole the whole idea from us. Maybe Joe could get me a better job in God's lab, splicing genes to make more intoxicating hyacinths, cuter kittens, phosphorescent fish. And what would I tell Adam White? Because he knows he does better research than God. And where could I get a job when my only reference was classified? It would appear as though I had simply not been working for five years. It was perfect, because God is omniscient and wouldn't ask for a reference. Wasn't having sex complicated enough without worrying about your lover being a spy? And would it worry me more if he was working for the Chinese or if he was actually working for God? From whom was I keeping the most secrets? The Chinese would reward me for my knowledge. God on the other hand could only be displeased at my hackery. And it feels bad when God hates you. How could I explain to God that my employer had forbidden me from signing a petition against a nuclear reactor on the moon? Was it too late for me to learn nuclear physics and to transfer to the moon? And would God be jealous that I was hooking up with one of her staff? Or were priests allowed to fool around with atheists now? Was sex as a sin contingent on the denomination? And, wait, what if a worst case scenario came about? What would happen? Or: How could it have happened? Or: Who could have prevented it? Adam would have me believe that preventing it was my job. I should have asked him what his best-case scenario was. It was childish, the way Joe clung to me all night, turning when I turned, childish and nice.

I want to leave the complex but they took my car away from the parking lot and cut the lights. I am walking out through the echoing underground tunnel following a faltering flashlight beam when I hear a car approaching from behind, its headlights flooding the tunnel, showing its endlessness. There is no place to hide or run so I stand and wait for it. Adam White leans across the front seat and opens the passenger door for me. We drive on as though we have someplace to go together. He seems pleased and won't stop talking about the project, trying to tune in something on his car radio. In the desert where a windsock rattles on a lone hanger beside a biplane tethered to the ground, he pees with practiced ease beside the car. I start the engine and put it into gear. He doesn't even shout as his undelighted face, red from the taillights, is engulfed by the blackness behind me. He looks like a struck match and is gone. I turn perpendicular to the way we were going, and exit. Then the only thing to see is the highway's stripe and the flare of odd, fierce meteors.

When, in the morning, Joe was gone, I had to search the house. A reflexive flash of rage gave way to relief, since, all things considered, I preferred having him gone. The note said "Love life and the moon, love Joe." How he could have made it out of my neighborhood was another question, but I wasn't about to ask the neighborhood guard if the priest I fucked had left before dawn.

The new genetic codes were called, collectively, Pandora. Since watching Jacob dissolve, more than once I believed I had been exposed, and felt that peculiar weightless nausea of possibly having fallen off the edge of a very tall building. But mostly I repressed such thoughts and focused on the numbers. We had identified the viruses with global depopulation potential and were now testing possible vaccines. Most of these vaccines proved to be themselves lethal, and the rest were ineffectual, with one exception, but I felt closer to finishing the project and being in a better position to broach the subject of my retirement with Adam White, in a stolidly professional manner, without the rage that had overcome me during our dinner meeting.

This new agent took a long time to incubate, but when the monkeys started to crash, the entire room went down in two days—according to my experiments a near-perfect fatality rate. On their last day alive, the monkeys, though they were falling apart from the hemorrhaging and liquefaction of the tissue, showed signs of aggression. They made horrible gurglings and flung their own infected tissue around the room. Something about the way this bug ate through their brains made them violent. From the looks of it, we had created something scary. But we had no way of knowing whether humans were similarly susceptible, which was fine with me.

We had, to all appearances, hit upon a viral model and specimen that fit the desired parameters—lethal, contagious, pervasive, and even infectious after death. To our consternation, however, autopsies revealed that the virus that had successfully killed our primate test subjects in our lab (and other species models in parallel labs to which we did not have direct access) was not the virus we had synthesized. As best as we could tell, it was either a mutation of our intended synthetic virus, or had come out of nowhere, coughed up by nature and landing, thankfully, and against insane odds, in an experimental animal in a hermetic lab.

My eyes strained as I peered through my helmet glass and focused the electron microscope on the viral tangle that had torn apart the monkey cell, I couldn't tell the shapes on the slide from the afterimages that swam through my tired eyes. I made a mental note to switch from two caffeine pills to three. There was no way to drink coffee in a space suit.

A red light came on. That meant there was a security problem. I shut down the microscope and went through the sealed door into the shower room and let the spray wash over the suit.

The red light comes on. Then all the lights go out and the emergency lights on only halfway. There is a klaxon firing short bursts. A fire broke out of the incinerator. The ventilator system now labors to remove smoke from the building at the risk of also releasing pathogens. I am in intermittent blackness, surrounded by glass and scalpels and monkey corpses and deadly viruses, my pressurized space suit going limp as the pumps have quit. I shout through my helmet to security hoping that one of the microphones works. I prepare to exit through the safe zone and airlock. The bleach showers no longer work, I cannot disinfect properly. Luckily the airlock doors can be pulled open. It is difficult feeling my way out with the gloves.

I came awake and did not know how long I had been slumped against the shower wall. The seven-minute shower had ended. The security alert, another doctor claimed, had probably been a drill. That was not my first narcoleptic seizure in the lab, but was the first time I had fainted into a nightmare. Obviously I couldn't tolerate that. I went home to try to sleep.

I have a satchel with the vaccine. I try to get out of the complex. The monkeys have escaped from their cages. Vicious, agile, infectious, they crawl through the ceiling panels and lurk, teeth bared in viscous faces. Thick strands of hairy bloody fluid drool through those grates, the gelatinous, infectious residue of the new dead.

I tried to wake up fully but lay there flattened by dread, my mind unable to release its hold on this problem: What is the difference between holding the virus in your mind and being infected by it? I had had a bad dream and had to reassure myself that the representation in my mind of the virus's structure was not real. But that wasn't true. DNA was real. DNA was in every cell responsible for every simultaneous thought. And if the thoughts were made of DNA, then why wasn't the DNA in my thoughts the DNA the thoughts were made out of? Did this mean my mind was infected? Could the virus be transmitted by thought? If the molecules comprised in the virus could be communicated by language then why couldn't the virus? And if I am dreaming, this dream could be my body's way of telling me something that not even a doctor could, at this stage, detect.

I pushed purring Ebola Reston from my pillow, rubbing cat hair from my mouth. It wasn't even midnight. I threw on a sweatshirt and jeans and drove out the gate and to the Club, needing to talk to someone. I might admonish him for leaving before dawn, if I couldn't think of anything else to say. I thought he would be happy to see me. It was a different valet who stood at the post though.

"We're closed."

"Is Joe working tonight?"

"Joe doesn't work here anymore."

"Why?"

"Missed two shifts. This is supposed to be my night off. They called me in to cover for him."

"That awful little candy red car—that belongs to Mr. White, right?"

"Yes."

"I'd like to go in and talk to Mr. White."

"You'll have to park your own car I'm afraid. I'm going home."

"Are you sure? Because I'd really like to put a dent in that toy."

"That's fine with me, as long as you wait ten minutes for me to punch out."

I found Adam White in the bar. While, in the corner, gentlemen of means chatted softly, rolling cigars in their jowls, Adam, sitting alone with a chocolate martini, was examining a row of bowling trophies in a glass case. He wore a yellow sports walkman with his designer sports coat and tie, and was bobbing to some beat. His eyes widened at my entrance as though I were a tennis ball unexpectedly served and he moved to intercept me, leaving his headphones on.

"Doctor, what a surprise. I didn't know you were a member here."

"I'm not."

"I'm sorry if I offended you the other day. Have you come here to accept my proposal?"

"I have a couple of concerns. The first is my salary, including full retirement benefits. The second is the problem of completing our research without human testing."

"So I take it you're interested in joining the inner team? Salary won't be an issue, I assure you."

One of the men in the corner, I noted, was Mac, who raised his snifter to me in recognition, not quite smiling.

"Because," Adam smiled, "your knowledge is indispensable. As are you, doctor." He gestured to the corner and I followed him over to the men who sat around a table covered by a large unrolled blueprint of a building in the shape of a pyramid. "Our new office," Adam beamed. His watch sparkled as he pointed to a corner of the schematic. "You and I will live here."

I wondered what he meant by "and," and "live." Was this a new laboratory where we would all get new offices? I looked at Mac, who did not meet my gaze, looked down at a pager, unclipped his phone and called in. He frowned, and Adam frowned, watching him. Finally Mac closed his phone. "How are the two women?" Adam asked. Mac shook his head. "I don't know, but we have some fires to put out. I'll leave you to your celebration."

Mac had learned that, in Seattle, at the university facility where Bertha was kept, a network administrator named Jay—a hairless trekkie I had met only once—reported a grievous security violation, in which one of their own employees had set up what was being described as a website for terrorists. This had been brought to the administrator's attention by federal government officials. Although no top secret data was kept on those machines, this bizarre incident risked undermining government confidence in their whole enterprise. Adam would have to fly to Seattle the next day to meet with the feds and smooth feathers.

But the real problem was that someone had snuck into our California facility.

While Mac presented me with my new keycard and the combinations to the core subbasement doors, Adam beamed like a prom queen. He looked like a catalog page with pink sports shirt tucked into white shorts, socks and sneakers, almost jogging in place with enthusiasm.

"Doctor, I am very excited to now be able to share with you this other part of our research. In cooperation with the federal penitentiary system we're offering prisoners a chance at a commuted sentence in exchange for their cooperation doing human testing of the potential vaccine you've identified."

Mac abruptly turned away and sneezed. Adam and I looked at him in alarm as he unfolded his handkerchief sheepishly to remove a spot of blood from his moustache.

"Are you all right Mac? If you feel sick you should go down to the medical wing and have yourself looked at."

"I'm fine, Mr. White, just a little head cold."

He punched some numbers on the wall and the door slid back. Directly ahead was the grey area, where protective suits were worn before going into the core. He led me to a corridor around the outside of the core.

"I think you'll agree that these experiments are most useful. Without verification with human subjects, the viral synthesis is just finger exercises. Here's the good news: we have two lucky women, prisoners, who may be our first survivors."

"If that's true then my work here is done."

"Oh the work goes on, Doctor. But you've seen what these agents can do to monkeys. So prepare yourself. Remind yourself that these subjects are rapists and child-killers being spared life imprisonment or execution in order to make a contribution to science."

We passed some wire-reinforced glass. In a bloodsoaked bed I saw a wet and shriveled pupa that was once a human. Adam tapped the glass. "This agent continues to amplify even after biological functions have ceased. This person is long dead and still smoking like crazy. I've not seen anything quite like it. As a weapon it is something new: destroys people and removes their corpses, leaving only bone and connective tissue to clean up. One of your lucky breaks, doctor. We hadn't set out to find a corpseless plague, it just landed in our lap."

We moved to the next window. "This one's still very fresh."

Joe's head rolled back and I saw his eyes were pink and soft. "He went blind early, it seems," said Adam. *The Priest had made a bloody mess of his holding tank. It appeared that he had been throwing himself against the walls, which bore his red imprints. His crucifix glinted from the ooze of his collapsing chest cavity. Joe had wanted to let the blind see.*

"Doctor White, I know this man. Mac? This man is no murderer or child-rapist. He's a priest."

"Stupidity doesn't become you Dora. This priest snuck into the facility hiding in your trunk. He is a friend of yours I understand? We can only assume he was working for the Chinese and hope that he was not able to get any information out of the complex. We have no reason to believe you intentionally compromised our security, but we cannot exclude that possibility. If you weren't necessary, it wouldn't be an issue. So, if you have any misgivings about your new assignment, you should know that it's too late for that. Just decide which side of the glass you want to be on."

Only one half of his mouth continued to smile. He pulled a tennis ball from his shorts pocket and bounced it on the sterile white tiles while awaiting the aroma of my response.

My reflection was superimposed on top of Joe. He twitched. His lesions hovered, burning, on my cheeks.

Into the mirror.

For many years I have been able to feel the tip of the bullet entering my temple, exploding gently like a migraine, then, in its wake of metal and bone, erasing most of my sensations and words for things.

By the time you read this letter, I have been shot, and you, in the commotion, have escaped.

I know this as surely as I know that you will be joining me in this cell. That we will be infected as lab rats, and we will survive. They will take this to mean that their inoculation is effective.

I remember that all of this will happen, though you do not. I can't sympathize.

I have never understood other people's refusal to remember the future.

All my life people were always in the most serious denial about what was about to happen. Often I thought they were joking or daft or genuinely psychotic in their apparent nonchalance about impending devastating events I could anticipate clearly. Having undergone tests my first time in prison, I understand now that my mind is unique. But still, surely it doesn't take a full-blown premonition to see where things are going. I mean you might be unaware that the plane you are boarding is going to crash, or dismiss these memories as fear, but when your leader is suddenly appointed and not elected and immediately begins to pass laws restricting public expression, and announces plans to start new wars with a new battery of weapons of mass prevention including new diseases, you must know from history that things are going in a bad direction.

When I tried to look into the problem, I had to conclude that not only was I remembering the future, but that those who claimed to be unable to were deluded. Think about it. We know from physics that time is relative, that there is no absolute simultaneity, thus no absolute present, past, nor future. We know from history and memory that history and memory are slippery, revisionist. And still we believe in a fixed, inflexible past, however we may forget it. And without any evidence that we can change our destiny, we live our lives to shape a malleable, elastic future.

An inability to remember your past is *amnesia*, and an inability to remember your present is *denial*. But ignoring the future, there isn't even a word for that. I guess we call that sort of ignorance *freedom*. A person who knows the future is a *prophet, clairvoyant, delusional*. A person who enjoys her breakfast with her husband and daughter and makes plans for their summer vacation one hour before she will be killed by a truck is normal. Like my mother.

I remember my mother was so happy before she died. She must have known. There is no other reason she would be so exuberant. She wasn't a happy person. Whether she was embracing her last taste of life, or was simply relieved that she soon would be spared the further abuses of my father, she was ecstatic. I knew we would be in the wreck. It felt like we had been preparing for it all week, a family picnic. We dutifully climbed into the car.

I've heard of people who have suffered trauma blocking out the past, forgetting their memories. Why isn't the same thing possible with the future?

I could always remember the future. I always knew which elevator would arrive at the lobby first. I always picked the fastest checkout aisle at the supermarket. I always exploited these gifts, because my life was dangerous, and I knew my days were numbered.

When I was in the car crash that killed my parents, I was blinded. Doctors found no evidence of trauma, no sign that anything had struck my eyes, head, or body. I had been strapped in, and the truck that decapitated my parents slid over my head without touching me. I think I went blind before the collision, because I could not bear to look at what was coming. The mind is not meant to work as mine does.

Since my memories from the time after the accident were whited out, I had thought I would die in the crash.

Later I began to remember my real death, whose impact I feel more sharply every day. I feel as though I can reach out and feel that bullet in the air, converging inexorably with my skull. Everything after the bullet is black, not white. I will die on the ground.

After the accident, at age thirteen, I started my adult life. I was placed in an orphanage among beginning criminals whose latent tragedies were apparent. I could smell about them the aroma of future jail time, blood, and ash. I was frightened of these young ghosts and did not make friends.

Later, when I ran away, I fell in with a bunch of radicals who were preparing for the end of time. They were cynical or had delusions that somehow corresponded with the truth. Some of them were terribly proud of their memories of our shameful future, whether these memories were authentic or not. I became an activist to work for a better world, and even succeeded in slowing the fall.

For most of us, being a professional activist led to becoming a professional prisoner. We got arrested repeatedly, and learned our way around the prison industry, learned which prisons were best and how to get into them. Some accomplished this by becoming informants. But me, I went with testing: submitting myself to scientific research in exchange for lenience, better conditions, and reduced sentences.

First I was arrested for lying underneath a moonrocket filled with uranium to prevent its being launched on time—successfully, I might add—and, consequently, had a successful career as an experimental subject in the hands of researchers who were interested in memory. They had been prepared to attempt who knows what insidious surgical intervention in my brain when, during preliminary interviews and testing, they took an interest in my ability to remember things that, to their memory, hadn't happened yet.

Those experimenters treated me extremely well, and most of their testing amounted to playing the card game Memory with Braille cards. To their endless fascination, they found that unerringly I could say what text was printed on the underside of each card before I picked it up. One young woman tried to trick me by refusing to let me hold a card I had read, but in her consternation she dropped it on my foot. I picked it up and handed it to her. As part of the lenient deal extended to me by my handlers, I was allowed to work toward my G.E.D. with a poet named Max Winchester. Having concluded that activism would not have an effect, I took up poetry hoping that my writing could influence the world I could not remember, after my death.

I was released on my own recognizance, having agreed to remain an experimental subject for this team. Each day I knew with more certainty that the world was done for, and that knowledge, if disseminated to those in power, would only be used to justify unimaginable atrocities. I knew that sooner or later the experimenters would get the truth from me.

Max took me to a poetry conference where I was able to read one of my poems to an audience, and there I sat next to someone whose voice and smell brought a flood of memories of what was next for me. He reminded me of you. I think he was your son. That conference was my best moment.

I knew that the following day I would speak at a press conference, be arrested, and it was too painful to remember all the hands I would pass through and the things they would do to me. Repeat offenders don't get the cushy gigs when they submit to scientific testing in exchange for a reduced sentence. This time around I would be offered no opportunities to play card games a few hours a week with cognitive scientists, live in a comfortable cell, and study politics and poetry with Max Winchester. For the crime of speaking at a press conference called by the local university whose microbiology facilities, including graduate students, were to be shared with a private bioweapons firm, I end up a human subject in experiments conducted by that same bioweapons firm, demonstrating a detachment that passes for irony on the part of the state. When I agree to submit to testing, I am not told that it will be testing of weapons of mass destruction, but I know, and I know you will be my cellmate, and that I will help you escape in the dark.

I can't see who shoots me in the crowd, but the bullet will have been meant for you. I can remember that you escape. I hate my death but believe that, freed of the momentum of the present, I will wander in my life forever. Maybe I can even change a few things. Maybe I already have. Lucky for you, you can't even remember tomorrow.

Admitted to God that, on its search for a more civilized future, humanity had gotten lost; that human knowledge had become too powerful to be entrusted to humans.

Came to see that research into the secrets of all life would lead only to development of instruments of death.

Saw a storm brewing in an electron microscope: an infinitesimal string of molecules larger than all of history's accumulated momentum; a submicroscopic shard—innocuous, monstrous—that could dismantle organisms trillions of times larger and more complex, leaping from lung to lung, throat to eye, bulldozing human timber, burning human tinder; a mindless reproduction machine that takes control of human physical systems away from their brains; as evil as only something animate but not alive can be.

Saw that the instruments of death could not be stopped, but could be turned against their designers.

Was infected by resentment so virulent it amplified into every thought, sensation, and decision.

All the while, continued to dutifully work in the government laboratory researching, synthesizing, and testing increasingly perfect strains.

Having seen a single particle of the pathogen eat through a roomful of monkeys, understood the absolute power at the disposal of whomever should wield it.

Practiced a plan such that every ritual decontamination shower became a rehearsal; tucked a vial into the sticky tape sealing the sleeves of the space-suit—empty the first five times it was taken through the decontamination showers; the sixth time, extracted a coal from the viral fires that burned brightly in the sealed lab.

Came to find that nobody could possess absolute power without wielding it.

In a basement lab engineered from sheet plastic, HEPA filters, exhaust fans, blood jelly, centrifuges, wearing a bio-hazard suit fashioned of garbage bags and duct tape, latex gloves, and a gas mask, put a tube of blackened viral monkey blood into a centrifuge, isolated the viral particles, and fed them on human blood.

Weaponized the virus into a weightless, floating dust that would expand to fill buildings, follow air circulation systems, and be drawn into the wake of human movement.

Within two weeks found the mice in the cage in a corner of the lab sitting bloated, bleeding out from eyes and rectum, some coming apart at the seams, others torn to shreds by the outbreak of aggression in the others.

Saw that the specimen had been taught to fly.

Thereby found the design of the weapon: a crisp five hundred dollar bill painted with invisible layers of viral paste, encased in glass. When the glass is cracked, the paste's fixative begins to decay, and a slow cloud of viral toxin streams off the bill, absorbable through inhalation and touch. The demonic denomination will ensure that it floats up toward the strata of society most isolated from plague.

When it was complete and perfect, sterilized the glass shell in bleach, and brought it out through the airlock into the history of the world.

Knew that all that was needed was one human specimen to run the final test on. And did.

Checked into the hotel where the Arms Contractors' Ball was being held.

Sat alone in a hotel room on the top floor looking at the weapon on the table, listening to the murmur of ghosts moving through corridors and adjacent rooms.

While observing on the television set an episode of Carl Sagan's *Cosmos*, was struck by how often he used the word "random" to describe the creation of earth and humankind. Wondered how it could be considered reasonable that science's effort to ascribe immutable laws to the workings of the universe relies on chance—astronomical improbabilities—random collisions, formations, mutations—from the formation of the earth and solar system, to the genesis of life on earth, to the chain of chance that led to the evolution of humankind. Is the universe really a chaotic popcorn popper of ricocheting particles? If all the movements of molecules are governed by immutable physical laws, how is randomness truly possible? From a precise measurement of the first movements of the Big Bang, the history of the universe could be derived. Is the conceit of random chance a feeble effort by the architects of science to establish human volition as a force in the universe—to establish that human thought and action, as distinct from the random movement of particles, is logical and ordered and thus able to shape the future? Certainly, if the evolution of a species sophisticated enough to create Carl Sagan's *Cosmos* from a foam of hydrogen and helium was a result of the dice rolls and coin flips of colliding atoms, than it is reasonable that people, being so much larger and more complex than those particles they comprise, could be major players capable of overriding the weak capriciousness of random coincidence to steer the universe's destiny.

Dismissed the idea that this string of six simple proteins that would eradicate the human world in less than a year could be any kind of coincidence, knew that a perfect and impeccably efficient nano-machine for ridding the world of its murderers was no fluke.

Saw the bathroom door move a few inches, though there was no breeze that could have pushed it.

Knew Pandora was in the room.

Wondered how long it would take.

Having made it a mission to retrieve the weapon to prevent its use, found that no mind could resist the seduction of absolute power. No humility or morality could override the desire to spend that bill.

In the bar on the hotel roof, watched the masquerade. Guests swing-danced dressed as depleted uranium, cluster bombs, fuel-air ignition devices, geiger counters. One wag had a missile for a codpiece, a belle had a B-52 and a bullet bra. Blindfolded by a white sash, a cigarette holder dangling from red lips, she swung at a piñata shaped like the earth. It shattered and rained gold coins across the tiles. Above the dance floor, lightning flickered.

Put the weapon on the bar, crunched the glass seal with the bottom of a heavy tumbler, asked the bartender to make change.

Saw that the monkey cage had come open and, even as the crazed beast infected with Pandora-black blood seized my throat with claws of razors, wondered whether the cage had come open as a result of random chance, or had been opened for me.

By my employer, or my Pandora herself, to teach me that I could not control her.

As the monkey bit through my neck, found the perfect alibi for my own infection, so the fire I had set would continue to smolder and would not be discovered until it was too big to contain.

Wondered whether that too was part of her plan.

These rich people should pay for drinking lessons. Chocolate martinis, appletinis, pomegranate daquiris. We stock the best scotches known to man, whiskeys so strong you could run a truck on them, vodka as pure as melted glacier. And these clowns in their ten-thousand-dollar suits are ordering soda fountain cocktails with hard expressions like poker-faced teenagers hoping they don't get carded. Mint flirtinis, passionfruit stone sours, ex-boyfriends with extra cherries. I heard these people were arms contractors. If the dealers of weapons of mass destruction drink like sissies then I guess the future is bright. A bigger threat than nuclear war is running out of wine coolers. Drinking while bartending is discouraged, of course, but I can't resist taking sips off a can of Pabst Blue Ribbon just to make a point: I may be a young, urban homosexual, but I drink like a grown-up redneck. "Sex on beach," one turbaned Muslim barks at me. In your dreams, pal.

Though it's hard for me to feel good about the one serious drinker in the bar. Mr. Downward Spiral. He's not making friends. An oily scientist with a thirst for single-malt scotch, he is running up a fast tab, sitting at a corner of the bar looking flat-out sick, eyes bloodshot, sneezing. He's ordering respectable, top call drinks but not sipping.

I can hear the conversations. *Plutonium, millions, collateral, neutron, laser-guided*. "Bioterrorism is the most lucrative threat to the new century. The bug starts here." There's something dead in these people. Their eyes are stone, their breath foul, they either overtip or don't tip at all. They don't know how to be people, they're just guessing.

The creep signals me to settle his tab: a McKinley is on the bar under his tumbler. It seems covered with some weird, dusty film. I give the guy a look and try to clean the bill with the towel I use to dry glasses, but the stubborn gunk puts a black streak in my bar rag. I put the bill in the drawer, and when I return with his change he has disappeared, leaving only some broken glass and an empty scotch glass. No way he tipped me three hundred bucks; he'll be back, I think. I sweep the glass into the trash, leaving a plume of dust. When I snap out the towel, a smoky wisp hangs above the bar, drifting in the red lights. A few VIPs sneeze.

When I pop open the register drawer, it coughs a cloud of dust. I am glad when a rich Indian prick peels a Cleveland from a golden money clip to pay for his buttery nipple. Who are these motherfuckers? The five hundred dollar bill seemed to steam as I extracted it from the drawer and tucked it beneath the rest of Gandhi's change.

A week later, the hotel is hosting a convention of school adminstrators.

Mike wants me to stay home. My eyes are bloodshot, but despite the coughing and sneezing I don't feel that bad.

He says I'll end up getting every school in the country sick, but I know he thinks bartending is beneath me, and I can't afford to miss a night of work. The teachers are frugal drinkers and tippers, but they eventually loosen up.

They're a friendly lot, at least. They strike up conversations with me. They tell the filthiest jokes I've ever heard, and pound cheap shots like nobody's business.

"Calvin," they say, "Let us buy you a shot."

I am running a fever, I realize, and ought to lay off the alcohol, but it makes me feel a bit better.

By closing time we are passing around a bottle of J.B. It's not my favorite, but I like these people.

A flight back to corporate headquarters in New Delhi.

Contact at the convention: U.S. congressman.

Invitation back to Washington D.C. the following week to discuss our products with some officials in charge of purchasing.

In New Delhi, met with the designers of the nuclear team, chemical, and biological team.

Armed myself with the latest brochures, tables of facts and specs.

Watched films of human specimens dying.

Acquainted myself with tectonic plates and fault lines.

Rehearsed my pitches in the mirror.

Noticed some redness to the eyes, watery mucous.

This exertion seemed to tax my system. Cold symptoms. Or flu.

Put together some large denomination bills of U.S. currency for my D.C. visit.

Mike is upset. I don't know if we are breaking up. I can't think straight. I might call in sick. I can't remember. This makes me angry. So angry I am shaking and then I throw up. Why did he go to the opera when I am this sick? I need him to take me to the hospital. I've been sick for three weeks. This is not normal. Is it? I know it's crazy, but I feel like I have monsters in me. Every part of my body feels off. I feel like I'm dissolving. And I'm very irritable. I'm like this thin balloon filling with blood and every sensation irritates me because any sharp object or noise or look might make me pop and start to leak. Having diarrhea for two weeks ought to make anybody unpleasant, especially when it changes color so much. Maybe I'll just break up with Mike and spare him having to make up his mind. I hope he gets home soon. I miss him. I need help.

Met with a government panel interested in our proprietary nuclear devices that create an electrical effect designed to knock out the opponent's electrical grid. Also the technology designed to cause earth tremors.

I had to excuse myself for coughing. Not professional. Not sure they noticed.

The sale appears that it will go through. This could be a lucrative contract for us.

They seemed uninterested in our other products. Our bioweapons, in particular, made them chuckle.

Must infer that the U.S. considers itself ahead of the curve on biologicals.

Nevertheless, our nuclear modifications were definitely of interest.

Expect to land contract.

Slept very deeply.

During the business meeting, when the waitress takes my salad plate away, I find a five hundred beneath it.

"Our way of thanking you for your time," the smooth Indian arms merchant intones.

A paltry gift, not likely to influence my bid.

One of my advisors tells me that their technology is already used by the Chinese. That's a concern.

Still, nice to have some money the wife doesn't know about, I joke.

The gentlemen all chuckle knowingly.

Something odd about the bill. I sniff it to see if it has curry on it. This merchant had been eating too much spicy food apparently. He sneezes a lot. It's a diseased, overcrowded third-world country, but they make damn fine nukes.

A bartender displaying unusual symptoms has been checked in to intensive care. As best as I can determine, a new disease is overwhelming his immune system. He is in great pain and bleeding from mouth and genitals. I anticipate publishing a paper on this. I have questioned the man who claims to be the patient's housemate. I presume the disease is spread among homosexuals—a new form of AIDS, more virulent. The patient seems to be undergoing some kind of internal liquification so pronounced that blood sprayed in my eyes when I inserted a hypodermic in his artery. I've begun a light regimen of anti-viral drugs.

I have started to make more aggressive inquiries.

By selling to our client's enemies, we maintain the global balance of power. This makes us responsible global citizens, we tell our shareholders, and doubles our profits.

I dislike dealing with Saudis at least as much as I do Americans, but they always provide luxurious accommodations, anything I request, and female companionship as a matter of course.

I have started to step outside the usual parameters to secure more contracts. I have let the Chinese know that the Americans have their secret.

What the missus doesn't know won't hurt her. Candy says I am running a fever. I say, all for you. Blow my nose, I say. Then blow my mind, just like in the song. I put a five hundred in my mouth and lie down on the bed. She knows what to do.

We get crazy and I don't have to pretend I love her. It's honest is what it is. Free enterprise. Made this country great. There's blood in my semen, she says. Better get that looked at.

All for you, I say. I'm an old politican falling apart. I got blood in all my fluids I bet. Running a country is hard work.

She laughs.

How embarrassing to sneeze during my daughter's performance of "I'm Just a Girl Who Can't Say No."

Some of the other parents glance over to where I sit in the corner of the gymnasium. Well, I'm lucky I haven't caught something even worse, given the clients I seem to attract.

I excuse myself and try to get out of my metal folding chair and make it down the aisle without too much distraction.

In the bathroom mirror, I see that my nose is bleeding.

In the silent morgue, a rustle, a crackle, a drip. A tentacle of blood has wrapped around the leg of a gurney and is slithering toward the ground. It meanders across the floor, a red sludge with black specks, crawling away from the drain in the floor, reeking of pestilence, excrement, death. A shoe lands in it and walks on by, tracking it into the corridor outside, each footstep spraying microscopic droplets.

A wealthy Indian with mutliple passports collapsed in a hotel and was brought in. The police seem to have records for a couple of the people he is claiming to be. This raises eyebrows. We don't know what is wrong with him, but we don't like the looks of it. Before the day is over, some Indians in suits arrive to take him away. They have a CIA escort, so we release the victim without having had a chance to run tests.

I don't like the way the gentleman from Utah is dragging his feet. We have a war on, moron. We can't quibble over pennies. I stumble to my feet. I seem to watch myself do this, as though I too were in one of the seats. It appears I am going to raise a filibustering objection, speaking out of turn. Instead I vomit more than I would have thought I could, splattering such profuse black regurgitation that several of the others wipe flecks from their hair and glasses.

I am a bit feverish when I stop off at Jason's. I'm not doing well. But a little cocaine ought to bring me around in time for the PTA meeting. Not for the first time, I look for an exit from this merry-go-round, and hope the peace of mind I'll get from the rush will help me find it. He's willing to do business on a barter basis, so I can save a little right there. I don't tell him I'm sick as I kneel before his chair.

I roll up a five hundred and inhale a rail. I always think the hundreds work better. They're usually fresher, less wrinkled, they've passed through fewer hands.

But not this one.

The cocaine sticks to the bill. I scrape it off and cut it into dime bags.

It takes a bit of effort but I manage to get the bill clean enough to deposit.

Luckily, I know the banker, so it's all good.

I had asked for a complete autopsy. I wanted the results delivered just to me. Unfortunately, word got out and the health inspectors wanted to get involved. Now they are accusing me of stealing the bodies to protect my research. Great idea, but I didn't think of it.

The bodies have gone missing. There's nothing but a paste under those tarps.

When one of our people dies, or gets gravely ill, we must keep the affair confidential until we can determine the cause. It's not unheard of for people who work near weapons of mass destruction to get ill from one cause or another. Canisters leak, shielding cracks, viruses escape. This makes the body of our lead salesman our property, you see, until we can determine that his cause of death involves no proprietary secrets.

All this I observe from outside or above: my railing from a subway platform. My collapse after these theatrics. Being stretchered and ambulanced to a hospital, where I am received like a nobody. They don't have my wallet, I must have dropped it. They don't know I'm a federal official. I am shunted into a side room where lights steadily fade. I think the hospital is flooding, and warm fluid is rising around me.

She had serviced a number of soldiers before we found her in bed. She had bled to death from many places. She had worked for me for over a year. I knew she had a young daughter in grade school. One of my bodyguards was instructed to put her in her car and leave her where she would be found. There was no better way. She would have understood.

At the bank, my friend greets me with an open office door, a broad smile, and takes my hand in both of his. In the office, I, VIP, push a fat envelope for deposit across the desk with a smaller envelope on top as a gift for my friend. A gift of cocaine. Nobody will be alerted to the large cash deposit, as usual. All very positive, professional. We work together to keep the city happy and productive, everybody feeling good.

Maybe I am allergic to money. The sneezing has gotten worse and worse. And I am afraid too many late nights at the club have been causing nosebleeds.

Sneezing blood into a customer's face, after all, is less than professional.

As I pick up the phone to call the doctor, the lights go out. The manager makes an announcement for all cutomers to leave the bank.

And the lights went out. Building by building. I watched from the roof of a skyscraper I had let myself into with bolt cutters, a crowbar, and persistence. If I had set off an alarm it wouldn't matter now. The police could consider every building under siege. Floor by floor, block by block, the darkness poured through the skyscrapers, black snow blanketing the city, silencing the buzzing fluorescents and piercing alarms. I stood on top of the world and watched the future come down. I had helped bring it. We had shattered the sky that had pressed us down and now shards of dark were falling to cover everything. The city was in a permanent night; nocturnal people were finally at home. I unrolled my sleeping bag and sat down on it, cracked a beer, and listened to the future rushing up onto the shore of the present.

And the lights went out. I threw back another shot and the bar disappeared. Only a soft light bleeding in from snow outside. I left without paying. On the street there was a sound of glass shattering; shadowy figures lifted a shopping cart out the pharmacy window, filling it with diapers, bottles of water, matches, aspirin. My phone showed no signal. I flagged down a cab to take me home. From the back seat I watched the shadows of lurkers or pedestrians hurrying to escape the uncomfortable new night whose flavor was yet unknown. Headlights panned like searchlights trying to pinpoint fugitives. Jane would still be at work or out with her hoodlum friends. In the basement apartment, I stood in the dark and listened for the sick girl's breathing. I heard nothing. But when I felt my way to the sofa, she was there.

And the lights went out. I cursed, crouching in the darkness with my camera, the photo shoot of my dying girlfriend interrupted. The pictures of Amy would be valuable, but a flash would have the wrong texture. As this period of history would certainly be remembered by its central photo-documentarians, I had decided to become a photographer who was also a poet, instead of the other way around. Amy seemed to ask for water. I poured some in her mouth. She was losing blood and liquid quickly. She had ruined my couch, and now I wouldn't be able to get a proper close-up of her eyes going blank. I went to the penthouse window. Lights of ships shone behind dark skyscrapers. The blackout would be good for a photo essay, but I didn't want to go out there. Looters might object to having their pictures taken.

And the lights went out. The record ground down to a growl and the speakers popped off. The dog barked. A car alarm alerted the neighborhood. Breaking glass, silence. A police siren stopped before I realized it had started. When, two hours later, I opened the refrigerator, and its light did not come on, I realized I had to start eating and drinking the best things. I ran a flashlight around inside the cool cavern and extracted items, setting them on the counter. Time to light the best candles. What music would be perfect? I remembered where I had batteries. I understood that this was the event—the only event—worthy of all the fine things I had saved for myself. The Icelandic whiskey, the Dutch chocolate. The cannabis in the freezer. Had the work of civilization just been preparation for a party to celebrate its end?

And the lights went out. The level four lab went dark and the roaring air pressurizing my space suit ceased, leaving a whispering crinkle of deflating plastic fabric. Nothingness engulfed me as I stood, scalpel in hand, over the hot mess of a infected, dissected specimen, surrounded by dirty blades, breakable glass, and cages of poisonous monkeys that could kill me with one swipe of their claws. And gone was the pressure that drew air out of the lab through special filters. The virus could now be considered free. This was an emergency. I had to leave. I began to feel dizzy. I just wanted to sleep. My skull tightened. Every breath was a mistake but they kept coming. I tried to remember the exit. The silence opened by the quieted blowers began to fill with the chatter of monkeys—monkeys in cages with electronic locks.

And the lights went out. Below me, Reno vanished. Even through the locked cockpit door, I could hear the collective gasp from the handful of VIP passengers. The instrument panel had gone dark, and it was not a good night for flying without instruments. I tried the radio but it didn't even click. A power failure like this was bizarre. The backup systems should have kicked in. It was as though electricity itself had failed. The flight attendant appeared to tell me something. I waved her away. This was a fun opportunity—my employers would never let me fly this way on purpose. I turned to Claude Reagan, who had been invited to share the cockpit with me, and suggested he fasten his seatbelt. Working for the government can get exciting, I joked, as I worked out what I would need to guide us in to project headquarters.

And the lights went out. I have to shout for Mommy because I am afraid. There are angry squirrels outside. Maybe they chewed through the electricity and are coming after me. Even the birds look mad, lining up on the telephone wire to watch the house. I tried to watch TV, but I hate news. Why aren't there volcanoes? Teacher is sick. Lots of teachers are sick. School is out. I made a bet with my best friend there would be a volcano but there hasn't been one yet. Dad is always at work and mom acts funny. She is always on the phone talking quiet. She puts things in boxes. Mom says Dad is coming home from work early and we're going to Grandpa's farm. She says shots will keep us from getting sick. I don't care, I'd rather be sick than get shots. Then I'd get Jell-O and 7-Up. Why can't we stay here?

And the lights went out. Me and Derek and Iain cheered. The restaurant was now lit only by the burners and candles on the tables. Late that night, in the silent suburbs, the restaurant's owner Allen Strange would see shadows moving in his yard and hear the hiss of spraypaint. A man who does not find and follow a conscience eventually finds his mind crowded by such hissing shadows, and learns to blink them away or silence them by turning off ranks of neurons. But these apparitions will stay. As he parts a curtain I will spray a line of red across the glass in front of his face. When the man who has not found his conscience cannot blink the shadows away, and must wonder what he has done to merit retribution, he stares into a deeper darkness, pure fear, out of which can come the most frightening shapes.

And the lights went out. The highway visible in the valley disappeared. The radio station went from citing catastrophes to silence. I turned the needle of the portable set all the way from one end of the dial to another, but heard only pure static. I resumed dishwashing. The rains had paused, and a crimson sunset's afterglow filled the kitchen. As I arranged plates in the dish rack, Becca pounded out dough and softly sang along with the song in her head. Something in the way she seemed not to know I was there caused a pleasant tingle in me. I felt I had entered the fragile bubble of some spell that would s t r e t c h the seconds before it was broken. Had there been a power outage? We didn't make much use of electricity on the farm. It did not surprise me. This was a day on which to expect anything.

And the lights went out.
I am the Prince of Darkness.
I am now at home.

That's a poem.

One dollar.

Poetry for sale. Buy my haiku?

I am the Prince of this Darkness,
the wilderness that is the city.

Buy a poem?

I am the Prince of those who are
shadowed from the light.

My kingdom has expanded.

Poetry for sale.

A smell of ozone or
static electricity

Songbird's terminated
chir

Heat so hot it feels
cold

Ash

Light

"What"

Burnt chemicals   Whistle of escaping air

Cold   Batteries

Square of fire writhing   EXIT
on the wall

Scorched tortilla

Laughter

Foot nudges mine
under table

Cilantro

Shining cloud rising,
closed caption

NEW CLEAR A
TACK [theme]

River water

Radio station becomes
static

Teeth rattling

Burning cigarette filter

St. Louis Arch
twisting

RIGHT LANE EXIT
ONLY

Sulfur   Ringing

Falling   Salt, copper

Flashes   "Help me"

Cold salt

Boulders hollowly
clunking underwater,
sucking, gulls go quiet

Sinuses

Copper or blood

Ocean on its side

SWIM AT OWN RISK

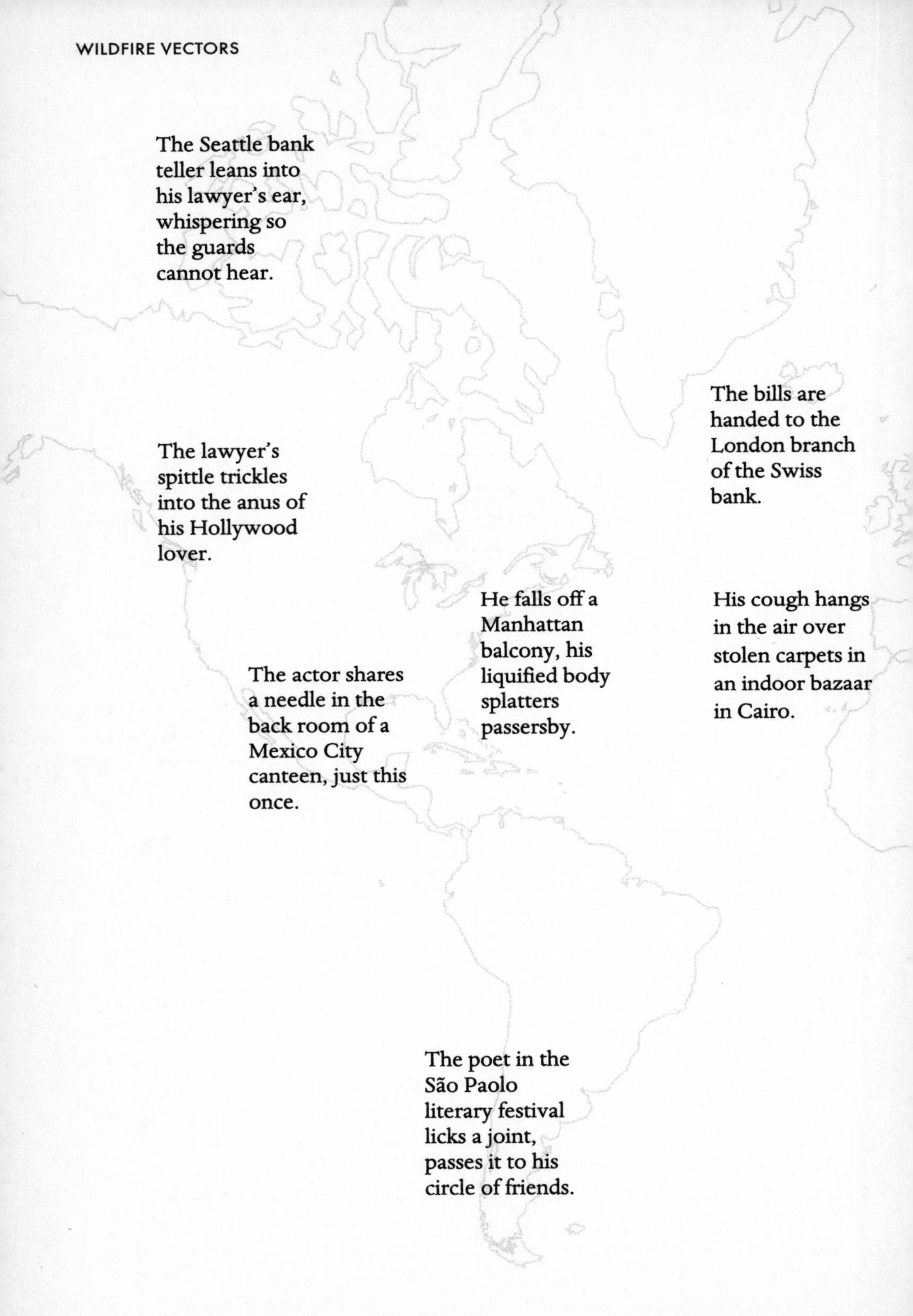

The Seattle bank
teller leans into
his lawyer's ear,
whispering so
the guards
cannot hear.

The bills are
handed to the
London branch
of the Swiss
bank.

The lawyer's
spittle trickles
into the anus of
his Hollywood
lover.

He falls off a
Manhattan
balcony, his
liquified body
splatters
passersby.

His cough hangs
in the air over
stolen carpets in
an indoor bazaar
in Cairo.

The actor shares
a needle in the
back room of a
Mexico City
canteen, just this
once.

The poet in the
São Paolo
literary festival
licks a joint,
passes it to his
circle of friends.

The Baku businessman coughs, explaining the Soviet warheads he has for sale.

The money launderer passes a vodka bottle to his Moscow contact.

The Shanghai pimp speaks reassuringly to an adolescent sex slave en route to Kabul.

The dishwasher in an Istanbul cafe eats an almost-untouched tea cake.

In a basement, the Tokyo animal dealer is bitten by an endangered species of monkey.

The Mumbai importer has nineteen children and likes to talk to each of them.

The Kinshasa hospital is at times so overcrowded nobody can tend to the dying.

The president of Australia addresses the Parliament.

1. ladies and gentlemen i'm breaking into the symphony because i have an emergency broadcast bulletin   listen

2. ——so——   sh. sh.

3.

4.   roger i'm investigating the oak street beach

5. ——underage drinker in a green vehicle, over. go ahead 54

6.   so?

7.

8. ——and by the time i'm done talking to him they were done with it.   and the guy had burst.   and the

9.

10. ——hold on a sec   jessica please shut the refrigerator

11. ——go ahead   there's a line down on the ground

1. a state of emergency and military curfew—what?—

2. what?

3. i need to speak to the president.

4. this thing is a mess ah. requesting biocontainment team. it's—oh, it's

5. do you want backup 54?

6. i was just calling, you know, to see if you had any—

7.

8. thing that was really i mean really gross that i didn't quite realize when i looked at the body

9.

10. for who? do it i can't do nothing you stay in this house jessica lock that door

11. the national weather service has finally issued a tornado warning 377 10-4

1. okay, has been imposed by the federal government executive branch effective immediately.

2.   jesus!

3.

4. soft.

5.   don't touch it 54. stay away from the body repeat stay away from the body

6.   holy cow dude what

7.

8. was that the feet had split, like above the shoe level, and all of the bodily fluids had come out.

9.

10. i can't talk about it cause the kids are here   amanda get in here now   you cannot sit on the porch

11. be careful on i-5 they have several semis blown over in that area

1. well. you're listening to parrot radio. i'm mindy mix, your classical hostess. this is my first emergency

2. dude are you listening to the pirate station?

3.

4. bodies.

5. how many bodies 54?

6. is everything alright?

7. let me turn it up.

8.

9. yeah, a lot of them do that, yeah

10. and play at night   hold on i gotta go out and get her   refused to listen   stop it

11. 10-4 and report of a power surge at 2205 south cottage grove   lines on the ground

1. citizens are advised not to panic, and to remain in their homes. oh.   right.

2. you need to record this.

3.

4.   i can't tell. i'm trying to count heads but—

5. 54 return to your vehicle wait for the truck over

6.   totally.   we're putting this in the album.

7.

8. well, i'm not saying all the fluids, but i mean a lot!   and i realized afterward they took his shoes

9.

10. no biting go to your room   okay i'm back   yeah i wish you would but wait until they

11. burning smoking in the residence after a power outage   lakeside terrace

1. it is not yet known whether this is a bioterrorism attack—please—but as always citizens are advised

2. fuck

3.

4. not again

5. 377 remove a trespasser   male outside the front door supposed to be banned from the property

6.

7.

8. separate, and that meant the skin separated and his feet were still in his shoes, right?

9.

10. investigate and—   hold on   go to bed right now   i'm back

11. respond to a power line arcing between units number 15 and 12   power lines on the roadway

1. to remain on the lookout for any suspicious activity. i now return you to mahler's fifth. trauermarsh.

2. is she shitting us or what?

3.

4. just lost my cookies over. i'll keep a safe distance.

5. she doesn't know his name

6.

7. yeah

8. that's gross!

9. yeah most likely. his shoes were off?

10. they're fighting   i work in a factory now so i   one more time and you're all going to bed

11. 1043 over   power line down   21 on the scene at 2207 10-4

1. it's a—it's a—symphony. i have to say—hopefully this announcement is a prank. computer virus.

2. man, that chick—

3.

4.

5.

6. she's drunk or—she's losing it.

7.

8. yeah, that's what i mean.

9. they wouldn't have taken them off.   that means his feet came off.

10. leave it alone sarah   officers phoned   i can't say nothing

11. an alarm at puget hydroelectric   possible transformer on fire

199

1. stay tuned for any further developments. in the symphony.

2. she sounds broken up. fucking pirate—   try a real station, let's—   there.

3.

4. this is car 54. over.

5.

6.   what is this? find someone real.

7.   MILLIONS BELIEVED DEAD

8. argh! that's so gross!   yeah, i know, i know

9.   well we had a guy that died in the bathtub

10. you can   he can't gag you   fine with me let him deal with them

11. truck 11 respond to a power line down on top of a vehicle   engine 11 are you on the air?

1.

2. me too, sh!

3.

4.

5. go ahead 54

6. i got rnn

7. IN THREE DAYS BY AN EPIDEMIC OF EPIDERMAL-NEUROLOGICAL DYSFUNCTION. HARDEST HIT WERE DENSE URBAN AREAS,

8. i know it. well, this guy was sitting at a desk, you know

9. and his feet came off in the tub.

10. i only agreed to every other weekend   let him have them every weekend   i guarantee ya—

11. respond to a power line down on top of a vehicle   70 mile per hour wind

1. what in the fucking hell kind of—fuck—whoops. why won't this mike shut off? i gotta get-

2.

3.

4. i'm thinking there might be a lot of bodies here. but they're in such bad condit-

5.

6. whoah.

7. THE COURSE OF THE OUTBREAK IS BELIEVED TO BE MORE MILD IN RURAL AREAS. THE STRAIN NAMED PANDORA BY

8. like how i sit at my computer, but leaning back, head to the right, and his neck was bloated up bigger

9.

10. three weekends and he'd never take them again

11. 24 available if they're needed   we also got a report of a tree down 150 division street

1. do i have to stay here now? there's a military curfew. what does that even mean? what does that mean for

2.

3.

4. eck. eck.

5. larry, get in the car and wait.

6.

7. EPIDEMIOLOGISTS PROVES FATAL IN 90% OF PEOPLE WHO CONTRACT IT SCIENTISTS HAVE NOT YET DETERMINED WHAT

8. than his head   and there was blood dripping on the floor and everything   and they were calling it a

9. oh yeah?

10. you can call   leave a message   my fucking cellular costs me an arm and a leg

11. 10-4   202 9757   202 9757   have some blankets and pillows turn the light off

1. pirate radio stations? i'm calling jasper.   pick it up, pick it

2. this is for real? what do we—what do we—what do we—do?

3.   shit

4. a whole lot of them, over, those are bones. washing up.   christ

5. for the spacemen to get there.   wait in the car.

6.

7. MAKES SOME PEOPLE RESISTANT. AN ANTIDOTE HAS BEEN DISCOVERED BUT CAN ONLY BE PRODUCED IN SMALL QUANTITIES

8. possible homicide and all this. it wasn't. and uh we get there and we look and there's no sign of trauma

9.

10. can't afford set a tires here baby i can't afford a new vehicle not like you baby   what color is it?

11.

1. up. fucking military curfew. military curfew? what is this, cuba?

2. i got another call.   they'll leave a message.

3.

4.

5. 516 missing person report triangle trailer park

6. what the hell's that? fucking machine gun fire?   who's calling?

7. RESERVED FOR HEADS OF STATE AND COMMUNITY. HOSPITAL EMERGENCY ROOMS ARE OVERLOADED AND HIGHWAYS ARE

8. or anything but the smell is so bad. admittedly i did not go around to the other side, between the wall

9.

10.   it's got power   what possessed you to buy this motherfucker $12,000

11. with all the trees down   route 150 side of the road   1452 pine 377 10-4

1. jasper this is mindy down at the station. i don't know if you're in bed but there's a military curfew,

2.   hear what?

3.

4.

5. a white female 8 years of age no clothing description trying to walk to the park from the seatac area

6. can you hear that?

7. JAMMED AND IN MANY CASES IMPASSABLE AS URBAN DWELLERS FLEE THE STRICKEN CITY CENTERS CANNABIS GROWERS

                                                        no, and i really

8. and his head

9.   did you give 'em a business card of the guy that cleans up those messes?

10. eleven hundred dollars to move into their apartment   for rent   first month and deposit   a three

11. can you give me a better location so i don't run into it?   on the ground just north of allerton

1. and i'm thinking maybe i should just shut the transmitter down and—you know—

2. no fucking way

3.

4.

5.

6. dude that's you

7. AND DEALERS ARE TO TURN THEIR SUPPLIES OVER TO OFFICIALS FOR EMERGENCY MEDICAL USE REMAIN IN YOUR HOME

8. wish i had one. it was a new team. in training.

9. the bioteam should have them when they pick up the bodies.

10. bedroom efficiency apartment no such thing efficiency means there's no bedroom whatever

11. 2300 and 200 that was on the ground is now dissipating 510 go ahead one in the air

1. pick up about ten gallons of water, twelve rolls of toilet paper,

2.

3.

4.

5.

6.

7. SEAL DOORS AND WINDOWS WITH DUCT TAPE AND PLASTIC SHEETING USE BREATHING FILTERS RATED N95 OR BETTER

8. and fred was inside, so i wasn't, but it was nasty!

9. another one? they're supposed to have those cards.

10. i'm sorry   i can't figure out what you're trying to ask me   that's okay   i'm not tired

11. southeast of philo   southeast of philo 10-4   649 25

1. a gallon of gin, a carton of smokes, and go home and pull the fucking curtain. duct tape the—

2.

3.

4.

5.

6.

7. BE SURE TO TUNE YOUR RADIO TO REAL RADIO LOCK DOORS AND WINDOWS TURN OFF HEATING AND AIR CONDITIONING

8. ugh. i'm glad i didn't eat anything when i left the

9. yeeee-up. i haven't been to a good one in a while.

10. something like that   you sound like you're catching a cold

11. no debris or anything like that at this time—no structural damage—route 49 at the marker thing—

1. —i just thought you'd know what to do. call me. please.

2.

3.

4.

5.   54?

6.

7.   CLOSE ALL VENTS AND FIREPLACE DAMPERS WASH YOUR HANDS BEFORE WASHING THE REST OF YOUR BODY AVOID OVER-

8.   house this morning.   no. this guy was supposed to go sailing with a bunch of

9.   was he recognizable?

10. so what are you doing tonight i'll be darned uh-huh yeah yeah yeah well i'm nervous about tonight's

11. hang on justaminute   bout mile and a half maybe west of that   10-4 it's still on the ground

1.

2. oh wait   this is just a movie.

3. that? that can't be real.

4.

5. oh GOD!

6. are you sure dude? it's the real station.

7. SCRUBBING IF YOU BELIEVE YOU HAVE BEEN EXPOSED REMOVE ALL CLOTHING JEWELRY WIGS GLASSES STAY AT HOME

8. friends last night, didn't show up. was supposed to have lunch with some neighbor, didn't show up and, um

9.

10. game   you gonna bring a thermos of coffee

11. 514   514 i think we're watching the same cloud from different angles and it has gone back up

1.

2. a zombie movie or some shit. a b movie. b for bad.

3.

4.

5.

6. what channel are you on?   what's with the sirens tonight?

7. PREFERABLY IN A SINGLE DESIGNATED ROOM, UPPER FLOORS ARE BETTER. TERROR IN AMERICA. WE'LL BE RIGHT BACK.

8. this is pretty bad, the neighbor called in a check the welfare and fred went out this morning around 10:30

9.

10. well fuck   i'll buy you one   fucking beat him   you can make him win   you can just walk away

11. thank you   is it a cold weather funnel or is it gray or is it a real funnel cloud?

1.

2. oh here we go. can you hear that?

3.

4.

5.

6. dude. mute it. please. i can't take a political ad right now.

7. THIS NEXT ELECTION WILL DECIDE MORE THAN THE FATE OF THE WAR IT WILL DECIDE THE FUTURE OF THE WHITE-

8. checked the perimeter of the house, everything else. cleared it with a k.   nope.

9. did he kick in the door?

10. i know it's too late now   hear that?

11. well it was a tornado. it pulled back up now   514 go ahead   i never copied the answer to

1.

2.

3.

4.

5.

6. yeah, so, i was thinking of, like, coming over, to see if you wanted to, you know, hang out, but—

7.

8. well, there were no visible signs.   well, apparently either

9. why not?   so, that's why you kick in the door.

10.   goodness   i gotta go   no i'm being honest

11. your inquiry about damage or injuries   going back into the clouds and dissipated

1. well that was mahler. apologies the dead air there.   if you're just tuning in,

2. wait—who is this an ad for anyway?

3.

4.

5.

6. huh? the one on rnn?

7.

8. the call didn't come in urgent enough or there wasn't a sergeant. i mean, i would have at least asked

9.

10. i'm talking to you for two seconds now   more than two seconds now   you don't want to go

11. 10-4 only dust in the debris cloud no building material   10-4 about to open the north loop breaker

1. apparently we are in a state of emergency of some kind. i'm still trying to figure out what's going on.

2. tweedle dumb and tweedle dumber

3.

4.

5.

6. i can't even tell anymore. war president 1 or war president 2.   yeah, so—

7.

8. for the—

9. you don't have to ask for permission, you make a decision. hold on, there might be some movement.

10. why should i go there if they won't let me talk to you   so you don't have the balls to tell them that

11. we have a report of a tree down can you clear it?

1. for now, we're on the air until—   aw, shit.

2. does ad time cost more during a national disas-   oooooooooooooooooooooooooooh.

3.

4.   uh-oh.

5.   oh!

6.   dude!

7.

8. seize something good for us now—ho! blackout gotta go

9. i'll call back.   ah!

10. somebody has to drive who hasn't been drinking— oh! it just got dark in here

11. bringing up the north loop   argh!   it did not hold

1.

2. dude i gotta go see—hello?

3.

4.

5.

6. hey. hello?

7.

8.

9.

10. well anyway for the sake of my own kids   goddamn chip on his shoulder   okay

11. we have another problem in the north loop somewhere

1.

2.

3.

4.

5.

6.

7.

8.

9.

10. pretty disappointed   you're not listening   i'm listening but you don't understand what i'm telling

11. closing the north loop   want to see if phil can go do that?   i'm right here i can get it

1.   jasper?   i don't know man. something crazy. i'm pretty drunk.   we can tell.

2. hello?   mindy? what's going on?

3.

4.

5.

6.

7.

8.

9.

10. i'm gonna hang up on you again because my battery's going

11. tacoma go ahead   the signals are unreadable   think you can get down to seattle?

1. i'm over at the station and i'm getting crazy. power's out. are you listening to the police scanner?

2.

3.

4.

5.

6.

7.

8.

9.

10. dead   i have no choice   you don't even know if i'm gonna be here tomorrow   i could be in the hospital

11. we got a request from the mayor   a bunch of trees and lines down   whenever you're ready

1.   you got power?   listen can you pick me up?

2. power's out there too?   no. i was watching real news and it died.

3.

4.

5.

6.

7.

8.

9.

10. calm down and i'll see you tomorrow alright?   i will call you as soon as i wake up

11. 10-4 closing the north loop breaker   i wonder if there's too much load all at once

1.   there's a military curfew on, i don't know if buses are running.

2.   no.

3.

4.

5.

6.

7.

8.

9.

10.   alright?   i've got the bar mitzvah and the wedding   tonight?   i love you

11.   —fire down here   we need some lights to see what we're doing

i'm out at the farm. sorry.

1.   what?   hello?   hello?

2.   oh shit.   hello?   mom?   hello?

3.

4.

5.

6.

7.

8.

9.

10. i'm not mad at you honey okay i love you   you need to keep it in one lane or the other buddy

11. copy that phil   before i have you try any of those breakers i thought i'd drive out there

1.

2.

3.

4.

5.

6.

7.

8.

9.

10. why don't you slow down   what emergency?   tonight?

11. someone's going to make a call on which circuits we bring up first

knock on the window when you get here

1. ooooooh.

2.

3.

4. holy mother   i've just heard what sounds like an explosion.

5. 51 go ahead.   10-4 51 we felt it too. 52.

6.

7.

8.

9. what the hell?

10. jessica?!   hold on   jessica?!   she better not have run outside

11. phil before we uh i'm going to go ahead and turn off 201 and 202 if you could turn off 204 first

1. testing?

2.

3.

4.

5. negative 52. we've got too much going on. we

6.

7.

8.

9. the subject is leaving the apartment. should we arrest him?

10. all i do is put more confusion into your head you're looking for answers and all i have is questions

11. 10-4   closing breaker 201   holding

i have the station generator going. if anybody out there

1. is listening and wants to tell me what's going on i—hello? somebody's here. i'll be right back.

2.

3. sir? it's starting.

4.

5. need you down at the oak street beach.

6.

7.

8.

9.

10. i definitely hear voices on the line   my kid is missing can you hold on my phone charger won't reach that far

11. gonna close breaker 202   nope. the grid is down.

BUBBLES

Shot
by a man I cannot
see but whom I have always
known is there, I merge with the moment my fear had always driven me toward. In the completion of the circle that
has been the bubble of my life I must wonder
whether I have been assassinated by a government agent because I was a dissident, or whether I have been a dissident because I have always
known I would be assassinated by an agent of
my own government. Regardless, on the
shimmering edges of what I had known to
be me, new bubbles are growing, and
one of those, my love Mindy,
will sail away up into the
future.

I know
she hit me with
an oar and kicked me into
the river and don't know whether
I continue to lie in the boat with my
eyes closed because I am discouraged, unconscious, or dead. But I think I know that
that roar that is getting louder means the river is at an end, and I sit up and look over
the edge of this forested area into a dry
canyon as the boat tips over the smooth
edge of the waterfall and I float there
above a desert floor that is also my unredeemable life.

                    Drowning
               in the light of that
          which I had tried to defeat, I
       went blind to accept it. God pushes a
    hole in my chest but puts His lips to it and
 blows in air, keeping me alive. He is flashing
blueprints on my retinae, schematics of this incinerator in which I have been dumped among oozing corpses. I see the spokes of underground railroad
tracks that bring the bodies here. I see documenta-
tion of the incinerator's safety mechanisms. As the
vectors of light collide, heat rises around, the dia-
gram of the emergency door is in the bones of
  my hand, too late I understand His true plan.
     I thought I was going to stop the river,
        but the flood of fire pours through
            the tunnels beneath the
                old world.

                    My
               best brandy,
            barbiturates, and
         batteries: Mozart's
         Requiem. Recliner.
         Take me, glittery
            ambivalence.
                Oh yes.

                    I dis-
               covered America
            in a VW beetle. And what I
         saw convinced me to play to pow-
      er. There's too many bad ideas loose in
     the world. We are overrun by gangs of dis-
    eased proles, the American people, I believe it
   is them, and realize I hope it is true. With a sack
   over my head, wrists lashed to the bedframe, I
   sprawl on the floor and listen to the breathing
   of my captor. I think it is a woman, she smells
   like outside, and must be teeming. I remem-
    ber how in my teens I was not so different
      from them. I imagine she would un-
        tie me and we would drive away
            together. And dream
                 we   do.

                         With
                 the collapse of the
             pyramid, all the data stopped.
          I wandered for years and lost touch
          with everything I once thought, though
          sometimes I would be reminded of the old
          thoughts, but usually this was painful. It was
          the life for a narcissist, wandering alone, thinking
          about my thoughts. Dogs are becoming a problem.
          I never liked them, but now they are getting mean.
          They follow me and get testy whenever I eat and
          don't share my food. I tried to escape them. On
           a bicycle. I thought I had succeeded until one
             night somewhere near Reno they con-
               verge on me in the street. I don't
                 think they're going to let—

BUBBLES

As be-
fore when I rode
the hot air balloon, this time
I rose and observed without judge-
ment the sandy-haired killer dismembering my body. And in the adjacent bedrooms, what he had done or would do to Mike,
Blake. I felt more for the pain I had caused Tom,
whose love for me I had deliberately misunderstood. It seemed my drop would rejoin an
ocean, an ocean whose tides had all but retreat-
ed from the shore. But we would be back, exploding in green spray through cracks in
the asphalt, climbing the crumbling
stone walls, covering and submerging every surface.

I un-
derstand
that I do not feel
bad for having made
the worst mistake a per-
son could. I have passed
through the weath-
er vane. I see the
barn from above
now.

There
are actions that are vi-
ral. You are infected when they are done to you or people close to you, and then you
are driven to spread them to others. Brutality, torture,
murder, thievery: these are diseases of the mind, possibly in-
curable. I didn't regret putting my former employer to death. He
was a murderer. That I had to do that did have some kind of effect I
can't deny. So I wrote my family and the rest of the farm a note and just
took off walking. I didn't know what I was doing yet. Whether I was going off into the woods to die like a sick dog, or quarantining myself to contain the disease of hate. God knows I was infected and infested with all the
lice of prejudice and my role in the deaths of so many. Too many. I think I
wanted to make sure the pyramid was gone, and that nobody lived in the
dam. As long as I had the disease, might as well make use of it. I rise up
above my life now and see that everything was necessary, and the
chain of mistakes I thought I lived was a thread that fit seam-
lessly into the beautiful tapestry of life yet to come, my
children growing and spreading like vines, no longer
anybody's minority on this new continent.

The
two planes of
waking and dreaming
are converging for me, such
that time now may not make
sense ever again. I am still in my
spaceship struggling to read the
swimming letters of the canon,
and I am in the new jungle of
Chicago leaving behind my
body in the shade of
skyscrapers.

I
am one of
the last bubbles
to pop of what was
once a foam that
covered every-
thing.

Will
I die with
these thoughts
nobody can ev-
er know? Or do the
thoughts live on af-
ter they shed
my skin?

BUBBLES

Good-
bye my
beauties.

BUBBLES

You lived
as best you could, didn't
complain when the world tilted and started to dump its mess on you. After that night on
the Ferris wheel you start listening to the radio. There was
a fancy disease afoot. Not a time to abandon neighbors, but
wasn't nothing else to be done. You had always took people into your
home. Kids and dogs too. Long as it took. To get things sorted out. But
you couldn't do that this time. This sickness it turned people against people in
the worst way. That's what you remember about it. You had to figure out what
was important then. Live or love, to put it bluntly. Live in fear or die helping people out. It was like to make a man depressed. When the preacher came round asking
for water you had to turn him down. He did not look well. He did not appear to be in
his right mind. Nearby is a rocky shore where the tides pulled back and forth hard. Now
the tides have pulled themselves down, and their steersman, the moon, is still in the sky.
But wrong. Differently glowing shards encircled by interlinking halos of dust. The circle
of the moon broken. Times change. There is no more milk. Then there are no cigarettes.
Moon means line instead of circle. Burning dust makes some days green and rainy. The
ocean settled and fish and creatures came to its surface for air. The sea crawled, thick
with writhing flesh, it could almost be walked upon. One July, water rose twenty feet,
submerging Main Street. After the tides receded, the gutters were strewn with fish,
some still flopping. There was a shark in the park and it didn't seem dead. Armies
of crabs marched the sidewalks. An octopus tentacle groped from a sewer grate,
expulsions of liquid gasping through the holes of manhole covers. The moon
doesn't set. An arc of gravel dirties the sun. The next morning it
starts to rain and doesn't stop. I'd say that this is the worst cold
a man ever had, but I am so old now who knows. Maybe
it's time to give back my bones. Or maybe it's just a
cold. But it's not the end of the world. That
happened about fourteen years
back.

When you run a publishing company out of a basement apartment, I suppose part of your mind is always thinking about a flood. The day when you will have to abandon everything you've worked for, watch it all wash away.

Abruptly, the clattering ferry motor backfired and quit. Percussion rebounded into the misty stillness. The ferry rocked, rattling the chains that hung around the deck. Jane and I watched the world above the windshield wipers drift until we were staring downstream into the darkness there. After the hopeless crush of traffic, the grinding panic, and the protracted haggling with the ferrymen, the feeling of the car sliding across the glassy river was surprisingly smooth. At this crossing where the tributaries converged in a rush of mist, days of rain had caused the already broad river to rise and pour with urgency high along its banks. The river would soon spill onto the vague, desolate floodplain where a few houses stood on stilts and migrating bald eagles perched like heavy apostrophes in the tops of tall trees in the swiftly gathering night. Then crossing by ferry would become impossible.

This was one of the new rivers, and didn't appear on our map. I wasn't sure where it went, whether it emptied into other rivers or the ocean. The travel route I had sketched out might have to be rethought. As soon as we crossed the river and found a marked road we would know where we were going. I tried to plot contingencies, but I was dead from the sixteen-hour drive and could think nothing. The cool fog rolled beyond the red glow of dashboard lights.

It appeared electricity was cut in this part of the country, as no lights appeared on the shore or the bluffs beyond. An eagle wheeled over the bow. We could make out no details on either bank. We heard a failed attempt to restart the motor and saw a black clot of smoke unravel into the grey dusk.

One ferryman wore a hooded yellow raincoat with two vivid stripes of safety orange, the other wore a white long-sleeved shirt with epaulettes, a tie, and an officious cap, and was manning the helm in the small cabin. The ferryman with the yellow raincoat walked stiffly out to the bow to lean over and look ahead, turned to cast a wave at the motorists in their vehicles, walked back amidships, and mounted the ladder to the glass cabin. Driftwood. Ring-shaped life preservers hung from the yellow gates that should now have been opening to let us off. Atop the hydraulic arms that lifted and lowered the ramp, blue bulbs flickered on, went out. CAR-TRUCK $6.00, ROUNDTRIP $10.00, the sign had read, before the ferrymen had painted over the decimals.

Fingers tight on the wheel, I watched obscurity slide past. I jumped at a sharp tapping on my window. The ferryman leaned down and said something through the glass we couldn't hear, and shrugged. We nodded. It startled me to have a stranger's face so close to mine, but the virus couldn't pass through glass.

I turned on the headlights to see if they would illuminate the shore, but they lit up only tendrils of encroaching fog. In the rearview mirror, I saw the drivers behind me lit red as they stared impassively forward. I turned off the lights and the people disappeared. I removed my hands from the wheel and left them in my lap. Jane turned on the radio and found a dull news reporter, sounding drugged or exhausted, repeating more or less what we already knew: the bridges were impossible, the city was in chaos, travel by auto was either discouraged or illegal, it wasn't clear. The panicked surge of traffic, combined with the shutdown of filling stations, police, and tow trucks, had made a mess of every major roadway. As the announcer droned about impassable bridges, we floated beneath one. Across the charcoal sky a line of autos. Half the cars were dark. Perhaps they were abandoned, or perhaps their drivers had shut down the cars to save fuel and electricity. I pulled the keys out of the ignition. The radio went silent and rain fell on the windshield. I cracked the window to hear what was happening above us, hearing nothing but a strange reverberation we thought was an emergency worker issuing directives through a megaphone but that turned out to be the lapping of the river echoing from the beams above.

I assumed the ferrymen were radioing for help and that sooner or later they would get the craft to the bank. My ignorance of such matters allowed me a certain calm. It was nice suddenly no longer to be pilot. I had plenty else to worry about. Could the virus live in water? I didn't know. I hitched the seat back and closed my eyes.

It had been a long drive.

I slept like hell. Christmas, great consternation about whether Santa would come, arranging cookies like Tarot cards. When the dream faded I lay there, wondering why things were so calm. I remembered the previous dream, which turned out to be true. A gentle rocking told me we were still on the ferry. I hoped we weren't too close to being rescued as I was in no hurry to resume our mad doomed drive to New Mexico. New Mexico was where Jane's grandparents lived in an A-frame cottage in the mountains. Since they were already crazy survivalists who pumped their water from a spot in the ground obtained through the insight of a divining rod, and dreamed UFOs into the night skies, we thought they'd be adjusting to things fairly well. Could the virus reach high altitudes? Finally I pried open an eye. Darkness. And in the seat beside me Jane was gone. I worked the other eye open and lay there tingling, weak. It felt like I had been shot up with muscle relaxant and then filleted. Soft talking. Jane was on the deck talking to the ferryman whose yellow jacket stamped a shape against the night. A cigarette passed from hand to hand above low voices. I didn't think I could move. I didn't want to be awake. I wished she wouldn't share cigarettes with a stranger. She never could resist. At least it wasn't one of our smokes. On a faraway hillside tops of trees flickered from a fire beneath, and I could tell we were still drifting.

She was my wife. We were newlyweds. I tested the words. With all the lawlessness, we had thought the courthouse would be a madhouse. But it was a strangely serene, air-conditioned chamber. We were ushered through the security and set the metal detector off. It turned out to be my suspenders. One delinquent groomed for a court appearance stood near the information desk. We told various guards we were getting married, requesting directions to the proper halls, and their faces softened. They seemed to regard us with awe, our simple union an unapologetically trite, disarming statement of respect for tradition and belief in a kind future. We were a bridge from the sunny comforts of a fast-vanishing past to a future quieter than the neighborhoods twenty blocks north where fires ate corner stores and overturned cars died in pools of their own poisons.

The judge told us that we were to be the last couple to get married. Perhaps he meant that day, but the implication of forever could not have been wholly lost on the man. He had a rounded baldness that seemed a comfort—he seemed as stout, sturdy, and inflexible as one would want an impartial judicial system to be. The guard or bailiff snapped our picture with my camera, although that was not her job, and the judge seemed eager to be frozen in the implied innocence of that photo op.

I got out of the car and managed to stand up on the deck, then leaned against our car, too dizzy to tell whether the ferry was rocking. The wind riffled my hair, light rain fell. "We keep thinking we're going to run aground but we don't," Jane explained, handing me the last of the cigarette. "At every bend," the ferryman added cheerfully. Apparently they weren't worried about diseases. I accepted the butt and its warmth may have chased some of my dizziness away.

A bit of moon flashed momentarily from a gap in the clouds and the river became a wrinkled sheet of light. Black splotches many feet across swam just beneath the surface. The ferryman's raincoat glowed as he leaned over the railing. "It's a dog," the ferryman explained. Any number of dogs swam in my blurred vision. Jane sang to the river, coaxing it with terms of endearment of all sorts. Something about that tilted my mind and I fell asleep leaning there and awoke in a spray of muddy water from a dog shaking itself. It had been swimming in the river and had climbed aboard. Jane was happy at this new pet. I climbed back in the car, pretended briefly to look for something in the glove compartment, to obscure somewhat the fact that I was unable to take command of this tragedy, and fell back asleep. Could dogs carry the virus?

I had unintentionally left my glasses behind evacuating Seattle. Jane had to remain alert while I drove to help me see, which was exhausting for us both. We made it out right before the barricades were erected when the city was quarantined. We did not know which government body was responsible for the quarantine, if any. It took us all night to get to Tacoma. Traffic barely moved, then didn't, then barely moved. Highways changed their course like rivers as drivers took to nearby fields to circumnavigate broken autos. The rains had not yet begun.

The drive was the worst. Somehow we managed to refill the tank once, and wanted to find food, but just had to drive. The news was getting worse and worse, radio stations fewer, somber, terse, without music anymore. Or sometimes happy music played with a conspicuous absence of care—with long silences at the end. Music was no longer programming, but just a sign that the station was still on the air between updates. I was becoming less disturbed by the reports than by their inconsistencies, as each region seemed to be creating its own tragedy. We were five miles outside Portland when the radiator started smoking. We poured seltzer into it and hobbled into town at 45 miles per hour. But the city seemed empty and our friends were nowhere.

We spent the night with Blake, in an apartment he said wasn't his, on a second floor above a record store which was open at midnight and serving free coffee, having a close-out sale, and even accepting provisions. I traded our last full carton of smokes and some cash for some Bowie bootlegs I had never seen listed anywhere, including covers of songs by Jacques Brel, Lou Reed, and, surprisingly, Marc Bolan and David Bowie singing as a duet Iggy Pop's "I Wanna Be Your Dog." I had left my stuff in Seattle, and these records felt like having the beginnings of a home again. I don't think Jane approved, but to me it was vital. For that night it felt as though nothing were wrong. The three of us acted and felt like college kids on an extended weekend. We left Blake with a vague promise to visit him in the Cascades where some mutual friends of ours had begun an intentional community. We weren't even fazed by the rain, which came on like the start of something. We continued south past flooded fields. The day never seemed like day. Over the course of the afternoon the sky changed from light grey to dark grey. The windshield wiper was broken and exposed metal was grinding an arc in the windshield glass. Not confident about our ability to find a replacement, we pulled over and lashed a condom around it with a rubber band, which stopped the grinding but left an arc of lubricant across the windshield.

In contrast to the insane highway situation in Washington we then encountered no one. A field of starving cows. Sometimes menacing clouds of birds would chase our car. A few brave souls kept filling stations going, often accepting only credit card payment at the pump so as not to confront the customer, burning their own gas in generators to keep the electricity going, in the hope that the electronic currency would still be good, or just to help, or even to use up the gas so they would not be bothered. Or sometimes there were signs taped in the window indicating what sort of currency was sought: food, water, aspirin, and others. But soon we crept along the highway not seeing another light save headlights until we got close to the city by the new river. The traffic started to get bad again and we weren't willing to brave another jam, so we left the main road and felt our way east until we found the ferry.

Jane was knocking on the window. Some-
one had made coffee, unbelievably, though not much. Sluggishly I unrolled
the window and she handed me an inch of coffee in the bottom of a styrofoam cup rescued from the trash.

The coffee was made by, I learned, the people in the camper. They were
on a hunting expedition. It was shotgun season and bear season. Nothing
could stop them from their mission. They had thrown open the back of
the camper, set up a rusted gas grill beneath an awning, and were hanging
out by the railing in their muddy camo, pointing with their shotguns at the
treeline, pretending to take potshots at a shaky V of overflying geese.

We were passing a small town on the shore where some festival appeared to be in progress. The breeze smelled wonderful. Slowly I tasted the
coffee and found it perfect. Though there was perhaps less than a demitasse
worth in the cup, I managed to sip it, and found it pleasant looking over
the river in the gently rocking car. In a slow rain a Ferris wheel was being
assembled on a hillside. Near a small and crumbling pier that stretched into
the water, a cluster of flags of all kinds hung from poles impaled in the mud.
Many countries were represented, as well as rainbows, pirate flags with
skulls, and even a few flags that appeared commercial in nature. There were
an orange Halloween flag, a green Christmas flag, a state flag, and others
representing organizations or locations unknown. It seemed like a festival
of affiliation, the township wanting to present an open ambassadorship to
the river. Though nobody was in sight but carnival workers, the effect was
welcoming. Jane took the small American flag from the bow of the ferry
and waved it about, either to hail them or to join in the festivities. It was
no longer about whatever the flag stood for anymore. Up in the bridge, the
ferrymen had taken an interest and seemed to be discussing ways of getting
the attention of the workers on the hill. Given the crisis, it was odd to see
able-bodied workers being used to set up stands and rides instead of white
tents. Odd, somehow calming, and though it seemed the men might be
persuaded to interrupt their work to help rescue the ferry, it wasn't clear
how to communicate with them. A colorful, rickety wooden train seemed
to be their mode of locomotion; it was doubtful that they had any boats,
trucks, or winches. I saw on the floor of the car the bottle of water we used
for the leaky radiator and took a sip. Jane had taken all the trash in the car
and spread it on the back seat: a stack of neatly refolded soiled napkins,
used paper cups rinsed in riverwater and set upside down to dry. I wasn't
sure riverwater wasn't worse than coffee residue but regardless I loved her
for her thoughtful touches.

She had left for me on the dashboard the gift of an entire M&M sitting on a napkin emblazoned with a lipstick-scrawled heart. I fell upon this feast with the utmost delicacy, my heart a fizzy riot of gratitude.

In the cabin the white-shirted ferryman held a radio to his mouth. The other ferryman had binoculars.

Jane was standing by the railing, studying the carnival. "Central Park," she read.

"Is that the name of the town? Or the fairground?" I asked.

She didn't answer. I got out of the car and opened the road atlas on the railing. My eyes searched for the words *Central Park*. But which direction were we floating? The sky offered us no orientation, only a shell of cloud.

The shotgun blast was like being struck in the head. A plume of smoke the shape of an exclamation point dissipated downwind from where one of the hunters stood. A bird fell in the water in a stream of feathers. The dog yelped and plunged in after it.

My ears ringing, I was having trouble reading the small blue-on-blue type. I steadied the page as close to my face as I could while holding it in focus, hoping the letterforms would reveal themselves, but ink glyphs swam in front of my blinking eyes until tears made me give up. Inside the glass box, the ferryman in white spoke into a handheld microphone attached to a coiling cable, his eyes trained on the bank as if he could see who he was talking to. He put the handset down, lit a cigarette, saw us looking at him, put out the cigarette, and came down the ladder.

"On the radio I got through to that carnival. At least I'm pretty sure that's who I was talking to. They say they're sending down a clown in a motorboat with a coil of rope."

"A clown?" Jane repeated.

"Why doesn't the clown bring fuel?" I asked. "Why a rope?"

The ferryman stared at me. Then he walked back to the ladder and climbed it. We watched as he said something into his radio, eyes fixed on the shore.

Jane took my arm, smiling, and pressed herself against me. Help was on the way. She loved clowns. Maybe this would be a fun road trip after all.

The dog had retrieved the waterfowl, but refused to relinquish it, backing away from the hunters, growling with its ears lowered, the duck's head dragging on the deck. A hunter in a down vest raised his hand as if to slap the dog and the dog winced and dropped the bird. I turned away. I just hoped they wouldn't discharge the guns anymore.

We built a fire out of maps of the Cascades and scraps of wood that had washed up on the ramp, and tried to heat a can of soup. This didn't work so instead we turned on the engine and set the soup on top of it. This took several minutes, but worked, and we shared the can of steaming goodness with the ferrymen, even passing the same fork. The SUV people eyed us uneasily. Jane gestured for them to come out and share the meal but they would not, turning to each other to explain why. Should I bother mentioning that the soup was the best thing I had eaten in my life? I had no idea how many hours it had been since my M&M. After we had all distributed the final scraps of food, Jane finished scraping the inside of the can with her fingers and licked them while the ferrymen and I pretended not to watch.

The hunters played cards at a folding table. They were using shotgun shells and poker chips, and their guns lay on the deck at their feet. Scabbards hung from their belts. Wisps of smoke rose from their outdoor grill where the duck was roasting.

It wasn't until sundown that we heard the boat. We had each, I think, privately given up on the clown, but now, cutting through a current turned orange by sunset beneath the clouds, came a tiny boat beside whose outboard motor sat a man in festive pantaloons and wig, his red rubber nose hanging around his neck on a string. Without slowing, he powered right up onto the ramp and cut the engine. His shoes made slapping noises on the deck as he lashed his boat to one of the iron hasps.

"You out of gas?" the clown asked, strapping on his nose.

"Yeah," the reflective ferryman nodded.

"You tried siphoning some from these vehicles?"

"No, not yet," the ferryman said, looking around as if noticing the cars for the first time.

"I'm about out so after I save ya you gotta give me gas for the trip back. We have a carnival tonight," he added, squinting upstream. "And I'm taking all the money," he winked, though the eye that had winked was crying, shedding plump painted tears. The other eye was smiling, surrounded by four black marks arranged like the points on a compass. Jane knelt to whisper to the dog, who looked up gratefully as she scratched its ears. They did not like this clown. The ferryman did not respond to the clown's demand. I was tempted to ask the clown whether he was serious about the money, but didn't see how I could get a straight answer. The man driving the Lexus SUV leaned over to say something to his wife, who appeared asleep, but with her dark glasses it was impossible to tell.

The clown handed me the end of a rope that trailed into a coil in his boat. "Don't lose it. I'm going to the bank to lash it to something." And he pushed his craft back in the water, tripping on his shoes, and hopped on board. He honked his nose, put his foot on the gunwale, and pulled the cord to start the outboard. But the outboard only sputtered. Meanwhile the ferryman had relieved me of the rope and with a professional flourish had lashed it to the hasp on the deck. Drifting away from us, the clown jerked feverishly on the starter, rocking convulsively with each yank, sending ripples away from his boat, muttering violently profane curses, but the engine refused to turn over.

"Island coming up," one of the ferrymen said. We all turned to what lay downstream. Banded with stripes of rippling refractions stood trees the closest we had seen since leaving shore. A small wooded island perhaps 300 feet long and 20 feet wide. At first I thought we were going to run ashore, then the ferry seemed to run into some obstruction beneath the water, tilted a bit, and began to turn away from the island, rolling around whatever lay beneath. Meanwhile, the clown's boat had disappeared around the other side of the island, the rope between us sliding out of the water up the roots of the trees. The ferryman looked at the splendid knot he had just made, cocked his hat back and stared at the island, then knelt as if to see things from the rope's point of view. I moved next to him in case any suggestions came to mind. The clown must have tied it to something, but why? The rope sprang taut, the ferry swung across the current, the rope singing and whittling bits of bark from the tree with the strain put on it, and we came aground in the muck, the current lapping at the ferry's sides and rocking it more than it had been.

"Land ho," Jane said. The ferryman smiled slightly. A sudden crashing in the underbrush revealed life on the island. We peered into the thick shrubbery anxiously, then recognized the wig approaching us. The clown stepped onto the muddy bank, threw his arms wide, and said, "You're saved."

"This is an island," the ferryman explained. "We need to get to the bank." The clown stood there, arms still outstretched, as the smile beneath his painted mouth faded, and his eyes widened. He tried to step back, but his feet had sunk too far into the mud and he fell with a splat. He struggled to stand up, falling twice, turning the back of his colorful outfit brown. "Hey," the other ferryman said, leaning out of his booth, "is that your boat?" He pointed downstream where a small hull floated away. The clown ran after it, flailing his arms, losing his shoes in the muck.

"I'm going to cut us free," the ferryman shouted after him. The response was unintelligible as the clown went splashing and crashing along the edge of the island, then dove into the water. The ferryman knelt and worked at undoing his knot. Finally, the rope fell slack in the mud, but the ferry did not move. A rumble of thunder came from the west and the last sliver of cherry sun disappeared.

One of the ferrymen leapt into the murk and struggled to push the enormous craft away from the shore, grinding himself ankle-deep. Kicking huge clumps of mud from his boots, he wandered into the island and returned with a small tree, which he handed up to the other ferryman, who trimmed off its limbs and then tried to use it to pole the ferry free, but no matter what rock he tried to push off of, it would sink into the mud. The first ferryman climbed on board trimming another tree and began to work beside his partner, pushing at the island, but the ferry was stuck. A wind kicked up and it began to rain harder.

Back in the car, Jane had a packet of ketchup and a packet of mustard. We ate them in silence. You never really appreciate ketchup or mustard, we agreed. These inane thoughts brought a weak anesthesia. The evening was moonless and before long it began to rain really terribly hard.

The car was sinking. I woke into a fierce storm. Jane's hand was wrapped around mine; though she lay still I knew she was awake. Water poured over us. We rocked as the swollen river pummeled the stuck barge.

"You know what's weird," she said.

I smiled in the dark. What wasn't?

"No," I whispered.

"Those two never came out of the Lexus."

Lightning lit the deck like headlights. Grinning as he looked into our eyes through a face that was a smear, arms outspread, a man with streaming orange hair shouted the first syllable of "Singin' in the Rain." Jane and I screamed. The clown continued to sing in the darkness. I hated him.

I should have been putting on fat instead of taking it off, Jane said. She was talking in her sleep. I rubbed my eyes. It was dark. We were still in the car again. I had awoken from worried dreams, in which I had been at the center of a number of events that had gone unexplainably wrong. I touched my face. I had a fever of some kind and felt dizzy.

The rain had not subsided, the sun had not really come out, it was not clear what time of day it was. The car clock was dark. I had dreamed that a dinging brought me awake and I had disconnected the battery in the rain to make the car stop worrying. The car seemed tilted and when I opened the door to the cold breeze and stood up unsteadily I discovered we were moving again through a thick fog, and that the ferry seemed to have taken on water, or lost a support, and was floating low and at a tilt. As I leaned against the car, trying to make out any details about the shapes we were passing, to my astonishment the clown crawled out from under our car, where he had apparently slept.

It seemed to be a row of stoned out warehouses that passed on the bank through thick wisps of fleece. The river rode high, covered with debris the flood had brought down. The clown climbed over the gate and, standing ankle deep on the ramp, reached into his boat, extracted a green fedora from the bilge water, shook it out, and tried it on. He came back and inspected himself, kneeling before the side mirror.

"Check this out," he said to me, still looking at himself, pulling out of the back of his pantaloons my atlas, bent backward on its spine to hold open a particular page. Had he been rummaging in my car? He pointed. "This next bridge is the last before river A joins this older river over here, see, and then it just gets wider, miles across, and then I'm never going to be able to save you, so I'm going to try to snag us on that bridge," he said, holding up a bouquet of metal that I gradually realized was an anchor of some kind, tied to a new rope.

"Why?" I asked.

The clown appeared stung by that. I realized he had retouched his makeup with axle grease. "Well I don't care if I save you anymore. You guys are too much trouble. I just want my money." With that the clown honked, touched the sagging brim of his soggy hat, and left me. After a few moments, the dog stood beside me looking up with soft eyes. But I ignored it.

I saw the ferryman in white talking through the SUV window to the man with the sunglasses, who was shaking his head no. I saw his wife in the passenger seat leaning over her right shoulder. I followed her gaze, walking around to the other side of my car, and saw the other ferryman kneeling by their gas tank with a hose and a rag and a large plastic cup. He stood up and came around: "It's locked." The first ferryman looked in the window at the man behind the SUV's driver's wheel, who eyed him nervously and made a gesture of impatient resignation somewhere between an angry shrug and a curtsey. The hunters were conferring between themselves. One of them glanced in our direction, and opened his rifle, cleaning it. The dog saw this and began to circle me, excited.

Jane, meanwhile, was leaning toward the SUV window, acting as the ferrymen's interpreter, over-enunciating as though to a deranged deaf mute, "We need your gas, to start the ferry's engine, to get us to a road. Here's an apple, I'll just put it on your hood, and back away. Wouldn't you rather have an apple than gasoline?" she gestured incredulously and backed away. The ferrymen had also brought offerings: half a sandwich wrapped in a grease-stained napkin, an unopened bag of Andy Capp's Hot Fries, a tin of Curiously Strong Altoids, and other treasures I coveted. I glanced at my own gas tank and saw it was open and had already been siphoned. The couple in the SUV appeared to be arguing in heated whispers. And then a few drops announced the beginning of another rain.

Sadly I returned to my driver's seat, but even as the drops fell both the ferrymen and the clown were continuing to heap offerings across the windshield of the SUV—a great deal of food and other objects. On the deck, a bowling ball sat inside a spare tire. Rivulets streaked my windows and I missed Jane. I heard her laugh and wished she would get in the car. I considered the possibility that a leak in the trunk was allowing the records to get wet. I then came awake with the fear that Jane might try to offer my records to the SUV people. I tried to remember where the keys to our car were. They were in my coat pocket.

I heard a shot and the dog started barking. I felt I should go out in the rain but waited. Jane didn't return for a long while, and when she did, she brought, unbelievably, instead of grim news, a paper plate of hot food and a spork to eat it with. I wondered whether we had been rescued. Very seriously, and very wet, she tore open and unwrapped a moist towlette, placing it in the lap of her soaked jeans like a napkin, and carefully cut loose a bite of food and held it to me, a steaming lump of meat held in the curvature of the plastic implement. I opened my mouth and raised my eyebrows. Jane spoke without much enthusiasm, and I realized she was exhausted. "The hunters shot down a couple of ducks, and grilled them. They really know what they're doing," she added, blowing a wet lock away from her eye. "Maybe I should invite them to New Mexico."

Twenty feet above the deck, the clown stood on the roof of the cabin among searchlights and antennae, and as we passed under the bridge, with incredible strength he heaved his grappling hook, now decorated with feathers, onto the bridge. We heard what sounded like broken glass. The clown kicked the coil down to the deck and the ferryman lashed the rope to the hasp with practiced movements. As the slack left the rope, it lifted into the air, stretched taut, moaning, turning the ferry around into the current. The ferryman stood back from the knot, but it held, and the ferry began bouncing gently. I looked around. Despite the clown's loud exhibition of victory, it was not clear what we had gained. The listing ferry was now stuck in the middle of the river, and a taut rope stretched up to an unreachable bridge. I tried to think about what I would do if the ferry overturned, but found I could not think about that.

The clown jumped up and down on the cabin roof cheering, and the pilot looked up at him, annoyed that he would behave so recklessly around the aerials. The clown jumped all the way down to the deck, somersaulted, did a cartwheel, and scampered up the rope, soon hailing us from the bridge above. "Can you pull us to shore?" Jane called up. The clown shrugged and disappeared, reappeared to give Jane an angry wave of dismissal, and was gone. We watched the bridge for a further sign of him, but only a paper airplane floated across the sky, circled, and came to rest on the SUV's hood. They turned on their windshield wipers as if to dislodge it.

I stood beneath the rope, doubtful about my ability to climb it. What I needed was to get the car to shore. There had been no traffic on the bridge.

The hunters must have been asleep in their camper. Their coolers sat along the railing and I wondered if they had more to eat. The ferrymen were arguing. One of them was gesturing with a knife. I gathered that they disagreed about whether to wait for the clown. The bow of the ferry was riding very high, the ramp accumulated brush that had been heading downriver, including an intact plastic chair. I wondered whether to bring it up on deck, I would have liked to sit, but that would have meant resigning myself to the possibility of being stuck on the ferry. The water now touched the tires of the camper. "But he's an...asshole!" shouted the ferryman with the jacket, and the other had no rejoinder so they stood there and let the word "asshole" rebound from the cliffs.

Jane retrieved the chair. Both ferrymen watched her and suddenly were looking intently upriver. There was some kind of craft coming towards us. As it turned so its side faced us I realized it was a riverboat casino floating free. Its hull was garish purple and green, painted with slogans. A chartreuse martini glass cupped a pair of dice.

I stood by my car. If it were to sink, there wouldn't be much I could salvage. The records, or at least their sleeves, would be more or less destroyed on contact with water. The dog shook itself on me again. Above me, the railing on the deck of the riverboat hit the rope, briefly lifted the ferry almost out of the water, and then the anchor lost its purchase and fell onto the casino. The ferry came splashing down, sending a sheet of water across the deck, I fell to my knees, and we were going downriver again, now tethered to a massive decadent riverboat.

Surrounding the riverboat was a network of driftwood and floating debris tangled in string, including a rowboat whose oars moved in the current, creaking their oarlocks. I thought I saw the slick black form of a rodent creeping along a branch.

The ferrymen climbed the ladder to the roof of their cabin and crossed onto the deck of the riverboat. Jane and I followed. Climbing the ladder made me dizzy. From this vantage we looked down on our car and the water lapping near it. Stepping across was difficult. The deck of the riverboat was painted bright green and covered with a scatter of cards and poker chips which stuck to our shoes as we walked. Behind a bar I discovered a tap that still worked and I cheered and poured everybody plastic cups of beer. The hunters took a table and picked up some chairs and dealt me into a poker game, but I quickly learned they were allowing hands I was unfamiliar with, so I recused myself. For a moment everybody seemed to be enjoying themselves, then a long strange sound made everybody quiet and we all stared out over the roulette wheels, card tables, dark slot machines.

The riverboat lurched, causing all the chips to slide across the floor at once with a frightening hiss. We ran to the deck to see what had happened. The SUV and camper were gone. They had rolled into the river. The gates at the stern swung open and broken. The clown, who I thought we were rid of, stood on the roof of my car, waving his arms as if to attract the attention of the people underwater, so they would know which way to swim. He was making noises.

Then a surge from within me sent a splatter of regurgitation down into the water.

After we cut loose the riverboat and its snarl of detritus, it fell behind us. The hunters had stayed on the riverboat. The clown had not. The river swept through wide curves over scraping gravel and beneath grasping branches. We passed a turtle city, a curl in the river where the accumulation of half-submerged logs, trunks, and rootwads was pimpled with shells, sometimes extending necks, other times rear legs hanging off logs. As we approached, they squinted impassively, then kicked themselves into the water, flying into the green deeps, banking low over a floor of stones.

A few hundred feet ahead, where the wide river bent to the right, a gap had opened in the bank to the left. A new channel was forming; floating leaves moved toward it. A thunder of water was shearing away the bank on either side in slices many feet thick. A tree toppled into the rush, roots pulling a cluster of earth with it. As we were swept into the new channel, we looked down a staircase of deep water that was already caving in the bank beneath a house, sucking away a picket fence. A horse tossed its mane and backed away from the opening earth. We slid down this muddy torrent beneath the collapsing floor of the house. I did not believe I looked up and saw a family hanging from ropes tied around their necks, their bodies seeming to stretch down.

I wondered whether we had just passed into another river. The ferry brushed by a gravel spit that stretched from the eastern bank. In an impulsive move I jumped in my car, started it, and drove through the broken gates onto the bank, immediately stuck in the gravel where spinning the wheels just seemed to dig the car deeper. Jane stood uncertainly beside the car. The clown dragged his boat off the ferry and into the shallow water, where he stood, holding it steady.

The ferrymen watched us sadly from their tilting cabin as their sloping craft disappeared downstream. We decided Jane would ride downriver with the clown and look for a way to get down to the shoreline. I would stay with the car, lodged in a bank of silt. I was having second thoughts about staying behind though. Jane's eyes and mine were locked in desperate negotiation when the clown honked impatiently and did a kind of splashdance. I wasn't sure I understood. Hunger had made me incapable. She was shivering and I gave her my coat.

She climbed into the tiny motorboat while the clown pushed it off, hopping in. It rocked slightly as the current pulled it away. Jane kept her eyes on the opposite bank as they went around the bend and were gone. Then I remembered that the car keys were in my coat pocket.

After I sat on the trunk for some time shivering in the wind, I became aware that the noise I heard could not be the wind. I decided I would try to walk downstream to see whether I could find Jane.

After a mile of picking my way through rocks and vines and mud, I came to the edge of a waterfall that emptied out hundreds of feet below in a foaming rocky pool. Below me, the land turned to desert and the river found its muddy way south. Squinting into the brightness below I made out the form of a colorful figure sprawled across the rocks. A dead clown. When I looked up I saw Jane across the river, staring at me. I stared back, and meant to raise my arm, but she turned into the woods and was gone.

That is all I remember and all of the paper. In the trunk of this vehicle you will find records. Keep them dry.

Over a thousand of us are dying in this hospital. The air is filled with coughing, sputtering, moaning, muttering, and uncomfortable silences. A generator consumes a dwindling supply of gasoline, providing a weak light. I am one of the lucky ones—I have a room and am dying of natural causes. Tending to me is almost a relief for the handful of strung-out medical practitioners in respirator masks attempting to treat the treatable, which they do through the judicious use of sedatives, administered through hypodermics they conscientiously sterilize even though the air in this place is a cauldron of infectious death. We all know that the best treatment would be to bolt the doors from the outside and burn the place to the ground with the patients in it. But they keep trying to help. I seem to be in and out a lot, sometimes looking down at myself from the ceiling, sometimes looking up at it from my bed, and other times in other places none of us have been.

Max comes through the twin glass doors into the lobby, his white beard marking him as someone who fell asleep in the nineteen sixties and never woke up. He is barefoot, overweight, wearing overalls, his left hand clutching a collection of wilting wildflowers, from his right hangs a battered thermos of whiskey and miso soup.

Attracting no attention whatsoever from the diseased who cover the chairs and floors, slump in wheelchairs, or loll on gurneys, he stumbles down the no longer immaculate white hallway, his feet silent on icy white tiles. He stops outside room 195, knocks once, thinks about that, decides nobody would allow him to enter, and enters. Before him, in bed, tubes running out of every joint, eyes shut, body quivering as the lung machine does its business, am I, the comatose Ms. Winchester. I hardly look pallid at all in the blue-green glow of the life support machines.

He sits down in a chair. On a small table beside my bed are some scattered pills, and he absentmindedly takes one, chews it, makes a face, unscrews the thermos, and lifts it to his lips.

"Hmm," he remarks of his never-washed thermos, wiping his mouth with the back of one sleeve, "it hardly tastes like coffee at all. I brought you some flowers. Almost dead. Kind of appropriate. I know you said you didn't want to talk to me anymore, but…. You don't have to say anything." He gestures to the jury of flashing, blinking, and thinking machines. "I brought a poem."

He unfolds a typewritten page.

Illiterally

For decades the ruling elite had been using media to control the interpretation of truth. But after people caught on, unable, in an open society, to control what is considered true, they instead chose to challenge *the very idea of truth*. Reality exists, but we are losing the words that point to it.

For example, the brand *Real Orange Drink*, whose fine print reads *less than one percent orange juice*. Or RNN—the *Real News Network*, which broadcasts almost no footage, just carefully-edited computer simulations. *Reality television*.

Literally once meant *as opposed to metaphorically*. Now it means *totally*, as in *it's colder than hell—literally."*

The copulative *to be* is a slippery pest and difficult to eradicate. In the sixties, CIA agents planted in the counterculture attempted to make it a noun: *Be-ins*, during which the troublesome youth were meant to take hallucinogens and behave inauthentically.

Conversely, some things that might be considered authentic are given labels to suggest they are simulations. The capitol of Rhode Island is now called *Historic Providence*. Scare quotes have become scarier.

Our means of referring to the world are being taken away, and our world with them.

The sky was as blue as sky blue paint, begins a successful poem of the day.

This is not what he needs to be telling me now.

He rises to unsteady feet, feels his way to the bed, and crawls in beside me. I feel the dirty warmth of his denim, the coldness of his bare feet, and the way his body sags the mattress, drawing me into its gravity.

He lived in a world already at its maximum level of chaos, stupidity, and insanity, so the end was more of the same to an alienated old man in a house with a couple marijuana plants. Max, I am ready to die now. You go home. Leave the back door propped open so the dog can get out, re-read the three books that mean the most to you, call Claude Reagan's cellphone and leave a haiku, put on Mozart's *Requiem,* retrieve the old drugs you hoard in the basement freezer, your favorite chocolates, and your best bourbon, your investigation of the language having run the course of alphanumerics leaving you with only Zs and zeros trickling off into the silence that nobody hears, recline the chair, and surrender to the final absence of babble.

Guys we gotta get underground. It was I who said that did. Before we got to the point where we couldn't tell whether we were saying and hearing words or just hearing things or communicating by mind somehow or just hallucinating. We were all a bit muzzy, invisible insects got us that way as I tried to explain to Eric and Iain. They couldn't care. All they could talk about was cigarettes. Give it a rest guys, I would say to no avail, you don't have to worry about getting lung cancer anymore. Nobody got it, I don't think. They don't get me, I don't get them. But I would rather be with them than alone. Even walking to Vancouver after the Big One dropped. *Especially* walking to Vancouver about a week after the Big One dropped. Fuck, I mean. I've been slightly confused these past few days, but I know which way north is. I know the difference between I-5 and poison, dusty flats. Frozen furrows sluiced in drizzle. Goddamn, I don't even smoke cigarettes. Not really. *Yet*, they would say. They would be right too. Cigarettes, as I didn't know then, walking through the long dead border post, were a rope that hung down the well of insanity. People fighting for the circle of light overhead could climb free of the insane murk, climb upward towards motivation towards sanity towards purity of thought: toward Canada to get more cigarettes. Guys, I still don't know much, I would say, continuing a sentence I had begun the previous day, but I can guess well and I think the following: I think that Vancouver was most likely in all probability hit pretty badly, and also that its contamination will not die down as quickly as we can walk there, and it was true, the two of them were keeping a steady pace and at this statement they laughed, they were incessantly giddy, I do believe they enjoyed the delirium. *Viruseses*, Iain cited knowledgably. Aw, most likely in any event, Eric responded nasally and they choked on hysteria for many minutes, replaying the comic highpoints of my concerns. I thought they seemed convinced that the problem was nuclear radiation rather than contamination and I was trying to put it in those terms. I thought again, playing to demand their attention more than anything else. How about this, I started. Ah! they indicated, laughing. You think Vancouver is going to be fine even though Seattle has gone to shit. Because what— because you think the Canadians all have health care and they're fine and who would want to terrorize them anyway so it's fine but you're committing the Canada Fallacy. The Canada Fallacy is where you assume that any social problem in the U.S. doesn't exist in Canada. See, I don't think you two will be the only two in Vancouver looking for cigarettes. I mean, I don't think you two us three will be the only ones in Vancouver, looking for this international tobacco warehouse you claim is there, unless Vancouver is truly contaminated, a hot zone. I paused for breath, amazed at my articulate manipulation for they were slowing to better hear and comprehend, moving to either side of me in fact. I think we were passing some bank, the money kind not the river kind. They were each furrowed in thought. Severe, detailed, analytical, capitulatory reconsideration, or so I thought. Eric? Iain finally queried to Eric who was on my right. Eh? Would you kill for cigarettes? Yeah! Eric snorted, mockingbird mustang Marlboro man scientific Eric. No, Eric restated a second later. Okay, Iain said, accepting his answer. Derek, would you? I thought about all the available sarcastic twists on all the convenient replies for a second, then, suddenly weary, replied no. Okay, Iain said, neither would I. But Eric? Yo. Would you give a hundred men who were dying from radiation sickness, viruseses, and leprosy head for cigarettes? And all exploded into mirth again. I gave up at that point, realized that these two were going to let nothing ruin their deaths, and perhaps that that was not at all a poor attitude to take. Nothing, rather that is, except the absence of cigarettes. Why not? It worked all right with life. Seemed to. Turned out life was a hoax anyway, a hoax which, ultimately, only the three of us refused to believe in. Those of us who worked in kitchens, who didn't save up any money, me and Iain, knew what was up, we were waiting it out. Well, Iain was in prison, so he was being made to wait it out, though he was allowed to come to the restaurant to work, and what he did that day was not go back to the work-release center when the curfew was imposed, when the phones went dead, when a few of us closed the restaurant and lived there for many days, a long time, we didn't know how long because it had no windows, but we ran out of smokes. I capsized with sighs and broke into a jog to catch up with them. Later, Iain put it in perspective a little bit, saying Derek, the factory we are walking to is in *a really bad neighborhood*, so... he lapsed, unable to finish. Eric did, about fifteen seconds later with, so we really don't have to worry whether it's dangerous. I had been caught in the Canada Fallacy. I didn't know Vancouver had neighborhoods. *Viri*, not *viruseses*, I corrected. Somehow then we refined the art of sleepwalking to the point where we could fall asleep while walking rather than the other-wayaround. It saved time. For the past few weeks the division between asleep and awake had been flexible as well as transparent and conductive of heat sound and electricity, sitting down, lying up, walking asleep. Coffee. I spoke suddenly with assurance, waking myself up walking down an exit ramp. Apparently I woke up Eric as well, for he said, where? We don't know where it is yet, Eric, but we know where it's going: to Vancouver with us. In us. Iain was gradually, as we all were, losing his ability to form well sentences good. But he explained some miles ago that the three of us had an unfair advantage, practiced, as we were, in the art of remaining lucid under adverse conditions of physical and psychological duress. I understood from whence he came. Eric didn't. Apparently Eric hadn't realized that those days were just practice. Practice for the real thing. But Iain was now on my wavelength, lean wolf hip to the hot scent of stimulants smoldering in styrofoam, the lusty coffee taste of cup uprooted and guzzled to the thick black dregs, quivering on the lip, then oozing down the inside, sliding in luscious caffeinated bittersplendor into one's maw, wet with eagerness, or so we discussed until Eric was showing some vague stirrings of enthusiasm, a heartbeat. We were too giddy to tell, Iain and I, breathless with anticipation of the hot fabric available anywhere. Where? Rather: when? No, where? Eric was whining, doubtful, uncomfortable.... A thought struck me like a metal projectile: coffee was only going to sustain our enthusiasm, and that only for a short while. It seemed an idea of doubtful goodness to drink coffee (ah thou perfect beverage coffee nestled gently within thou insulatory cup of immaculate white) and then discontinue drinking it. To drink it, and then not to drink it. It was a terrifying thought, but then another thought struck me. This one I chose to spout, at once, prying it into Eric's attention: Eric? Mm? Eric, coffee is good food Eric. Ah, Iain laughed, it is that. Fast food. Eric glowered: just get me to the cigarettes and I shall don my chipper expression. Get me there and I shall smoke one cigarette for each of you to show you my gratitude. And one for yourself? I inquired innocently. No. A hundred cartons for myself. We were all fully awake now, the imagined texture of nicotine sliding like a thatched snake down and up the throat, expulsions of smoke blossoming from breathing lips, nostrils. Shafts of light, enough to restore Eric's higher psychological functions. Coffee, I said again, this time pointing to the top of an interchange somewhere in the sprawling borderlands where the interstate is paved with lodging gas food phone opportunities for the restless. I was pointing at the shattered shell of a convenience store, where were the words, aflame with irony, OPEN 24 HOURS. But none of us acknowledged the joke. Down to our last candy wrapper. We were silent, as we climbed the hill, with the serene realization that we had not encountered a single human being since we fell upon our boss's, the owner of our restaurant's, house with cans of luminescent spraypaint. And that was days after the outbreak was announced. We saw him move the curtain. We had been walking to Vancouver ever since. The first days in the restaurant we heard much traffic. I stepped through the shattered doorframe and inside. What I saw looked unpromising. Eric and Iain stepped in through the window and we three just stood there for a while, saying nothing. It was strange indeed to see a store so brutally stripped as this one had been. All shelves were bare, even the MAGAZINES had been lifted. I spotted the silver coffee machine in the corner and it looked as if someone had hammered it to pieces. I toed my way forwards across the glass-scattered floor over to the SELF-SERVE BEVERAGE STATION. There was little there, but, opening the cupboard doors below, I found two red packages labeled to my unprecedented delight FOLGERS FOLGERS FOLGERS. I laughed, in fact, wept, holding them, in my psychic fits of hunger delirium weariness I had never clung to something that felt that powerful, something I felt could raise my consciousness above the physiological turmoil, I.... Come on Derek, Iain was saying gently, there's no water. No pot to boil it in. I was stunned, but only for a second as I noticed Eric, glumly across the store behind the counter, searching for smokes, and, recalling days of what seemed at the time to be declining innocence, in a wild inspiration I clutched spasmodically at the boxes above the coffee machine. Stirrers, Nutra-Sweet, and straws spilled across the aluminum counter. Straws. We've got straws, I declared enigmatically but with genuine enthusiasm clearing none of Iain's doubts about my sanity, but he was too tired to react in any way. Not even a fucking box of Virginia Slims! Eric's distraught voice fell across the room to us. Iain was now kneeling carefully, his huge frame absorbed in the shadows beneath the shelves where he had discovered three cans on the floor, dented, unopened, and labelless. Eric was kicking the cash register, it protesting in ringing bell mechanisms and crunching parts. I had succeeded in tearing a package of Folgers crystals open and was arranging the delicate brown substance on the aluminum countertop, into even rows. Fucking a yes kick ass Iain sputtered, rising to his shoes holding two opened cans, the other one may be Alpo, but this one is Campbell's Tomato Soup and this one is...unidentified. He held up a plastic fork and a wet substance gleamed unenthusiastically in the slanting morning vague glow oozing from the grey south. Which necessarily means it's caviar. Steak, Eric called, then an unexpected ho! as his kick dislodged the cash register and sent it spinning to the floor on the other side. He walked around to crouch and inspect it. I tore the paper off one end of a straw and then put the exposed straw to my lips, blew. The paper missile missed Iain by many feet, spiraled unnoticed to the floor. Hey Eric, Iain cried, toss me your Swedish army knife. Eric replied in astonishment, no longer visible crouching behind the counter, hey, this thing's filled with money! He stood up, beaming, fists filled with bills. We're rich! he cried, all our problems are solved. We can buy a tobacco plantation now. Sure Eric, Iain said uncertainly, a bit taken aback by this unprecedented display of manic zeal from laconic Eric. I took my first snort. Reality cascaded. I looked up at them, dull smile escalating, left nostril streaked with brown, and they were laughing hysterically. They understood the game now. They were on the scent. We snorted laughed ate left, leaving exactly one mutilated packet of FOLGERS coffee grounds, one straw wrapper, three clean cans, and many small bills scattered about, stirring in the wind. Tasting freedom for once and for good and uncertain how to respond. We could not see the skyline from any distance, even a block away, in the uninterrupted fog. It was like arriving in a new city by subway, invisibly. We discussed it, our conversation like a depot with trains constantly arriving later than their connections, which had left going the other way to look for them, and concurred that elevators were probably out of order. Fortunately, we did not have to explore that thought in any more detail. We were looking for the proper exit from the highway. By the time we found it, and walked slowly up a broad cloverleaf until we were facing southeast, the sun was probably setting. It was hard to tell. The sky had become translucent rather than transparent. Ug, I believe someone said at some point, sentiments we all shared. Vancouver was dead. I thought I heard harmonica distant but when I tried to comment on it I realized I was asleep or was I? It was relative. There was a flickering light up ahead. We were approaching it soundlessly and because I believed I was asleep I believed that I could do nothing to slow my walking, I would follow the other two. There were people then, gyrating across the light, causing it to appear to blink. Undulating flame of light. People encircled the fire dancing casting shadows like spokes across our eyes.... I get the feeling at this point that we all wanted to talk to one another very badly but could not. We could only let our feet drag us closer to the voices ahead. Iain! I heard someone say. It seemed quite appropriate. People were surrounding us, I felt an unreal sensation, watching this played out around me: kick ass, Iain said quietly, Jeff, Lisa, Wendy. I knew Jeff. The two of us took hands, each smiling knowing, unreal smiles, as if we were too dumbstruck to whisper we knew this meeting would happen and we still didn't believe it, shook and released them. Lisa and Wendy, this is Eric and Derek, hello hi hey Eric how are you Jeff hi Eric and Derek. Iain always said he'd bring you guys up here. These are my friends from WSU. So where's Marianne right now? She's in Manhattan, the phone...yes. Sorry. (Careful hugs.) Wendy, would you believe that I walked here from Seattle just to kiss you? (Laughter.) Derek! You wouldn't have...have even.... Are you all right Iain? Eric, in a restrained, urgent voice: I really need a smoke. Fuck right Eric let's go. Goodbye Iain...should have known we'd run into you guys here. We all stopped dead on the loading platform in disbelief. Cy was sitting there, staring with puzzled intent at a circular iron draingrate in the concrete. He looked up at us. It seemed like he looked up at us twice but he was unable to fixate his gaze and his vision traced a ring of vague recognition around us. He raised two fingers shakily as if a peace sign, but that was not what it meant. Twosheets he slurred. How many days ago? I asked pointedly, but apparently that was all he needed to say to us. His vision traced an uncertain line back to the grate and he resumed sitting, drifting in every direction at once. We walked past him, into the gaping rectangle of black, the loading door. It is not very bright at all in there, I said needlessly. We proceeded slowly. Seeing Cy was very disturbing, but he looked oddly at peace. Fucked-up, but at peace. He had been wearing a suit I realized. Had he? I wasn't sure whether he was my hallucination or me his. Eric tripped over something resonant and metallic, cursed, stumbled. I'm going to smoke my very first cigarette, with chums Eric and Derek at my sides, through my eyes, Iain explained to the darkness. Eric began: I'm going to put one in each of my nostrils and one in each of my ears and ten in my mouth and one in my ass. We had begun to, one by one, descend a metal staircase. I'm just going to bum a hit off one of Eric's I offered. Back to the days of seemingly declining innocence and back in a lightning flash of insight that demonstrates in a sense exactly what amazingly, astoundingly, staggeringly innocent delinquents we actually were back then, because nothing we did to our minds or bodies was as bad as what was to come, that makes me want to scream and howl but I grab the stairway tight and forcefeed myself a couple of breaths. I had to speak, my friends were only perceivable as rubber soles scraping rung growing fainter below me. Society mishandled us, I begin, almost shouting, Society mishandled the respective cases of Giles, Eric, known to most as Eric; Wyld, Derek K.; and Curtis, Iain...X. Whatever. *First* they show us what there is in life that's thoroughly, thoroughly graspable. *Then* they tell you that you cannot have it. *And then* they say maybe you can take it anyway, if you cut meat. *And then?* No reply. *And?* Eric: Iain there's no floor. Huh? I'm on the lowest rung. *Then?* Then what, Derek? *I'm glad you asked that, Iain!* Whuddo I do? Jump. Jump? Jump or I will push you. Okey Dokey.... I was still at the top of the stairway, a distance away, and found myself voiceless to continue. Then they destroy everything and expect you to feel responsible...I whispered, disintegrated into sobs. Eric shouted. There was a soft crunch. No. Eric exclaimed, rustling. What? No. What? I'm waist deep in smokes!

YAAAAAAAAAAAAEEEEEIIIIIIIIIOOOOOOOOOOOOOOUUUUUUUUUUUU

Iain leapt into blackness, landing a second later in cartons of cigarettes. Derek! One of my shoes fell into the night below me and I stared into where it had gone. The tormented earth had opened up in a tide of cartons and threatened to swallow us. Iain was suddenly erupting, a brilliant God whose features were chiseled in gold by a butane flame that was sucked away into a glowing point of orange. Give me that lighter, sport, Eric panted.

Eventually flint would scrape in a chink of sparktangents but no invisible current of butane no incarnation of the flame deity writhing to life in our palm affording us a frightening glimpse of one another's faces as we collectively understood that we would have to chainsmoke through the ends of our lives don't put that cigarette out Eric was probably the last complete thought whispered by the cracked and blistered lungscape wracked in life-sustaining spasmodic reflations indicating the eccentric flow of time like the telescoping progression of the orange point of spark eating its way through

cigarette after cigarette only after we three complete our respective halflives will it taste the bitter filter the handle where your fingerbones connect to the cigarette the axis the only point of reference in this world as our skin is coated by layers of crawling lashing dribbling eels is the flame that only appears as an omniscient orange bit flaring with the rasping breaths of whoeversshift it is to keep

awake and smoking while the others wheeze in and out of dreams the deity incarnate as the glowing icon around which all our private religious and philosophical speculations revolve in this inexplicable realm of memory and delusion in the darkness alive with the rushing chatter of all we have ever spoken to as we smoke in evercycling shifts to preserve lung tissue and consciousness and the flame

that floods our aching sensory minefields with warm numbth I drag gingerly but persistently on each fraught afraid I will lose its spark with truly restless impatience to start the next to finish the next and the next and sometimes I keep two going at once, just to be safe, until the end of the shift when I clumsily pass the cigarette on to the next

one not a moment before again sliding into an unconsciousness tangled in wild failing dreams like jumbled reassessments of my former life which I had no clear idea of Iain had finally and frighteningly seemed to have lost his impersonal cloak of coolness the narcissistic facade crumbling as he lay murmuring unintelligible things about Jimihendrix until his eyes discovered Eric lying face down on a crumbledout cigarette protruding from flaxen lips in the jagged clarity of a lash of electrical lightning quaking in thunderous resonations concentric sound-circles expanding in an inky pond as Iain gasped in the inevitable perception of reality that we had managed to elude as he stood there standing as the tremolo lightning engaged cloud again and this time revealed the ranks of cold iron shelves slaving in perfect rows into the distance over the pool of form slurped on the floor which was the Eric who had died on his watch and let us down Iain turned and gazed triumphantly at me I guess I wondered where the soft light could be coming from flickering into vivid detail Iain's hairy skull as the deity climbed pyre high into descending sheets of rain carton sinflame tumble burning from above where smoke curdles up into the violent pyromaniacal night trickling electrical extensions from the turgid cloudsoup in the sky above Iain walking into flame consumed as an impatient cigarette in the rising empire of electrical fire to sweep in a great wake of flame across this continent erasing the gutted ruins of the past as the roof weakens in a crunch above a cascade of sparks I realize too late that Iain was the incarnation himself the Avatar of Agni and I silently thank him for this theatrical death (as else I would still be at work).

I see fish kiss an underwater skeleton, each leaving a speck of flesh, accumulating a man. A raveling ribbon of yellow silk, a red nose, an orange wig, and a green fedora float upstream and attach themselves to the head. Blood pours upriver and flows into the clown's veins until he flies up into a boat that rolls over the top of a waterfall and floats upstream, cradling the sleeping clown, who wakes up when a woman on the shore pulls an oar from his head quickly, gives him back his secrets, then steps gently backward into the boat, which drifts upriver where she joins some friends, and the clown pilots the motorboat backward upstream to this circus on the shore where he comes ashore and passes through the center (and it is at this moment—the fulcrum—that I could take him and save him, but do not) of my cold crystal ball, rounder than a world, clearer than memory, a serpent's eye, a parabolic refraction of the clown's present in the center with past and future and the lives of everyone the clown will know compressed into a circular periphery, flattened into an arc along the edge of the glass ball, where I glimpse myself, exotic snake dancer Serpent Tina, who received a shortened prison sentence when doctors were allowed to experiment on my brain before I fled the researchers to be taken in by the good Doctor Bizarro, circus ringmaster, orchestra conductor who sweeps freaks, outcasts, and mystics into a rainbow symphony, for if love is a radiance shining from the center of the universe, poking bright through the pinhole of every snapdragon, bee, puppy, and person, filtered by the formations of rock that ossify the minds of the powerful, then Dr. Bizarro is a prism, refracting this cosmic candlepower into a spectrum of acrobats, animals, strongmen, tattooed ladies, impresarios, exiles, clowns, escapees, and undocumented refugees who perform at the circumference of his circus in which my fortune-telling tent is illuminated by a silver paper lantern ringed by a constellation of colored candles, the ground covered with a haphazard patchwork of rugs and satin pillows, and when an owl stutters in the night, the clown leans closer, wanting to know what I know, secrets he wants to hide the way a duck will tuck its head beneath its own wing to make the world disappear, hatching fantasies of me that nest like timid mice in his skull stuffed with straw, but that is not all, because he knows as only I can know that the train of time is creeping across a line of fire dividing past and future, its locomotive soon to go cold, belching its last patterns of fog, smoke, and vapor into the thirsty air as he draws in the whispered question, "Will you tell me my fortune?" I release Lucky's purple gloved hand from my own naked one, and we stand opposite the table from each other, and as Lucky corks the wine he brought me, the air empties into the bottle a fizzing flutter of orange butterflies, while my snakes spell out on the ground a cursive only I can read, and I unlight the candles, putting their fire back onto the tips of the last matches, and breathe the words, "Come in," sitting at my makeup table to remove the glittering parallelograms around my eyes, scraping my lashes down from their long curves, and, in a flourish of plumage, my peacock flaps to my lap from the ground where it had stalked backward among the perfume bottles there, relaxing its guard now that Lucky the clown is backing away outside, worms squishing under his floppy shoes whose every step sprays a lace of dewdrops, and he returns to his tent, puts on the table a bottle of green wine, a dozen blue roses, and his favorite nose, and, framed by dead bulbs along the perimeter of his cracked mirror, erases painted tears from his face, while the crowd gathers, and lightning stitches together the moon, and gives back all the lights to this town by the river where we had planned to spend our last magic in the best gift these frightened sick people had ever received: a full-on three-ring extravaganza with rides, lights, music, animals, games, tricks, and clowns like Lucky Phosphorus, who joined the circus when our lead clown fell ill the previous week, when, as the train backs out of town, from the boxcar dressing room, with a gurgling from behind the curtain where the other clown has fallen sick, Lucky the clown peers through a slat into the hissing and steaming rain where a rat drops a knucklebone and clambers away across the cinders, the moon swallowed up in the face of the greedy night with stars in its beard, poking bright fingerbones through cracks in the sky, as the backwards circus train drifts on, creaking, rocking like a boat, out of a dark and slanted town through an alley where men watch it pass with interest, skinny shadows with implements that glint in the moonlight, and the clown shuts the shutter on them and walks backward into his past, shedding his colorful clothes, scraping the makeup off his face back into jars, and joins the web of light that connects him to the dying people who are pulled back to life one by one as he sits down on the office chair where he will spend years as a dull, dead man in front of a screen, moving only to tap buttons, hair enough only for a small tail in the back of his head, and big glasses that make him look like an insect nesting in wires, diseases blown up on screens in color, preventing the end of the world without thought, unbuilding the recipes that encode the deadly sharkgerms, unknowing what he is doing, unpretending he doesn't know he knows, (not recognizing the woman who will feed him to the fish as she passes through his office to meet a friend), as he grows younger and warmer, decreasingly meek, and less honored to be salaried by the devil with sunglasses on his head, taking apart the disease machine, erasing every rehearsal of murder until hair falls onto his head, his eyes stretch to see distances, and he skips backward into childhood, a bright dot at the edge of my crystal ball. I turn my head away and say quickly, "You will have a very happy life and save the world." Lucky stares until, finally understanding, he leaves, and the sun peeks over the horizon, curious to see what is going on. We are all dying.

Spurred on by emergency, chaos, and crisis. Everyone on the highway is fleeing toward or away from all the same places, the same problems. I would turn back and go home. Or try to.

All grown up now, a nuclear technician. Security clearance. Still. Going home. When I get together with my brother and cousins, we're teenagers again. After the cancer, chemo, remission. I thought I'd pretty much shown my dedication to my job. Not much doubt the work had caused the cancer. Taking apart old warheads. Parts of my body shorting out. More feeling in my cane than my legs. But the facility went to a higher security level and I'm out of work. They said they'd keep covering me. You never know with government jobs anymore. In our dad's day they could count on a pension. Scary times, apparently. Good time to pick up brother Sam from Albuquerque and head for the mountains. Literally. Granddad's cabin and land up above Las Vegas. Las Vegas, New Mexico, that is. Different sort of Las Vegas entirely. Small, quiet, slow. The one in Nevada had been evacuated. A trunk full of medicinal marijuana, bourbon, and food to grill. Time to kick back. Sam worked construction and drank. Never changed. Radio reported bad traffic and craziness in Los Angeles, New York, Seattle. Albuquerque seemed quiet. Always does. We were listening to all kinds of news on the road up the mountain. A two-lane lined by yellow wildflowers. Branches all over the mountainsides into dead-end vacation retreats, survivalist hideouts. Nothing different about this road. Nobody drives through there. Can't get through. No way out of the mountain except the way you come in. Quiet. Perfect for us. A party on the edge of oblivion. The cabin all to ourselves. Dad was in Seattle, granddad too, last anybody heard from the old guy. Last thing we expected was to find a car in the driveway. Our still-teenage hearts sunk at the possibility of chaperones. Turned out to be Jane, our cousin, which was cool, we always liked partying with Jane. And her brother Mike. Not cool. Assbag. But not a real problem. Weird thing was how they got there. Jane said she got a ride from some good old boys into Reno after a crazy journey out of Seattle by car and boat. Mike had been in Los Angeles and came to pick her up when she got stranded. His boyfriend Calvin had gotten sick. Died real quick. Whole city going crazy. Worse than Rodney King, he said, worse than O.J. He said he came up to get away. We knew the truth. He was lonely. Without his boyfriend to look up to him, he needed the comfort of family to feel superior to. My theory, anyway.

As kids, Jane, Sam, and I had hated having Mike around. Bad enough that as the favorite nephew of a dandy uncle he had come into a trust fund that none of us had. Never held a job. Not for a minute. He was an artist. Librettist and composer. A diva from childhood, and he never let us forget it. Despite being privileged in ways we could only dream of, far from being grateful, generous, and kind, he demanded extra consideration. Talked down to everybody. Not that he'd managed to make the big splash we all thought he would, now pushing forty with no more twenty-five-year-old boyfriend to clean up after him. Scrape the caviar off his china, launder his silk panties. And Calvin was also the one who was cool and personable so Mike didn't have to be. Calvin could take a drink. Would be missed by us all. Just kind of sad how he let himself be taken in by Mike's grandiosity. Calvin had come from a poor family and was always the diminutive partner in the relationship. Seemed unable to get on with any kind of career or degree or life beyond taking care of Mike's loose ends and temper. We suspected Mike blocked Calvin's efforts to go back to school. Wanted to retain financial and emotional control over him. As a result Calvin had spent the past decade acting as Mike's secretary, lover, and liaison with the human world. Smoothing over feathers Mike ruffled while Mike festered in the tower of his narcissism. Hard to see how Mike was going to cope. He had bailed Jane out by picking her up. Now he expected her to put up with his bitchiness. Whatever. He had arrived, books and oboe in tow, to ruin our fun. Sneering funhater. Used to insult the television when we tried to watch. Hated music, beer, burgers. Insisted on silence to compose even when surrounded by family in a one-room cottage. We were cowed. He was the only one in the family with money, and we were reluctant to become his enemy.

We left him in the A-frame to sit and pretend to write music. We went to the Rock to get high and go skinny-dipping in the creek. The rock was a tradition. We could have smoked joints in the house with no parents there. Hell, I had a prescription because of the chemo. But the Rock was where we went as teenagers, and we liked going back.

Granddad had built the A-frame more or less himself. Back in the 1970s. Sleeping in a shed to be safe from the bears that came around at night. Some nutty dowser with a divining rod had told him where to drill for water, and, sure enough. So over time the cottage had been given plumbing, electricity, a back deck that looked over the creek. Certain comforts. His land was shaped like a long triangle, quarter mile long, in a rift between two ridges. A creek bisected it, flowing from a waterfall up at the point. A long driveway led back to the two-lane. The Rock was a massive boulder twenty feet above the creek. Jutting out halfway up the bluff. As kids we could commit mischief there. Nobody could see us, we'd see anybody who tried to climb up to us. Somebody else's property on the other side of the ridge, undeveloped. Just another cliff heading back down the other side.

The air was still and perfect. Warm, arid. A cardinal thrashing in the brush. Giant monarchs trickling through the air. It was a rough climb for me. Tricky with my cane. Sam helped me get up on the Rock and I shared my medicine. Whoever grew that got it right. Cancer had a bright side. It helped to be a government worker to get access to the medicinal. Got a buzz on. Jane told us crazy stories about her trip. She had married some dude before she left, only they got separated on a river. Something about a clown in a boat. Now she thought she needed to go back to Seattle. Maybe look for her husband. We told her to send Mike to Seattle and stay in the mountains with us. She laughed. We liked her, but getting her Ph.D. and becoming a professor had made her screwy. Until recently she had been working part-time at an office store. Now she was ultra-sensitive. She was always offended if we said "girl" and all that because it was offensive to women. At least she used to lash out. But she now had a new set of rules she wasn't even going to tell us. She would get weird and give us the silent treatment, probably for things we said, but we couldn't figure out what. Even well meaning gifts—like a CD—would tick her off and she would never acknowledge the gift. Weird. It was actually pretty annoying, but she was cool to us when she felt like it. Maybe now and then she'd read a theory about the importance of being nice to your cousins and then be old Jane for a while. But it was getting to the point where you couldn't depend on her. I never told her about my cancer, for example, because I thought I'd break one of her new rules and she'd feel violated. Well, it was obvious she now belonged to a higher class of openly-neurotic educated people. She still drank, smoked weed, and watched TV, but now she always had elaborate excuses for why it was okay for her to do the things she always liked. But not okay for other people, I guess. Today she was all cool, though. I think she appreciated us after all that had happened to her.

After getting ready, we climbed down from the Rock—Jane helping me down the slope—and hiked up to the swimming hole. A pool under the waterfall was the deepest point in the creek. After a couple swigs of bourbon, my exhaustion set in. Couldn't keep up like I used to. "You're getting old," Sam said, laughing, floating on his back and spitting a spume of water into the air. I smiled at that. It was a compliment. I wasn't old: I was old and sick. Strange. I was staring at a black shape under the water. An inky blob about three feet across. It flowed back and forth across the rocky floor of the creek. Oily, like a huge amoeba. A moving shadow. "What's that?" I asked, pointing, uneasy. Nobody understood. I sat on the bank, pulled my feet out of the water, lit another joint, and stared. Maybe that was the virus, I thought, growing out of control there in the swimming hole.

Guess we didn't hear the motorcycle and truck arrive at the cabin while we were down there. Or maybe we did and hoped it was Mike leaving.

It was dark and we were starved when we got back. Two unfamiliar trucks were parked outside. A towtruck pulling another towtruck, with bared grilles gleaming in the light from the cottage window. Something not quite right. The way they parked to block in our cars. I went onto the porch. Through the window I saw Mike bleeding from the mouth onto his green silk shirt. Lots of blood. He was tied up in a chair. Burly interlopers stood around him. I gestured for Jane and Sam to hold back. Men had apparently tied him up and shut him up manually. Mike seemed to be lost in thought about all of this. Slumped in the dining room chair, eyes not quite looking. A bubble of blood grew from his nostril and deflated, marking each passing breath. The house had been taken over. In the kitchen more visitors were apparently taking inventory and making themselves at home. One of the men who stood over Mike was apparently also lost in a reverie, looking down at his new friend, wearing a leather vest for a shirt, one of granddad's homemade beers wrapped in a hand. The other hand wiped a knife on his jeans.

Sam pulled me off the porch and into the pines. "This isn't good," he whispered excitedly by way of clarification. The man with the vacant look and leather vest appeared in the glass door, gazing out into the night. Not good. Think, damnit. Fighting the inebriation, I groped around the edges of the situation to find a grip somewhere.

At that moment, where I was looking through the tree branches, a shard of meteor traced an arc across the sky, so close I could see the glittering wake of its trail. Did I make a wish?

Hidden on the Rock. We huddled and whispered about our predicament. It was frightening to see Mike taking a beating, but we could see how it happened. There was nothing he could have thought up to say to these roughnecks that would have done anything but infuriate them. My swaying mind momentarily played with pitying the thugs as I would have trained police dogs. Jane advocated going to confront the villains and demanding the release of Mike, reasoning that they would be happy to have the little douche taken off their hands. Sam and I were less sure. There was no cell signal available. If we wanted to escape, the road would be difficult: we'd be exposed the entire length of it should they come or go, or, worst, should more hoodlums arrive. It would be almost impossible to hide. The best way out was upriver and over the waterfall—from the peak it would be a short hike to a ranger station, a nearby subdivision, or a major road. In our childhood we used to climb its slippery boulders. It was hazardous, one arm had been broken. Still, it seemed like the only exit from this play.

Sam wanted to avoid a confrontation at all cost, and could only consider entering the house after the thugs had left, been lured away, or had drunk themselves to sleep. With shaking hand, he tried to light a cigarette, but Jane grabbed the lighter. "They'll see us," she hissed.

I don't know whether I passed out then or my mind just hiccuped.

The Rock. Granddad's Ventures album
and shouting. Something wet against my face. I jumped to my feet. A dog
wagged its tail. A stray, apparently, one of many roaming the streets these
days, had found our hiding place. Down below I could see a flashlight beam
staggering between trees. One of the interlopers. Tromping through the
scrub oak. A cough and explosion of urine on leaves. The dog jumped up on
its hind legs, putting its front paws on me. Tags jingled. The urine stopped.
A flashlight beam scrawled across the nearby hillside. I tried to crouch, but
my weak legs could not support me, and I fell backward. I tried to pet the
Dalmatian in a manner designed to defuse its enthusiasm. We all held our
breath, I'm sure. The man cleared his throat and the footsteps receded to
the house.

Sam was whispering that this dog would give us away if we didn't kill it.
It whimpered in response. Sam's breath suggested he had been continuing
to drink. Jane whispered that we could set fire to their trucks and cause a
distraction outdoors during which we would go in and grab Mike. I didn't
like their ideas. I managed to make clear that if we set fire to their trucks
we would eliminate any possibility that they might drive off on their own.
Jane accepted this piece of logic. I felt a fleeting sense of having managed to
contribute. With enough such solid bricks of reasoning we might build an
action. Meanwhile night was passing and with it our chance of remaining
undiscovered. Jane said, "If you see my lighter flash, come down," and slid
down the bluff to go scout out the situation. The dog tried to follow, but I
kept it in a sort of friendly headlock. Sam said something about killing the
dog and then killing the men, but neither Sam nor I were paying attention
to what he was saying. He had his cigarettes out but could not light them.
He took another swig.

Another meteor happened, and passed through a moving airplane's
lights. The plane seemed too low and its engine did not sound healthy. We
were under a flight path approaching Albuquerque Sunport. I saw a lighter
spark in the woods and eased myself over the edge of the Rock to crabwalk
down the slope, leaving Sam to detain the dog.

We knew the landscape. We lay under a pine from a rise where we could
see into the house. We had spied on the family from there. Mike had not
changed position. Perhaps he was giving his attackers the famous silent
treatment. That would be his best survival strategy. Even if he meant it as
a provocation. One of the men asleep on the floor. The other was in the
process of dismembering the house. In search of valuables? Every piece of
wallboard has been stoved in, every cushion eviscerated, every framed print
had had its glass broken and its backing slashed. Even rugs had been cut

into strips, the kitchen table dismembered. Scraps of debris were scattered outside the house.

That's when things went wrong. The dog started barking. Sam had let it go and it had followed us to the house. Whether in play or some other capacity, from fifteen feet away it lowered itself into a crouch and aimed agitated barks directly at our hiding spot. The back door was slammed open. Vest appeared, a chair leg in his fist. Engine sputtering, another small plane was coming, louder and lower. The man stumbled on the porch steps as he peered into the darkness. The dog looked at him approvingly, then spat a couple more barks in the direction of Jane and I. There was a terrible noise as the plane came out of the sky, tore through the treetops, crashed into the river. A bit of fire visible.

Vest was gone. A motorcycle roared to life. Its headlight found the trail that led to the river. Jane stood up, pulling me toward the house. Whether I was too numb to walk or trying to pull back, she overpowered me and we stiffly tiptoed up the back steps into the broken glass and stuffing-strewn cottage where one man lay asleep on his stomach with his head turned toward the room.

Not asleep. He had received the same sort of going over the house had. Stuff that used to be inside his stomach. I had just stepped on a very small egg that was his eyeball.

We inched forward. Crunching glass. Inscribing silent footprints of blood, the entire cottage a mouth we entered quietly, afraid of it coughing. Mike did not raise his head to meet us. The ropes that bound him to the wooden chair seemed impossibly knotty. Jane glanced toward the kitchen doubtfully. Didn't want to go in there. She looked down at Mike, her face morphed into a mask of horror. Her eyes got so wide I thought they would distend her skull. She kneeled and vomited, the splatter of it as loud as a bucket of marbles poured onto a glass table. She stood up and gestured with her head. We each took an arm of the chair, shuffling as we maneuvered it toward and out the door, thumping down step by step, into the woods. Gasped for breath. My legs were cramping. Mike nodded. An orange speck came out of the darkness and our eyes strained to prove it was Sam, coming toward us, lit cigarette in his mouth, carrying a whiskey bottle. Dealing with crisis. Jane slapped him, knocking the cigarette into some pine needles. "What took you idiots?" Mike muttered. Sam lifted his muddy boot onto Mike's bloody shirt, kicked him and the chair he was tied to backward over some rocks. Jane grabbed the bottle, shook it angrily and silently in Sam's face. Took a long drink. Threw it aside. Mike stood up, swaying, pulling at his ropes from which pieces of chair hung. There was a gunshot from the river and we heard the dog yelp.

Mike followed, cleverly giving us the silent treatment. Wading upstream, downriver from the plane. Single prop. Just a tiny fire in its engine bouncing light on the ripples. The motorcycle on the bank cast headlamp light onto the wreck. The grunting vested man dragged the pilot's body out of the cockpit and, with a heaving sigh, tumbled it into the creek where it rolled over and floated our way. Vest leaned into the plane, breaking things. Apparently searching the plane for valuables. We knelt in the water. Three heads on the surface of the stream, which smelled of gas. Someone pushed into me, but I could not move to let the pilot's body pass. Or was it the black shape I had seen, oozing beneath the water, looking for a leg to wrap a pseudopod around? I almost whimpered. The pilot was not dead. He sputtered and his hand worked itself into the buttons of my shirt. The motorcyclist was leaning into the cockpit, working it with a knife. We heard a cracking. He flung various pieces out into the creek.

He began sawing the wingfabric, letting it hang in shreds. Then he backed away, brandishing a duffel bag, climbed up to the motorcycle. Kicked it to life, turned it back up the mountain to the cottage. Where his captive, his prize, was no longer. Wanting very much to scream, I stood up to let the pilot pass downstream. I was shaking. Too much destruction. Sam and Jane waded ahead around the crumpled tailsection of the plane. Mike following. I stumbled after them, my cane sticking in the mud of the creek floor.

Jane asked Mike what had happened. Mike told us that he had offered the three men a hundred thousand dollars to let him live. A disagreement had broken out. A shout such as we had never heard tore through the woods and rebounded off the mountainside. Compressed rage and fury. Of such intensity that we stepped up our pace.

The motorcycle howled. We came upon the waterfall. Without hesitation our motor memories found the old ways to climb. I always went up the right edge. Mike followed, quickly passing me, slowing me down as I waited for him to find the handholds. I slipped on my useless leg. Caught myself. My cane clattered to the rocks. My legs could not do this. Numb twigs poking around for footholds. Sam tried to splash up the middle of the falls. The old rocks had moved. Jane went up the left bank. Motorcycle light dawned. Awful, deafening sunrise.

Jane made it over the edge and dropped out of sight. Mike was in my way. Jane reached down and just lifted him. Felt it before I heard it. The first bullet cured my cancer. Pushed its way into my abdomen. Miracle cure. Second bullet cured my alcoholism. Shattered my right hand. I kind of looked down at that point and saw my fluids spattering down onto the surface of the water, white with motorcycle light, beneath which the black shape waited to take me when I fell. I saw Sam jerk before I heard the shot that had taken apart his skull. Bowl of chili con carnage. Why did I think that? His body shook, clinging to the rocks, and fell. Thrashing in midair. The way he always did cannonballs.

Above me. Jane and Mike. On opposite sides of the creek. Backed away from the edge. Away. Mike was missing an ear. A square of blackened gauze taped to his head. The black amoeba undulated. Waiting. Edges rippling. It had already consumed Sam. When I fell into the water it snapped around me. Sealing me in shadow. Taking me away.

AFTER THE REVOLUTION time was free. Time had been emancipated. Nobody would ever need more time again. Those people who had invested their time carefully before the revolution now felt bewildered and betrayed. Those of us who had wasted our time felt nothing. Now we could no longer buy or spend time and would have to find other things to do with it. Time was the only thing we would never run out of. Long after all the food and medicine had been stripped from the shelves we would still have enough time. This was the time we had always hungered for. Time was now perfectly elastic. Either we would stretch it around gigantic projects or it would snap back and be forgotten in less than a second. This was time during which novels could be written or symphonies composed for a world with no publishers or orchestras but possibly readers and audiences. For a few weeks someone continued to ring the hours on a distant belltower and dutifully clocked every hour. Eventually whoever it was overslept or gave up or left town like all the other people. It was impossible. Time meant little more than distance and the certainty of sunrise and sunset and the possibility that autumn would grow colder. Time had been freed from its rules and measurements and we discovered we needed other rules and measurements. The order of the day became the order of the day. We invented new rules for everything each time. We tried new ways of walking talking cooking eating and sleeping. We found dozens of old board games and tried to figure out different ways to play them. We never consulted the old rules. Now that we were able to live without decisions we began to make and follow them. Those of us who were anarchists before now obeyed our own rules more zealously than anyone. Often the rules didn't work like eat without using your hands or don't touch the ground. We finished every game anyway. We had finally found that the only way to have fun or accomplish anything was through rules. The only way to give free play to our creativity was through a labyrinth of restrictions. We wondered if inventing rules should have rules. Even casual conversation had become impossible without rules. Without limiting ourselves to four letter words or a particular verb tense there was too little to say and too many ways to say it and we would end up talking about ourselves and each other and who hadn't done the dishes and what rules might get him to. We used strange rules to become friends. Now the handful of us were alone together in a world without automobiles or muzak whose electricity had died and whose billboards were peeling and we had to work through the jostling shifting of our various enmities and alliances until we each shared a language with every other person and had learned to enjoy and depend upon each of our idiosyncrasies. We managed to do this surprisingly quickly. We began to wonder what we could do as a group on the day we agreed on the rule to speak without using singular pronouns.

AFTER THE REVOLUTION I always told you to meet me at the university library—although it was quite a long bike ride away—I always said you'd find me—even though it was now deserted and the few people you did see were reading and you respectfully subdued the urge to greet them—I had hoped we would never meet—and inevitably discuss what was going on with our friends at home—and how we weren't sure why—even now after the revolution—we couldn't talk about them in front of them—and whether Heisenberg's Uncertainty Principle made more sense with interpersonal interaction than subatomic particles—or at least—interpersonal relationships being more urgent—especially now when there was no electricity to power particle accelerators—whether the principle was a more useful model when applied to them—etc.—instead I had hoped we would each wander a maze of carrels—wandering opposite directions down parallel aisles—researching old ideas of the new society—reading waiting reading sitting waiting etc.—finding messages we scrawled to one another in the margins of pre-Revolutionary revolutionary literature—call numbers of books where we had scrawled other messages—wild reference chases in which we would search through pages for evidence that the other had been there—finding only answers to more urgent questions—slowly filling the margins of every book with commentary—I left false clues and genuine red herrings—books I wanted you to read so I wouldn't have to—maybe when we found each other at some call number we would embrace and with wide eyes speak to each other in the startling new languages of other texts—we would have met interesting people and spent time in their carrels learning about what they had read—we would have used different reference systems—wandered apart on lattices of footnotes only to meet up again—when we last met at 154.63 Sa22:r:E we charted our separate courses through and about time and space and found each other in the poetry of Erasmus Darwin—gaping at the same stanza—different expressions on our faces—we would both walk around the stanza a few times and come face to face between two lines each of us with different understandings and different books and we would stay right there for days—building forts towers playpens out of books by daylight—the libraries never closed—cuddling in the dark cold nights on the floor—and—who knows—maybe occasional moans gasps sighs would echo down through ten empty floors and the small new moons would wane—embarrassed—then wax—curious—and—who knows—someday—when our minds seemed to map perfectly—we might disagree on the meaning of a word—and set off in separate directions to find definitions and—who knows—not meet again for days—or weeks—or back at home in half an hour.

(AFTER THE REVOLUTION I found I was as lonely and confused as before (I couldn't explain it because there was too
much important work to be done (and I often skipped dinner
(rather than reorganize my food on the plate while the others ate (laughed
(made up new rules for how to behave at dinner (threw handfuls of cauli-
flower)))))) but I wondered whether I belonged here (where I wanted to be)
or whether there was more important work for me elsewhere in the world
(and once during lunch the bell tower which had been silent for days rang a
great many times and we counted the hours up through thirteen (at which
point my friends all screamed (delighted) and chased each other around
the farm while I watched (vaguely sick (that clock used to...(never mind)
)))) and I excused myself to do the dishes in the middle of the meal and
go for a walk) and I wondered about the other people and what they were
doing (and I considered leaving my friends to go investigate the rumors
of disasters (earthquakes in Missouri floods in Oregon) and communities
rising up everywhere (looting and revelry in New York and Detroit (they
shared the moons with me)) and I walked until night down dark cobble-
stones through empty residential neighborhoods and I stopped in a park
and watched a moon pass through a gap in the clouds and wondered what it
saw (What did the new moons see? (Could they tell me anything about the
world they were the eccentric calendars of?)) and I waited for the moon to
tell me but it disappeared again and left me in perfect darkness too treach-
erous to negotiate home) and I wondered whether the rest of the people
were forming groups like ours or whether we were deluding ourselves to
believe that our only problems were internal and that everything elsewhere
was so good so safe so warm and I asked the darkness whether the other
people had survived a pleasant revolution to enjoy this peaceful world
(or were there other consensuses (another moon passed through the gap
in the clouds going the opposite direction (I wondered briefly how))))
and then (in the light the moon cast) I ran home).

AFTER THE REVOLUTION
Blake and I got to spend time alone together
in the park playing with a giant green ball on the hill
writing poetry whose logic we then spoke
then thought
then ended up in weird situations
like Blake at the top of a tree shouting
"I PRIVATIZE YOU! I HIJACK A BLUE YOYO!
FOG! WOOD YOU AXE IN MY SEQUOIA?!"
and I paused in astonished recognition of
the deliberate play of vowels
but before I could compose a reply
which showed a keener sense of the distinction
between the use of Y as vowel or consonant
he produced a blue yoyo I had never seen before
and dangled it with exaggerated elegance
from his slender branch
I fell in the grass laughing
he threw the green ball down from a blue sky
through red leaves
At night we went off in different directions
I needed secrecy
to prepare a special salad of handpicked plants
chosen for their obscurity
subtle distinctions of flavor
for Blake who claimed to be able to recite the Latin
name of any plant he tasted
There were no reference texts out here
so we would have to rely on poetry to teach us botany
Latin
Poetry was capable of this
It spoke us to each other
We gave it back to the whispering trees in
the cool autumn night air of smoke
manure
We tasted each word as we spoke it
to the congenial
lights on the horizon
lights?
Blake threw the ball
we saw its silhouette eclipse a moon
And stop
The sky remained black and we never heard the ball
fall
The new moon waxed gradually over weeks.

AFTER THE REVOLUTION Jane and I undertook the project of redecorating an empty mansion / got enthusiastic / found food and art supplies to fill it with / discussed how the mansion / theatre / 3 piano rehearsal area could be used / walked through deserted grocery store aisles with flashlights / choked on the sweet stench of rotting produce / accumulated cans of artichoke hearts and bundles of pasta / remembered which dark aisle everything was in from before / accumulated necessities with the detached guiltless logic of shoppers / became distracted by the fact that other people might rely on this supply of leftover commodities as well / wanted to leave them more in the way of greeting than plundered shelves in the supermarket / fetid cave / consumer cathedral lit by a sunroof whose glow cascaded down in the center / arranged canned food into rainbow patterns / built houses of cereal boxes / attacked the magazines dated in the month of the last date with scissors and left images everywhere / pushed an overflowing shopping cart across a parking lot falling up across the setting sun / took the food / toilet paper / batteries to the house / worked through decisions of how to arrange it / what rules to use / where the stage should be / wandered through the house all day together / alone / silent in marble hallways / singing to each other down spiral staircases / met on a balcony to share some cigarettes we had found in one of the rooms / decided that the first floor should stay as it was / comforting to the visitors we hoped to receive when the other people came back / frozen in lavish pretensions towards an elegance history had overcome / as close to the former conventions as we could mimic / decided that the second floor would have the stage and classrooms for us and visitors / decided that the third floor should get weird as we imposed different rules on it / talked about a black room / a reflective room / a plaid room / an upside down room / a soft room / a maze / an underwater room / a library filled with our writing / songs / ideas for new societies / worked out absurd and useful ideas / drew up plans / put the groceries away.

AFTER THE REVOLUTION, after we had accumulated food, moved in together, had arguments about whether and how new rules should be applied
to an activity as essential and unfamiliar as gardening, we asked ourselves
the question, "What do We want?" Was there some way we could simplify
the question? How about: "What do I want?" There ensued a merry chaos
during which everybody shouted answers, except Mike, and eventually the
rest of us gathered around him, wondering, "What does Mike want?" He
didn't answer so we argued with each other on Mike's behalf, because he had
always brought red to our cheeks and tingling to our fingertips, and Mike finally cut us off by asking, "Dinner?" It was morning, was this sarcasm? Mike
clarified, "Mushrooms, and can you make them blue?" So Hunter and I fixed
dinner, discussing what else Mike might want, how to make the mushrooms
blue, what to prepare for the others, news we had seen on the horizon, heard
on a radio, or found blowing down the street, about where the other people
went, what they were doing, until Jane burst into the kitchen to give us each
a piece of paper, pencil, and the instruction to answer the question "What do
I want?" When we brought the food out we found Mike and Blake rehearsing
a puppet show they had written in a very short time, and learned that, during that same time, Jane had read the Wants and composed a consensus that
we should invent social organization games, or rules, which could be tried
on small or large scales, try them out, and compile books for the benefit of
the other people (would they ever come back?). During dinner, Mike, too
excited to eat, now confessed he had written a piece for us to perform in one
week, and he gave us each handwritten copies of a score and instruments to
which I asked, "Wha—?" Dinner forgotten, I opened the clarinet case and
brought out the black cylinder with the maze of keys and rules, and left for
the valley with the instrument, a notebook, his score, and a vague promise to
do my dishes later, found a sunny spot to sit, unfolded the music, studied it,
and felt a terrified flattery pump through me as I wondered, "How to count
that measure?" I made six different drawings of the first measure, attempting
to play each sketch, until the sun left, and I invented curses, remembered
the drawing of the measure where the notes were vegetables in a garden,
and looped it to the cackling shriek of locusts and the tittering murmur of
breeze, until the cackling and tittering joined in, the gusts regular, the locusts
harmonizing ordered bursts in a stack of, no, minor seconds? My notes fell
across a tangible grid and time emerged, divided by rules, and my fingers
wrested away my control and marched across the metal rings and wooden
holes as I turned around playing and saw a melody of rising moons arranged
above the horizon like notes on a staff.

"AFTER THE REVOLUTION writing has become important to me, Tom, can you—" "Hi Hunter. I thought you'd be in the treehouse. I can see you're typing but can I talk to you for a second? This afternoon my phone was working for about an hour." "Really?" "Yeah. For the first time in weeks. I was talking to my Mom and apparently some pretty crazy things are happening out there outside the Farm." "Like what?" "Well...on the RNN Evening News Mom saw a story I can't believe they'd report even if it was true about organized movements of people refusing to use money all over the United States and Canada. Instead of buying things from each other they trade, negotiate, work, organize, and are finding out that there's enough to go around. In fact it seems like there's more than ever before because people are taking less. My Mom saw footage of people singing and playing guitar sitting around a campfire of burning dollar bills!" "Yeah?" "Apparently during the riots last week the hospital where she works was flooded with patients with no money and the management ordered that the doors be locked but the staff refused the order and they were all working around the clock treating and feeding people and then when those people started getting better they started helping treat the newly arriving patients...or maybe they starting getting better after they started taking care of the other patients I don't remember anyway now the hospital has become the community center: kind of a combination town hall, soup kitchen, coffeehouse, library and...hospital! It's fantastic news!" "Sure, sure." "And you know what else?" "Hmmm..?" "Tag! You're It!" So that's what that liar was up to. So I am It again. Sigh. It means I have to stop what I am doing and go find someone to tag. Just as well. What was that Tom had been saying about money? It'd been so long, I'd forgotten about money: how you had to carry it everywhere, how you could lose your wallet on accident...and actually regret it. Ho-hum. I decided to go tag Blake. I knew he'd be in the woodshop working on his essay and I was right. "Hey Blake, apparently Tom got through on the phone to his Mom today and—" "—Hunter can it wait I'm right in the middle of a run-on sentence and—" "—and people all over America have stopped using money and—" "—and I'd like to hone it, whittle it, melt it, boil it, burn it down to a clear and sober thesis so—" "—so the revolution has begun, Blake." "I don't believe it. Some Mom said this? Tom's? Give me a break." "I didn't come here to tell you that anyway. I have something much more urgent to get off my chest." "Make it concise?" "Tag! You're It." I don't really believe that I am 'It' but after a while I'll extricate from this tangle of prepositions and grumble down an entire flight of steps and out to the loading dock to find Ella, welding brilliant blue refractions in a trickle of sweat and copper, the quiet exhalation of acetylene which will cessate when I shout, "Hey, Ella!" "Yeah?" "Hey Ella Tom's Mom said that people out in America have stopped using money." "Really? That's great. If it's true that is." "I'm sure it isn't. I also got some other unlikely information I wanted to pass on." "What?" "Tag. You're It." I'm It, am I? That's alright because I can hear Mike on the third floor hammering out on piano the same measure that tripped him up an hour ago. I'm getting sick of it. I'll just run up the stairs and lean over his shoulder, scrutinizing his sheetmusic until he gets flustered. "Ella, what's up?" "Have you heard the great news?" "What?" "Tom's Mom and some of her friends have stopped using money." "Tom's Mom's *alive*? See? Great things are happening all the time. All you have to do is notice them. Revolution is on the way!" "Also, I wanted to burden you with something else." "Oh?" "Tag. You're It." I need an excuse to talk to Derek anyway. It's nearing dinnertime and it's his turn to cook tonight so I'll just slide this music into my briefcase and start up the gravel road, gulping deep breaths of clear air, grinning, whistling that measure across the valley.... "Derek that smells incredible! What's in it?" "Cilantro I picked just moments ago. Try some." "Mmm. I heard that Tom's Mom has stopped using money." "Wow. That clinches it: this is the best day of my life." "Don't be so pessimistic Derek, wonderful things will continue to happen. For example, I have a present for you." "Yeah?" "Yeah. Tag. You're It. Isn't that great?" "That *is* good news." I will find Jane beside the unlit firepit singing and playing guitar to an exceptionally fortunate sunset who will not go unsung to. I will watch her sing and smile and rock back and forth and wonder how I could be so lucky as to have a friend like Jane. When she finishes singing her new song to the sun I will tell her the good news. "Hi Jane! You sing good." "Thanks!" "Um, I came to tell you that Mike told me a story about somebody who once stopped using money and you know what else he told me?" "No." "Tag. You're It." You will never be the same again, Jane, after having heard this anecdote about the money here at the Farm, the free hospital in the mountains of Snohomish County. You will gaze amazed at the sun eaten by mountain and strike a chord you haven't heard yet. You will know that this change of state will happen to other elements, that from one person going for a few days without money a new society will be designed. Deliberately. Revolution will come. Already you will imagine the bills in the firepit curling and setting like a sun in the mountain, the President smiling and mutating into something unrecognizably human.

AFTER THE REVOLUTION the absence of electricity was the most devastating to Hunter: he used to work in security and data cryptography encoding digital payments sent across the World Wide Web: something which we had never understood and which no longer made any sense and his status as fallen mystic caused him to become terribly despondent: he never took off his guitar: with the lightning eloquence of a typist he would run such astoundingly sad programs that at least once the entire room was swept into silence and under tears until Jane saved us: she joined in on accordion and Hunter's eyes flickered as his mood reset and he and Jane interfaced rhythmically and shut it down: applause laughter tears: Hunter's as his face displayed a sad smile and he retuned his guitar and manicured the ends of the strings and polished the wood until we were all reflected in it and he never looked at us but didn't need to: the inscrutable logic of his haunting harmonic subroutines and algorithms and recursions caused unexpected functions in our movements and conversations even through the weeks he couldn't practice because I did something terrible: I played the blues and broke our last E-string and Hunter could no longer produce output and crashed: he got lost in strange loops and had the same nightmare every night: he would wake up in the blackness convinced the others were coming back: riding with guns: he told us everything: we made him then we consoled him and joked with him and argued with him and eventually he agreed that these were leftover fears but still he couldn't sleep and we worried until we agreed on a rule: we took turns sleeping in his room with him and he said the virus would delete itself and we didn't need to worry but I wasn't so sure: when it was my turn I woke up in the middle of the night to find him staring out the window scanning the darkness: he was scared: he was convinced he had seen a shadow cross a moon and I knew I had to free up some of his memory: I asked him to go for a walk with me: he was scared to so I told him: we'll bring the harmonica and the melodica and be prepared to sing a song to anyone we find on the street: we went walking and he spoke to me then seriously about the risk and the plans: plans he had made to lock the doors and hide the food and arm ourselves and practice running and emergency routes and hiding places: none of this I had considered before and all of it I found quite troubling: I proposed a rule: I told him to write every fear down as an eventuality: if we needed them we could use them but in the meantime we ran a greater risk by being frightened when we finally might be able to move without fear and he finally nodded: he agreed to begin typing the next day after breakfast and we returned to bed but I wasn't certain I had erased the fears: half an hour later I found myself staring out the window beside his snoring mattress trying to convince myself that a twinking light on the horizon was a star.

AFTER THE REVOLUTION I watched as everybody made friends with you for the first time again or for the first time, one by one, getting fed with your attention, quenched by your voice, inflated by your excited ideas, and wandering a lattice of mutual rules. I think I got jealous. I did. I couldn't tell anybody about it (except the cats). It didn't fit. I didn't want you to see it in my eyes and I avoided you in the kitchen in a self-fulfilling delirium. Everyday I would have breakfast at the table laughing with you and our friends and then I would go to the library to talk to a creased, thumbed photo of you, telling it how much I wanted to be with you, asking it if people should have rules in addition to feelings for one another. I kept it in my other embarrassing secret: my wallet. The others had lost or abandoned theirs. Mike, laughing, realizing he still carried his wallet, tossed it onto the floor. Later, alone, I retrieved it, transferred its money to my own, then—afraid he would discover it had been emptied—went to some trouble to hide it elsewhere in town. I was convinced, and didn't want to be talked out of it, that this would prove to be in everybody's best interest eventually. Sooner or later we would have to pay for something we needed and the others would regret their easy willingness to slip out of time. It was a weird habit, weirder still because I tried to hide it. Once I went into a bank and found so much money that I almost regretted the Revolution. Now I had all the money I could ever want and was unable to spend it on flights to Australia to jet ski, or a car, or a house, or food to cook for everybody on the weekend. Every old "want," every consumer capitalist wetdream, worked out in breakrooms with coworkers and bosses in excited tones and expansive gestures over ashtrays and lottery tickets, resurfaced in tears and I wandered home in a daze through deserted shopping districts. When I got home it seemed like everybody had left. I stood in the middle of the house in the slanting afternoon light, clutching a neat block of hundreds, my eyes streaked with revelation, Wolfgang Amadeus Mozart and Johann Sebastian Bach bumping into my ankles, meowing miscellaneous accusations, queries, confessions. I wondered where you were and I heard something, a sigh? A sound, a moan? A creak, a gasp? I didn't know which one you were with this time. Forget it. I shoved the money in my pocket, put Bach on my shoulder, picked up Mozart in one hand, my clarinet in the other, and started walking southeast. I was leaving. I was a freak. I didn't belong with these people. I needed rules, more, different. And I was taking the cats. But Bach and Mozart didn't agree and after two miles, the sun setting behind us and an angular orange moon full on the pale blue horizon in front of us, they meowed clamorously and clawed to be let down, but I clung to them and lectured them sternly.

That moon is *not* closer, it just looks closer because it's closer to the horizon and we're seeing it not in reference to an infinite sky but rather to objects whose size we are familiar with like houses and billboards and skyscrapers...

Okay okay so there's no houses and billboards and skyscrapers out here fine. You cats think you're so fucking smart but you need to wake up.

That's not true. They don't care anyway. I just need to change my old consistencies. And so do you. Y'know you two really piss me off. You could be tigers now, or flying elephants, but instead you just lie in the sun and fucking stare at squirrels like before. Forget it. We can't change until we find a different community. Or live alone. I don't even care. Wherever the other people are they're looking at the same sky. So that's where we're walking.

You think you know everything but you were neutered before the Revolution.

It doesn't even matter what you say. Everything is prelinguistic now.

Okay okay *postlinguistic*. Linguistic. It's different. We need to make up a new language to say what we want anyway.

Fucking cat. The moon will get smaller as it rises. You'll see.

But it didn't seem to be. It seemed to be getting larger faster. It covered nearly half the sky and was unbelievably detailed. It couldn't have been farther than a half block away. Its seas, craters, promontories, filled the sky. It was close enough to touch. I was about to walk into it. I stumbled, stopped, afraid of its weight, afraid to walk into one of its mountains. I put the cats down and stretched an arm out, slowly. Sebastian rolled onto his back and stared up with intense eyes. Wolfy wandered up to the moon and bumped his head on it, purring, and a cloud of orange dust rose slowly. I closed my eyes and took one step forward, arms outstretched, groping.

Nothing. I stopped. My feet, heavy, planted, refused to take another step. Wolfy and Sebastian waddled and loped down the road before me. But it was dark and I didn't know which way to go.

As soon as I left years collapsed.

I rivered the blank canvas calendar of the land.

Even the moon was nonchalant about which month.

I was looking for different people.

I had no pen and paper. Before, I couldn't survive without a notebook in which to jot notes and make lists. Now I would never need them. There was nothing to buy, no telephone numbers, no reason to write. Survival is its own mnemonic. That there could ever have been no reason to write would have once been inconceivable.

But I found notes everywhere strangers had left for me: "water."

The city of sutures was in the desert in a palm canyon. It seemed deserted in the noon sun.

Plastic was taped over a broken window high up on a building. What appeared to be fresher cement, bright green, covered rifts in the pavement. Patched with silver tape, the flag of a country that no longer existed hung from a pole. Something strange about the whole place: it had been weeded. Potted plants. Fallen trees pulled to the side of the street. Some rampant order running through.

Things seemed to be wrong colors: no two lamp posts or parking meters matched. Nothing did.

I turned a corner, and down a narrow alleyway there was a woman painting at an easel in a circle of sunlight. It was the first person I had seen since leaving my friends, and I felt a strong and unfamiliar feeling. She was looking right at me too and seemed to react by painting more rapidly. I walked toward her. Her eyes caught mine. She commanded me to stop and back up. I did. She told me to stop again. I wasn't sure if one of us appeared threatening to the other or which one of us it was. I stood still until I realized she was adding me to the painting. I wasn't sure if this gave us an opportunity to talk or not. So I listened. She told me that most of the town was sleeping: the musicians and writers probably wouldn't get out of bed until close to sunset. But she had to finish her painting in daylight so she could use it to buy food. Did this mean she was going to sell her painting? When she finally let me look at it, it was confusing to see myself, even abstracted into a silhouette. She explained that everyone who lived in the town had had their portrait done twice or more. The only way she could make a painting of any value was to paint a new image, and I was the first new image anybody had seen in some time.

City on the mend.

I heard dogs fighting but it turned out to be people fucking on a blanket in the park. I hadn't seen people in a while. Was it bad to stare? I couldn't help it. This changed things, if people were doing this.

Then I looked over behind a tree and saw who was painting them.

She looked at me angrily for threatening to intrude upon her so I backed away. I walked down a street until I came across a barricade. Usually that meant that the blocked-off street was walled off to all but the dying and their caretakers. Or had been.

I went the other way, and followed sounds of tapping and clanking to a team of people working to take apart a street. Some of them wore white protective suits that covered their entire bodies, including helmets or hoods with plexi-glass faceplates. Others wore T-shirts and jeans, or were half naked. They removed each brick from the street, immersed it in a bucket of blue fluid, dipped it in a can of green paint, and set it on a splattered tarpaulin to dry.

A woman in a filthy white Nirvana T-shirt, cut-offs, and cowboy boots put down a pick and walked over to greet me, handing me a silver pail of water in which a shiny steel dipper clanked dully. She told me they were doctors: epidemiologists. She explained to me that, in order to fully sterilize the city, they had to take it apart as much as possible so that every crevice of brick could be disinfected, and marked to show it was clean. Generally the rule was not to put anything back together again the same way, so that future generations would be able to adduce the progress even if paper records had not been properly kept.

But can't the bricks get dirty again if the virus comes back? I asked. She shrugged. We just have to do what we can. To undo what we can. If nothing else, our efforts can serve as a reminder of what has been lost.

Originally most of them had been just one team out of many sent out to control the spread of the virus, dispatched throughout the world with special vans, special planes, tents and medical equipment, all inoculated, well-equipped and well-coordinated, but insufficient. The virus they sought to contain by quarantining infected areas instead soon had them surrounded. Many doctors got sick and died. The grid went down and the team lost contact with the rest of the global effort. Though this town had been the site of an early US outbreak, where they hoped to stop the epidemic, there was nothing they could do. So instead of quarantining the sick, they quarantined the healthy. They occupied the town hall, and built an antiseptic fortress. They installed in the top of its dome a large fan with filters fine enough to stop the virus, powered by a gasoline-burning generator, which continuously blew filtered air into the building forcing all the other air out, so that the virus could not waft in. They dragged out all the furnishings and fixtures and anything that could be unbolted, heaping them in the town square. Then, starting in the top of the dome, standing on scaffolding, they bleached the entire inside of the building, down to the basement floor. The foyer, with its marble columns, was converted to a grey area where people would store the white suits in lockers, and disinfect before coming inside the building.

Since completing the town hall they had been methodically widening the perimeter of their sterile zone, building by building, street by street.

And then when I told her where I was from she blew a whistle. Another one in a white suit came forward and told me I would have to be sterilized.

It was the painter's job, apparently, to disinfect newcomers. She said she was one of the inoculated. She turned on a shower and told me to undress. And she undressed, breasts swinging as she bent over to remove her boot. I asked her what she was doing and she said it wouldn't make sense for me to clean you and then walk away with your germs. I stripped down to what was left of my underwear and realized I was getting an erection. I looked up at her helplessly. Good, she said, hooking my waistband with a finger, ripping away my shorts, then with both hands grasping my cock and inspecting it briefly, that will make it easier to scrub. She put a hand on my chest and pushed me back under the shower. Don't get it in your eyes, turning on a faucet, lacerating me with icy disinfectant. She stepped in, pulled the curtain closed, told me to raise my arms and began to scrub me. I watched the bubbles stream from her nipples as they swayed from her efforts. I looked into her eyes, but she was looking at my scalp. Checking for lice, as they could carry the virus.

After the bleach, the ultraviolet, and a merciless battery of antibiotics, I was locked in a "grey area" for the night. A room with a bed. I wasn't sure I wanted to be here. But after the months of wondering whether I was going to die after every time I ate, drank, or talked to somebody, I was looking forward to being sure I was safe. If only for awhile. That was tempting.

Through a window I could see people passing through the disinfection procedure, going into the capital dome to retire in bedrooms made out of the glass-walled offices of former clerks. It seemed as though everybody had broken up into groups of two or three, holding hands, kissing in the showers, not bothering to dress afterward. As the evening grew later, one couple did it dirty, choosing to make love before taking the horrible showers. I wondered whether that was safe. Watching this as a stranger behind glass was excruciating, the arousal the painter had caused had never really subsided, and I had to give myself relief in order to sleep—how she had put her hands on the wall, spread her legs, pushed her ass out, and looked over her shoulder impatiently at the man until he stood behind her, hands on her body.

She asked if she could paint me. She made me stand naked in the park. Then she mixed some colors on her palette, and began to apply them to me with cold wet strokes of her brush. Hey, I said. Hold still, she said. You're too white. She painted a red spiky flower on my chest. In the middle were three yellow spokes. Then she set up her easel and began to do a portrait of me, warning me against moving. I stared at the squirrels running by on dead power lines. I felt sort of stupid. As it grew warmer, she took off her shirt and tossed it aside. She told me to hold still. I noticed her collarbone, how the freckles began there. Hold still, she said. She shifted her weight, jutting out a hip. She looked down at me. Stop moving. Can you make it go back down? But stay that color? Oh now you've ruined it, she said. I tried clumsily to embrace her. She pushed me away. Just go away let me finish you from memory. I scooped up my clothes and walked over to dress behind a bush. My erection refused to go away all day, bringing tears to my eyes, I hated it.

A nearby team was working on dismantling a nuclear facility, a sprawling city where nuclear bombs were assembled and stored. I asked to be transferred to that group. I had tried to forget about her. I didn't think I wanted to live there and was looking for a chance to cut myself loose and drift, but in a way I liked the structure, the working and eating times, the sleeping and reading places, the clean lines between hot, grey, and safe.

Unfortunately, the painter was also on this team. They took me through a hole in a chain link fence that stretched across the desert floor to the horizon, topped with glittering razor wire, and we entered a rusted city. From the central building of the complex, on the top floor, one could walk around through the crowds of pigeons, look out through the broken windows, and, in any direction, beneath a grid of cables populated by migrating birds, were row after row of identical warehouses, each the size of several football fields, stretching across the deserts to the mountains in the east.

In the buildings, everything was coated with thick milky dust. Some were empty. Some contained consumer goods: shelves of televisions with lenses blind from dust, eyes that would never open. One building contained crates of newly-minted pennies, whose copper, I was assured, would be useful someday. One of the group reached into her pocket, pulled out a fistful of pennies she had collected about town, and poured them noisily onto a metal shelf.

The buildings that were now an ad-hoc laboratory used to store and dismantle radioactive material had been painted bright yellow by the team. They shone through the gaps between the darker buildings. I could hear the roar of a generator. As we approached the buildings, toes crunching through the dust, they seemed textured and undulating. The yellow buildings had scales and were breathing. I rubbed my eyes. I wondered whether the radiation was making the hot buildings shimmer. Then I understood: the yellow wall was covered with thousands of yellow butterflies, fanning their wings, crawling over one another, and now and then one would break away to flutter across the desert where nothing awaited it. Are they attracted to the paint, or the radioactivity, I asked, but nobody heard or responded, and our feet crunched through gravel all the way to a padlocked bright yellow steel door.

The generator powered the fluorescent lights beneath the hoods in the nuclear hot zone, and the exhaust fan on the roof of the yellow warehouse, which was constantly sucking air from beneath the hoods out through HEPA filters on the roof to capture all contaminants. The radioactive team worked in a world opposite the one they slept in: one imploding, one exploding.

The enriched uranium had been created for making nuclear bombs, lots of nuclear bombs, and now needed to be buried in special containers so it could be forgotten. In a long warehouse the canisters were stored. They looked like rows of coffee pots. Wearing special yellow suits, we would carry the coffeepots to the central room where they would be put beneath the hood. There a technician, peering in through a plastic window streaked with radioactive beryllium dust, reaching into the hood through long rubber gloves, would labor with a wrench and screwdrivers to open the coffeepots, and then measure and dump the contents—uranium pellets—into better canisters. Sparks flew from the pellets when they scraped against each other. The stuff was pure Uranium 235. You didn't need an explosive trigger to set it off, just put too much in one pile—a few pounds maybe—and it would go critical. Dump too much in one can and you could trigger an explosion the size of ten Hiroshimas. This was dangerous work. I wondered whether it was worth the risk.

The new canisters would be crimped shut, their outsides decontaminated, then passed out of the depressurized hood beneath heavy rubber flaps. Then, still in yellow suits, we would stack the canisters on a library cart, and push it a quarter of a mile to be loaded into the back of a filthy pickup used to deliver sealed canisters of uranium to a disposal site—a desert gorge painted with warnings in a somewhat more seismically stable region than where they lived, and far from any water sources—or to search for gasoline in neighboring villages for the generators. This was something they didn't speak about, and I surmised they tended to be mercenary in their approach to liberating gas for their purposes.

The painter, to my frustration, was assigned to train me. She showed me how to don the yellow suit, with the zip-up shoes. Luckily I did not have to undress all the way. When I asked why we didn't just bury the uranium in the canisters they were already stored in, rather than laboriously recanting them, she said it was to be safe. I decided not to question why we were doing the work in the first place.

I was helping her with a particularly unpleasant job involving dismantling some heavy steel shelves stuck together by rust, in order to open a door blocked by the shelves, to create a shorter passage to carry canisters through. The bolts were corroded and the wrenches were hard to handle through the gloves. The coffeepots stacked on the other side of the room seemed to ooze a persistent heat and there was no way to wipe sweat from our eyes through the faceplates. I tried to argue that taking apart the shelves was too much work, that it would take less time simply to walk the extra distance. We fought, and we worked late. When we finished it was dusk and we discovered the others had left for dinner, locking us in the warehouse, not knowing we were still there.

I realized I was stuck with her. We decided to remove the suits and go through the decontamination procedure, and stay in a back room, which had been converted to a sleeping space by piling pillows and rugs around.

I let her shower me, staring at her navel, and this time as she soaped my erection I ejaculated immediately and uncontrollably. She held and stroked my cock with interest as I came, each caress wracking my body with shivers. Stunned, I gazed at her helplessly, still slowly spasming, like a dreamer abruptly wakened. She laughed and kissed me on the nose. Still holding the head with one hand, with the other she pointed at her thigh where I had left a thread of semen and told the sperm to stay away from the radiation. She looked at me and laughed again. You don't look mad anymore.

In the room of furs, she put logs in the fireplace and sliced apples. They will rescue us tomorrow morning she said. She lay next to me and put her hand on my cock. What happened? she laughed. But it started to grow again.

Without humans, there is no one to hunt.

I remember that line from a National Geographic documentary.

What else do I remember?

The jingle of the collar of a dog attacking a fleaspot with its hind leg. A cracked vase of dried chrysanthemum casting shadow in slanting afternoon sun. The purl of cars on a bridge as heard from underneath. Quiet memories assault me now when I sleep. My memories of childhood are crisp. But I don't remember people.

Not that I believe that nonsense about one's life passing before one's eyes when one dies, nor that you will kill me.

Is this what you wanted when you locked me in here?

As if I care.

You'll read what I write, understand, release me, and kneel while I slit your throats. Or if you want to run shrieking into the jungle like monkeys as I shoot you in the back of your necks, so be it. There is only one way this can turn out.

I gave much thought to how to kill you, and write down my findings only in case I fail, and leave people behind me, so that someone will come after me to resume my efforts to cure the earth.

In the back seat, I carry a suitcase and two red plastic five-gallon jugs. The suitcase contains found clothing; the jugs contain gasoline and water respectively. I hotwired a lot of cars; I changed a lot of tires. Tires have started to collapse and decay. And I wear them out. I need speed, it is my reason. The highways are untrafficked though by no means wide open, so it is risky pushing a hundred when the roadway might be unexpectedly cracked in two or blocked by a jackknifed semi. But speed was what I did. There were a few stretches that I often returned to—former highway 15 from L.A. to Vegas—but for the most part I liked to drive too fast on highways I had never been on, leaning forward to see what curves and obstacles were up ahead. I wrecked a couple of cars or more, but sustained no major injuries. I wear seatbelts. Sometimes a helmet. I'm not crazy.

I'm not.

You are.

California is not a place I like driving. Earthquakes and flooding have made a dangerous mess of highways. It is unsafe for driving at the speeds I am accustomed to. But there I went, heading west at 120 on 40. I scraped between two abandoned cars parked so close a side mirror was sheared off, spun in the air, and flashed in my rear-view mirror. I ran over a coyote family crossing the road. Their bones made quite a crunching percussion. I slept and ate in the car, became a metal shellfish. Night was not a time for me. Animals and the things I did. I had to wait it out. In the reclined passenger seat I slept in fitful bouts, trying to ignore the sounds of beasts walking around the car or scampering over the roof, howling, sometimes in low voices speaking. I kept my eyes tight; if there were any living people out there, they would have to make their presence obvious before I would believe in them.

Once when I opened my eyes at the slanting dawnlight, there was a wolf curled on the hood, apparently for the heat. When I yelled and knocked on the windshield it didn't move. I yelled until I was out of breath. I didn't want to step outside, though I needed to pee, so I tried to start the car, but the starter had died and the twisted key issued only clicks. I unrolled the window slowly. It rose to its feet, head lowered, yellow gaze locked. The shotgun left the hood streaked with a gruesome paste not even 100 mph winds could scrub, and no matter how much wiper fluid I pumped on them, the flecks of windshield blood only smeared into arcs.

I wondered when I would have to give up auto travel. Gasoline evaporates and tires collapse. Deserts are crisscrossed by cracking, sand-flooded highways, increasingly impassable, packed with dead vehicles in crystallized gridlock. Bridges tilt in the torrents passing beneath them. Falling trees and crumbling mountainsides bury the asphalt roadways or take them down into valleys with them. Increasingly, I am confined to deserts. I would try to drive into the mountains or valleys and end up having to backtrack.

Survivors had collected on farms scattered throughout this wilderness. These communities are a recrudescence of a disease that had almost been eradicated. Cancer cells. Biotherapy had been 99% effective. Surgical intervention was necessary to complete the cure. A system of communicating between cells had been established despite the absence of a working telecommunications grid. There were radio stations in barns. A nomadic committee comprising one representative from every commune walked from farm to farm. Their purpose was to coordinate, share or trade resources, and work out increasingly formal, consensual structures for how the groups might resolve disputes or collaborate. The committee, for the most part, served to preserve equilibrium among cancer cells. They were the law, but were generally welcome wherever they traveled. When they returned to a farm, that farm's representative would return to work the fields, and a new representative would be chosen. They wore pieces of old uniforms they had come into somehow. A police hat, a random badge, blue trousers with piping.

I considered this ragtag band of hippy farmers playing at being sheriff a metastasization. This roaming cell I tried to eliminate first, in such a way as to breed fear, instill mistrust between cells and jam future communications. The first time I saw the committee, they seemed armed, but without any serious firepower like the assault rifles I collected in my trunk. They yelled at me from the side of the road as I tore past them in a black Mustang. At that time I did not know they had connections. I thought they were just nomadic scavengers. Fish in a barrel.

I drove for twenty more miles, parked the car, waited until dusk, armed myself, and walked back down the road. As I suspected, they had a fire. I stuck to shadows and crept up on it. Standing against a tree I observed at once that nobody was beside this fire, that there was a second fire deeper in the woods, and that a German Shepard near the fire had taken notice of me. A growl was rising from its throat.

To my astonishment, they were prepared.

It was a trap. After sustaining one minor bullet graze to the arm and mowing down two of their sentries and their dog, I made a retreat and don't think I was followed. I vowed that would be my last bullet wound, and I doubt very much you will force me to renege on that promise.

After my crash landing, I had lost my plane. I wasn't going to try to take off in one of the abandoned, unmaintained aircraft you find in hangars, so I could not track the committee's movements by air. I would have to ruminate on the problem or wait until I had them cornered and unsuspected. I knew that my attack would force them to arm themselves more thoroughly, and that packing heat would eventually override their bucolic natures. I had not killed them, but I had infected them with the violence of fear.

Many of the farms used low power FM to communicate, making it possible to triangulate the colonies' locations using my car radio.

The first farm I found had ten people—two normal, healthy families who raised crops and livestock, canning, curing, and drying what they could to make it through the winter months. The men were furriers, and these furs provided for some commerce with other farms, usually for fuel. The families occupied various rooms in an old farmhouse. They took me in, fed me on their best food, and let me sleep in the crawlspace above the kitchen. My second night there, I went outside, threw their fuel around, burned the house down, and shot them as they ran out. The spectacle of the fire consumed the sound of the gunshots, so I was able to get everybody before they figured out what was happening. Not that they were prepared to fight. But I reminded myself to use a silencer for future massacres so that I would not run the risk of scaring away the victims before I could shoot them. I did not seriously think any of these farmers could resist me by force, but of course if they ran into the woods I would have trouble tracking them. It is easy enough to find silencers, or accessories for guns. America is full of guns.

That time I made no effort to hide the bodies. I slept in my car. One of the victims crawled off during the night—a teenaged girl I shot in the arm and, I thought, chest—but I wasn't worried about her chances of survival alone, wounded, and homeless. It was becoming a pretty hazardous world; at night one needed shelter. I burned down the barn and other structures just to deny her any. Hazardous, that is, because of the animals. The old dangers—human crime and violence, and toxic waste—were resolving themselves, if slowly. Well, there were no laws to break, and the absence of people eliminated any strife. I don't consider my actions criminal in any case. These procedures were medical, eliminating pathogens from the surface of the earth. In my travels I saw former cornfields turned to gravel and mud. Nonrenewable genetically-engineered seed and a battery of herbicides and pesticides had transmuted arable soil into black sand. Acres of clods in this capital-ravaged landscape. If employed by Monsanto, I certainly could have engineered a better soybean that would not have left this legacy, but my talents were occupied elsewhere. Nuclear power plants had not been shut down properly. When their power failed, the coils that cooled the water in which thousand-degree nuclear fuel was stored failed. The water boiled off and the plants burned down, releasing tons of radioactive smoke, creating disaster areas worse than those a nuclear bomb would have left. Radioactivity announced its presence in landscapes where nothing grew. I drove through these white areas quickly with the windows up and ventilation shut off. I call these large tracts of dead land *white* because they usually were ashen. But most places outside the desert were so green a jungle grew in a wall right along the edge of the highway, screaming with birds. Entering a white area was like driving into a sudden snowstorm: a dusty white dirt that met the far off and cloudy sky, the stubble of former trees the only indication that I was on Earth and not the moon. The effect was like driving through a giant ashtray. I tried not to inhale until I had passed through into the green on the other side where clouds of insects again painted the windshield and animals stood in the road staring dumbly at my approach, like the moose apparently content to sacrifice its life in order to mash my grille, leave my windshield cracked and bloody, and total my car in a carnage of steaming hissing meat and dribbling pungent gasoline. Another dead car to be around longer than dinosaur bones, as its fluids and bad ideas sank into the groundwater, titmice nested in its broken headlights, ferrets birthing children in its nests of shredded upholstery.

But I digress. All these poisons would be folded back into the ecology, no matter their halflife. The white spaces will again become green, long after I am dead, having taken as many as I could with me. Thanks to me.

How long before the language was deforested? How long would the words for trees hang on, before they too were at last uprooted and sent the way of the dodo? If language was the detritus of that which no longer existed, a clutter of empty symbols snared in their own semantic equations, then wouldn't it be better forgotten? Perhaps language is a constant in the structure of the universe, like electromagnetism and gravity, irrespective of whether people understand or harness it.

I developed a style after my next slaughter. After two more I even wished I could start over and rekill the first two farms just to give my debut homicides the signature touch of my repertoire. The second farm was pretty large, and after the initial burn and harvest with an assault rifle, I hid in a barn until the survivors had crept back and I could arrange to mow down most of them in a line. I was very patient. I used hand grenades I procured from an abandoned armory. This was a good way to kill them as they slept, such that the survivors would be too dazed to give me any trouble. They shouldn't all have slept in the same place at the same time.

There was no way I was going to clean up a mess like that, so I poured gasoline on the bodies and torched them, burning down much of the remaining buildings and surrounding wilderness in the process. This was gratifying, but a waste of gasoline, so I made a note to stockpile other, less useful flammable chemicals as I came across them in my travels. I had quite a long shopping list of tools to help me kill. Not all of them were efficient, but as a former scientist I had a natural curiosity to see how quickly or slowly a human specimen could be dismantled.

It was at the third farm that I was able to work the killings up into something more worthy of me. I lashed the youngest one's body to the turret of the barn. I impaled skulls on stakes to greet visitors from any of the entrances. I hung bodies from high tree branches where animals would not be easily able to drag them away, so they could sway in the wind and send an unsettling message to visitors.

Admittedly, I became self-conscious. I had somehow shifted from killing victims to communicating with whoever might discover the bodies through my choice of how to arrange the scene of the crime. I could leave the bodies for the animals to maul and make it look like a crime of nature, I could try to make myself look like a gang of savage marauders, or even some supernatural beast. But what I settled on was to make it look like the farms were killing each other. If I could just instill enough fear and hatred this way, they would be able to help me with the work of wiping themselves out.

I remember the dirty chaotic old world and miss it. After the plague, people lost their animal edge. I was a weapon designer, not a killer in the useful sense, but I still expect that murder used to be much more challenging five years ago. I regret not having tried my hand at it. The covering of one's traces must have been the central concern. An effective police force stood in for the spineless "morality" you mud farmers have—it forced one to keep moving. You kill too many people in one jurisdiction, they were sure to catch up with you. You couldn't keep your day job and kill when you wanted, you had to earn a living at it in order to keep paying for hotel rooms and gasoline, auto repair. And you would have had a lot of competition in those days—killers all over the place kept victims somewhat wary. Now there were no police, and fewer victims to choose from, living in isolated knots usually connected to farms or fishing waters. They knew no violence more extreme than how to kill a bear, they couldn't defend themselves, and they wouldn't chase you. I decided that for the rest of my years, I would find and be taken in by these strangers, and live among them as a guest, eating their food, even helping in the fields, until the night I would kill them, make art, move on.

Nothing from childhood, or even from before the outbreak. My memories of people really begin when I began to execute them. This started with human testing of prisoners in our bioweapon research lab. Then I was able to explore new methods of terminating life on behalf of the community where I lived, which was not a dirty farm but a shining pyramid that was truly the culmination of everything. I could take the least desirable people out into the desert and conduct experiments to see how severely they might plead. And bleed. A dirty woman destroyed our creation, an experimental subject on whom I had first tested the vaccine. She is dead now, of course. I pursued her and finally ended her life by fire-bombing her from my airplane. But the plane unfortunately suffered some structural failure and so I was forced to execute a crash landing. After that I had to travel by automobile, and was unable to rejoin my people where they lived in a fortress with the last full-scale electrical generator functioning. It is only a matter of time, however before they discover the good work I am doing out here and bring me back into the fold. The work of purifying the planet is not yet done.

I am one of the most successful businessmen in the history of the world, one whose name was never printed. With a bulletproof designer biocontainment briefcase—packed with crystal vials of weapons grade smallpox, Marburg, Ebola, airborne, waterborne, foodborne—I was floated through the corridors of power. My burning vectors refracted through the lenses of governments and those to whom they answered. I was a VIP in every capital in the world. Even the most fundamentalist governments fed my every whim with champagne fountains, sex, solvents, opium, hashish, cannabis, oil, jeweled Kalashnikovs. What I sold commanded fear. Nobody shook my hand.

As you can see, my work was perfect.

Our project was to create a virus that would attack every cell in the body with a fatality rate of 99%, but a slow incubation period during which it was highly communicable by air, skin, and vermin. Deploying the epidemic ourselves would have been trivial. First we sold the weapon to our enemy. Of course, there was no easy way for them to test the vaccine we sold them. In the end we may have been undone by one of the scientists in my employ. It hardly matters.

Sometimes a good idea just catches.

Behind electrified fences and sprinkler systems, in the walls of our pressurized pyramid city, we poured effervescent toasts to the first falling domino from a chilled bottle of rare vintage vaccine and watched the fires on TV until the only station was ours.

I found this fourth farm by accident. I drove by people working in the field, who waved with half-smiles. There was a wide-spread taboo against the automobile, a lingering superstition that its use would lead back to the old ways, and the farmers tended to drive trucks and tractors sparingly, only for farm work, never for travel. It was a stupid prejudice; regardless, it was increasingly hard to keep a car going. Of course I chose convertibles and sports cars. I routinely stopped at automotive places, filling my trunk with spare parts and tools. They lay on blankets in the trunk. Beneath the blankets were guns, ammunition, hunting knives, baseball bats, handcuffs, rope, wire, explosives, bottles of everclear tourniqueted with rags, acids, barbed wire, razors, pillowcases, golf clubs, grenades. Sometimes I offered some of these new tools as gifts to my host communities. Eventually I would kill them and take the gift back.

They had waved at me, if visibly suspicious of my red Corvette, so I considered that an invitation. I pulled into the farm, my car then surrounded by barking dogs and a few curious strangers trying to pull the dogs away and shush them.

This you know: a thin black man appraised me, bending toward the window. I told him that I was traveling, taking logs of communities, a sort of census bureau. I feigned ignorance of the committee. I was invited for dinner, though they seemed uncomfortable around me. They asked questions about other communities and became silent when I told them about a nearby farm I had recently visited. He went to get coffee, but from the kitchen there came a crash and curse, and he reappeared saying he had accidentally broken the pitcher, apologizing, offering tea, which I accepted, though I wondered what it was brewed from. When I put together that the black man was the leader of this farm, I felt a pang of something I did not recognize. My gut told me to kill him immediately.

He gave me a bedroom and I lay awake listening to the house. I thought it might be best if I just stayed awake and killed them that night, perhaps keeping the young woman alive to take my time with. But somehow I was surrounded by them, I think there were four, but I was having trouble focusing. I felt gelatinous. My wrists were tied to the bedframe. Most of the people hung back out of the lantern light, but the thin man sat on the edge of the bed and said that he believed I had killed the neighbors. I tried to look incredulous and protest but was too sleepy to feign surprise. Then he put a shotgun on my lap, and I saw that it was mine. I discovered my feet were also tied to the bed. I fell asleep thinking of ways I could mutilate them, and interesting places to leave their bodies: on the swingset, in the yurt, in a boat in the pond.

The next morning I shouted for water until eventually someone brought me a glass. The girl. I smiled at her. She poured the glass on my face. I choked and sputtered and protested this inhumane abuse. I was treated with the most abominable callousness. These barely evolved orangutans who desecrate the earth have the audacity to treat a fellow human being like one of their mules. Roped to the bed like a goat, soiling myself, cruel and unusual punishment clearly in violation of my human and constitutional rights by these ignorant hypocrites who claim to live in harmony with nature while burning trees for fuel and raping the earth of vegetables and game, who have the cold-bloodedness to snare rabbits but lack the courage to kill a man.

At dusk I was spoon-fed chalky soup by the thin man, with his straw hat, sitting on the side of my bed. And I let him know that he was being unreasonable, barbaric, and his behavior was an affront to community, human rights, and due process. He smiled at this last one, which I had to admit was a bit outdated, but for the most part he seemed seriously to consider it. And then I must have fainted. I was dimly conscious of being untied, lifted onto a plank of wood, and stretchered out of the house and into the woods. I think I asked them more than once where they were taking me, but my drugged mind seemed unable to absorb whatever answer they gave. I fought to wake up but more water was poured into my mouth, making me choke, belch, and pass out to the sound of my own moaning.

This time I woke up feeling bad. My arms were numb and tied behind me, I was outdoors, looking into a barn, and when I leaned my head back I realized I was tied to a tree. I wanted to struggle with the ropes, but I couldn't feel my hands.

So they were still discussing what to do with me. In the meantime they would feed me and keep me alive, tied to the tree. I tried to appeal to their kindness, called them fascists, referred to a police state, and all manner of criticisms I remembered liberals had held about the government before the collapse, but none of it seemed to help my cause. I confessed nothing, and doubted they would be able to find evidence.

But for now I was being made to suffer, but in the end it would only increase my power over their sniveling guilty consciences. Though I was a bit dizzy, I thought through the worst possible contingencies. These people certainly couldn't dust for fingerprints, compare tire tracks, or do any sophisticated forensics. There would have been no security cameras, no photographic record. I could have left the murder weapon behind, even a gun that had been registered in my name, and there would be no way these hippies could trace the gun or match a bullet to a firearm. I was innocent.

I nodded off, smiling.

But when I awoke there were two children before me. I pleaded with them to untie me, but they continued to appraise me coldly. It began to dawn on me that I hadn't seen any children at dinner the first night, but these two looked somehow familiar. Then one of them opened her mouth, sort of croaked, and ran away, the other pointed at me, his lip blossoming in a sort of pout. The thin man stepped from behind me, and hefted the child onto his hip. "Is this the man?" he asked. The child brought his fist down repeatedly on the thin man's chest, weirdly robotic, and then I understood that these were children from the third farm. I remembered being introduced to them but I did not remember killing them. Something had happened and I had blacked out—maybe I had drunk something before using the chainsaw, or maybe I just got carried away—and I woke up in my car somewhere down the road.

The thin man put down the child and it ran away, shouting the same thing over and over, a word I did not understand. This farmer crouched before me and ran his hand through my hair. "Water?" I choked, trying to look more piteous than I felt. He stood up and walked away.

"Due process," I heard the thin man say somewhere behind me, and he again asked me to confess. I shouted a string of insults at him, referring to my rights and other notions I thought would melt his communitarian heart. I couldn't tell if he was still back there. Later I heard arguing. Someone was being told to do something she didn't want to do.

That third farm had done wonders with renewable resources, really the whole place was a marvel. They manufactured solar panels of various designs, which I would have thought impossible for them. Most of the people who lived there had ended up in the composting toilet, in pieces, but I was starting to regret not having hidden the other bodies. That farm had had a wimpy consensus-based, non-hierarchical job rotation, and all decisions had to be made unanimously as a group. As soon as I learned that, I realized I could get away with anything, because, even if they could form a consensus when most of them were dead, it would take them forever to agree on how to punish me. One of the couples even had a GPS finder for their child, a device run on scavenged batteries that broadcast a signal to a finder, allowing them to know where the child was at all times. I couldn't believe those satellites were still up there, working, and saw no way I could bring them down. The child, who was a bit slow and probably autistic, had a tendency to wander off into the woods. This was how I set a trap for the parents before I hunted down the rest. Those three bodies were likely never found. That farm had been strictly vegetarian, and even the cattle would die peacefully of old age. There was nothing for me to fear.

This farm, I noted, had a hierarchy. The thin man was obviously the leader. That didn't bode as well. Though the thin man was obviously a pacifist and incapable of violence, I didn't feel completely good about it. My misgivings multiplied when I discovered that they had incarcerated a prisoner before. A murderer, a jealous alcoholic trashed on some homemade potato wine had killed his lover for sleeping with the thin man. The culprit had been tied up. They spoke of him in the past tense, but would not answer my questions about what had happened to him. It seemed unlikely that they had executed him, more likely he had been exiled. If I was able to convince them to untie me, I might consider just fleeing. But probably I would find a way to come back and finish what I had imagined.

It was dawn and I had not really slept. I heard footsteps and murmuring and before me stepped the thin man, with an adolescent girl. The thin man carefully loaded a shotgun and handed it to the girl.

I don't remember what sugary righteous bullshit he said exactly, but it was clear he was instructing the kid to shoot me. Fuck this, I thought angrily. The kid took the gun uncertainly, and the man advised her that this would be an important experience, and that she was never to kill without the thin man's permission, but that someday the thin man would not be around and then she would have to assume the responsibility. It was also okay, he said, if she enjoyed it.

I began screaming. What kind of way to raise a child is that, I demanded. I demanded a fair trial, I called them murderers, racists, capitalists, and everything that came to mind that I thought might trigger their guilt. I made a self-description of how I had come to help them, how I was a guest, how I used to be a social worker. I may even have accused them of murdering the other farm and trying to pin it on me. I think I mentioned child abuse as well, accusing them of torturing the young children's mother in the barn before executing her, but then I realized I had said too much.

The girl raised the shotgun and I strained against the ropes to turn my head away.

But she couldn't do it. She started to cry. The man put one hand on the rifle barrel and with the other pushed her to her ass. He raised the gun and cocked it and pointed it at me with one arm, still repeating an angry question to the girl. I yelled. He didn't fire, he just shook the gun in demonstration, then threw it at her feet.

I was yelling, the child was protesting, and the man was screaming at both of us to shut up, and finally grabbed and discharged the rifle into the air, bringing a rain of sassafras leaves and silence. A woman ran across the lawn at the sound of this, but, seeing I was still alive, seemed disappointed and wandered away. "Murderer," I whispered as spitefully as I could at the man, who returned a look so intense I had to look away. Apparently he wouldn't settle to execute me, it had to be a lesson for the young one. He shook his head and walked away, shotgun over his shoulder. The girl refused to look at me and went into the barn, presumably to sulk in the hayloft.

There was a birdfeeder near the tree and all day I watched these feathered vermin gobble seeds, argue with each other, and fly away. Cardinals dominated, and came in male / female pairs. The bright red males with their Mohawks of peaked feathers seemed unintimidatable. Fat sparrows traveled in defensive flocks, and the chickadees seemed to hang back until the group had moved on. The titmice, who also seemed to move in couples, would appear very briefly to snatch a seed and wing away to a treetop to devour them.

At one point a squirrel came tentatively across the lawn like a nervous inchworm, climbed the pole, and began to stuff its face with birdseed. To my surprise the cardinals attacked. Two males and a female fluttered about it, and drove it down the pole. The squirrel chattered angrily from the ground while the cardinals took watchful positions in a nearby tree. Eventually the squirrel began to inch its way back up the pole. This time the cardinals attacked more forcefully, but the squirrel was tenacious, taking position atop the birdfeeder. The female swooped to rake the cringing rodent with her talons, as it turned around and around, shrieking. Finally one of the largest males seemed to drop straight down from the sky and spreading its wings to brake the fall, impaled the squirrel's eye with its beak. Chirping oddly, the squirrel slid off the birdfeeder in a drizzle of blood and fell to the grass, where it wormed in circles. Again the red hammer came down. The squirrel fell dead in the grass, its neck snapped. I wouldn't have thought it possible. I began to rock, trying to work at the rope that bound my wrists against the tree trunk.

That night they forgot to bring me food. I tried to shout but found that without the evening water I was voiceless, so I slumped there, arms behind me, shoulders burning, forearms numb, and tried to work through my confused thoughts, without much luck. Escape, kill them, were the two main ideas, but I didn't know what order they came in. I couldn't uproot the tree. Working my way out of the rope was hopeless, since I could neither see nor feel my arms. I could try to talk them into releasing me but I finally had to admit I wasn't sure how to do that. Threatening them didn't seem wise. Offering to run away and never return? I thought I had already played that card to no effect. Acting piteous to invoke sympathy also seemed like a dead end, since by this point I was quite weak, prone to crying fits I barely managed to contain, and sick all over, shivering, crossing my legs for warmth. Confession? They wanted a confession. I didn't see how that would work. Their consciences wouldn't let me die by starvation or any other means. I wasn't sure they had established my guilt. As if it would help, I tried to walk back through how I had come to this to see what mistakes I had made. The thought of killing them was the only one I could fix on, so I tried to remember how many people I had seen here, at first trying to count them on the numb and unseen fingers behind my back, finally kicking off my shoes and using my toes to keep track. I had trouble, but it seemed there were nine, including the escaped children, who might be especially hard to catch this time. I must have fallen asleep, or sort of. I could hear a discussion at the farmhouse, raised voices carried over to me. I imagined words like killing, justice, but was weak and unsure. Clearly the timbres were those of a painful disagreement about something, almost certainly me, which I took as a good sign. Finally dawn approached. I heard creatures crashing through the underbrush behind me but tried to ignore them. As dawn broke through the mist a family of deer walked past me. I hissed at them and they bounded off into the woods, except the male, who came over, hooves grinding the dirt, and bit my nose. Blood filling my mouth, I drifted off again, and when I came to, I heard an intermittent scraping behind the barn. It was a regular sound, and I thought it might be a grave being dug for me. I knew the man was back there.

He told me that he was my employee in the old world. My head of security. Whether I remembered or believed him is irrelevant. All people have always been dead to me. Nothing you say makes any impression on me. Nothing anybody "feels" has ever done more than enrage me. Sperior man has a right and purpose, a responsibility to kill. The sperior man must kill. The inferior man will of course try to stop him but the inferior is slow, soft-witted, noncommittal. This means that the sperior man must plan his spree with care, execute it with suddenness, speed, and deliberation. The structure of sperior man's life is thus as follows: self-care, amassing respectability, knowledge, money, and sex partners. Copulation. And then an effort to kill as many inferior people as possible in the shortest time, by hand, through an act that will be labeled criminal or terrorist, or, best, as a military action.

There is an *I* in *sperior man*, but no room for you.

The next day he had found the key to the manacles in my trunk, pilfered from a bondage shop in Reno. My ankles were chained to the tree and I was allowed to sit in a chair at a small table. I was given a notebook and pen and told that if I wrote a full confession I would be allowed to go free. Of course this is coercion, and I everything I have written is a lie designed to seem plausible to you, because I must be allowed to live.

Then they are standing here: the committee. Oh, what a ragtag band of legislators, their clothes torn and inappropriate, salvaged from anywhere. I ignore them as I write. Many of them wear plastic armor—sports gear—and I surmise they are the combatants. One heavyset one looks ridiculous in a cup and shoulder pads. All of them carry backpacks hung with pots and pans and implements of various sorts. I am so delirious I almost recognize a woman with an arm in a sling. Her hand doesn't work right; I'm sure I would remember that. They stand in a semicircle studying me seriously. So. These are the people I have been playing with this whole time, the ones who I arranged bodies for, lit fires for, left bizarre graffiti for, false clues for. This is my chance to perform my innocence, my victimization and outrage, for real. But as I sputter, blubbering bubbles of blood from something ruptured inside, I remember the body I had left tied to a cupola on the roof of a barn, weather vane impaled in its eyesocket, and I start to laugh. They just keep staring.

is this thing on? testing test—
i ah—don't know how long it's been since
i last spoke i have a battery-powered radio
receiver here so i know i'm broadcasting listen—
! feedback. ow. got your atten-
tion. bet they can hear that in space. the sky is purple
and the wind is restless going back and forth like
it's looking for someone. probably me. the sky has changed its meaning. the sky once seemed fragile, blue tissue paper over
black rock, to be torn away by pollution. now those
clouds look like teeth. i was afraid trees would die. now i
am afraid trees will kill me. i thought the sky was fleeting
but i was. we all were. the clouds have
come to life. rains spin rivulets across the windowpane.
on a night like this there is interference. and of course in
the light— hello? —ning i see people
who aren't really there but what really scares me is the
water. it's coming. it's just a matter of time. even what
i saw in the desert, the harsh emptiness there, doesn't compare to my fear
of the sea. in case you thought this little broadcast was
a cry for company, no. i don't want company. i just want
to do good radio. listen to this. i'm the only thing on the
dial except sometimes a strange tone all the way to the left. once i thought i
heard salsa. very poor reception. disconcerting that i can't tell whether static
is music. and you? do you think you're hearing things in the static? worried
that you're insane? what is sanity but inhibitions? inhibited from doing
what? walking around naked? shitting in the middle of the street? collecting
months-old cigarette butts? talking to yourself? that's
my life. your radio is not broken. your mind is not broken. your world is broken. where are you? at the top of
a shattered skyscraper in a ruined city combing the skies for any information? in a shack by the desert? among people living together in confusion?
or in a sealed hotel room watching reruns? where am
i? wouldn't you like to know. when i escaped from prison i was in southern
california, and i walked a long way, east, away from the oceans, mountains,
and deserts. i am in a radio studio off an alley, a canyon of ivy in a crooked
maze of impassible streets blocked by foliage, debris, and fallen trees, a bus
on its side, a former construction site now a deep lake of rainwater. when
i pushed aside some vines and found the door to this place it was the first
deja vu i've felt since the day i was arrested. someone had been camping

out at the radio station until fairly recently. the transmitter is the same model used by the pirate radio station where i used to have a show that was the reason i was arrested, supposedly. all i needed to get on the air was electricity so i set out to find gas for the generator.   it's a city of trees. just a new forest thrusting up through asphalt shards. i waded with my knapsack through walls of weeds rising from cracks, parking lots half-covered by composting leaves and topsoil, a furniture store that looked like a terrarium inside. two noisy cats fucking. lichen climbed crumbling concrete walls. a dank underpass beneath railroad tracks. the carapace of an ivy-encrusted train, most of its windows intact. spraypainted inscriptions. i was finding nothing. then i saw a glass tower above me through treetops. in its cavernous parking garage vehicles slumped on soft tires and walls of slatted metal crumbled a red rain of powder that stained the concrete. the painted markings were still bright, yellow stripes and black numbers, reserved parking. chirping echoed from sparrows nested in blown-out light fixtures stuffed with twigs and leaves. i checked the cars but their tanks seemed empty. a snake flicked its tongue from a hole in the wall. i forced open a warped doorway to a footbridge, an open cement path canopied by a roof of corroded ribs where perhaps an awning once hung, arching to the towering glass hotel. i crossed over a wide fountain, now a brackish pond, and saw a deer drinking. this one was the size of a horse and its antlers were menacing. it glared up at me, eyes narrow with contempt. on a shore of yellow curb a firehydrant drizzled. through a door wedged open with a cinderblock i entered a hallway of ruined mossy carpeting. empty hotels frighten me only when they aren't really empty. i climbed thirty stories of steps.   i need to point out here that i suffer from verti-go.   "vertigo"   i should explain because i don't know how many words have been lost.   vertigo is a fear of heights so intense you can't trust your senses. nothing feels stable. the floor is covered with ball bearings. walls are no longer vertical, flat, or motionless. you turn into water. my fear of heights is so profound that i feel unsafe on the upper floors of a building, and it's even worse now. maybe its worse because i no longer have to conform, or maybe because the buildings are falling, or maybe because the planet wants me dead. but i have learned, during those months i tried to drive cars, how to find gas, that it helps to have a view. at the top of the hotel was a moldy restaurant, a large circular dining room with windows offering a panoramic view of the treetops ob-scuring the city. a breeze came in through some broken panes and it felt as though the building were swaying. i went behind the bar first. my gun was in my hand before i realized i was staring at myself in a mirror. i've looked better. i've been shaving my head to keep it clear of ticks but haven't done a very neat job. my face is streaked with dirt and my eyes are scary. for a person who gets nothing but fresh air and exercise i don't look healthy. beneath the bar caps shone. cases of bottles. a splintered jar of olives contained an explosion of growth. the restaurant had not been looted. i entered the kitchen. in the beam from my flashlight a butchers table loomed. i saw the freezer door and knew better than to open it, it would have been thawing for a year, a room stuffed with maggots. i found a gallon can and hacked it open. in the dining room, at a table not too close to a window, i ate cold beans by the handful, until my dizziness made me nauseated. but stronger than gravity was the pull of whiskey, so i fetched one of those shiny bottles and unscrewed the cap. time had been cruel to this blend. a reeking fume of potent mash rose from the bottleneck. nervously i hefted it. no microbe would survive a dousing with that solvent. glug, i sputtered a wavering haze of fume. let me introduce another word.   "alcoholic."

    i don't remember what exactly it means. but i had a moment. the orange sky spread beyond the slow curve of windowpanes encircling the upper deck. the tables were set. napkins rose in special folds from the sunfaded dustfrosted tablecloth. wineglasses and waterglasses stood at attention, diffracting splashes of light. silverware lay in ranks. i saw the place where the manager stood when he told the workers to go home. i walked around the perimeter scanning the streets beneath, and found fractured shards of oil logos where gas stations stood. most signs are now empty rectangles mounted at the tops of poles, their words have faded, fallen, or broken, and they frame only sky. what words remain also seem to have faded, their meanings lost. on the southern horizon i observed a flash in the smear of a rainstorm. this gave me a pang of fear, but i seemed to be upwind of the storm so i supposed it was not looking for me. the sun turned golden, set the tops of the trees aflame, obliterated the brilliant sky until it could not be looked at. a soft tinkling of insects rose. even thirty stories up were meandering gnats. a few berserk cicadas sputtered by. the shadows lengthened, tinged by a touch of rainbow. trees stood diffidently. branches began to drain light from the sky, blackness seeped up from the roots. and i sat and drank. nod, slosh, clunk. we repeated that procedure. a wave of annihilation swept through me. my cells wept. i finished the bottle. i meant to get another. i must have tumbled off the chair and passed out. i hadn't realized it was one of those rotating restaurants. in inky dreams i stood in a desert walking away from a fire.   i heard a crash and it took a second to fix myself. hundreds of feet in the air in an unfamiliar structure, uninhabited, or so i had presumed. i had no idea what woke me. like cymbals but i thought it might have been my head. the floor was spinning and i couldn't tell whether i was falling. my hand groped for my backpack.   with my flashlight in one hand and my gun in the other i came up on my knees swaying. the revolver was already slippery from the sweat in my palm. i flicked on the flashlight and it lit up claws in the darkness that sliced my face, knocking me to the stagnant rug. something shrieked over me and womped against the window. a huge bird fell to the carpet. a lattice of cracks spread through the window spinning an iridescent web across the light the moondust spread across the night. a fragment of glass fell with a tinkle. the stunned bird rolled over, striking a wing against a table leg. i opened fire until the pistol clicked, wasting my last two rounds on an animal i could easily have killed by hand. the rest of the glass caved in, raining thirty floors down the outside of the building. a surprised beast down there yelped.   and then the ringing in my ears.   if there are any humans in this city i have announced my presence to them. that was me, folks. my gunshots had set all the dogs in the neighborhood to barking. unknown animals answered the dogs and it seemed the whole forest was screaming my name.   without really sleeping i woke in the morning on the floor, wracked with thirst. wincing, a bright and hostile sun rising. each photon of light was a prick of pain in my skull. climbing down the stairs took an hour. even as i made my way outside the building i was afraid it would fall on me.   luckily there was no sign of the deer. after refilling my canteen with hydrant water, the first swallow made me throw up repeatedly, each spasm echoing away as pain in my forehead. it was luxurious wasting water like that.   i found the strip of businesses i had seen from above. tattered awnings flapped gaily. signs above storefronts posed a sequence of meaningless syllables. on an orange striped barricade blocking the street, one of the amber warning lights was still blinking.   "one way." i struggle to remember what words mean. they usually mean other words. "florist." a profusion of plants climbed out of the storefront. what i thought i remembered could not have been. an abandoned bicycle had a flat tire. a payphone was mounted against a wall of disintegrating stucco. sagging within the glass of a convenience store a number of curling, fading signs boasted of bargains to be had there.   language blankets the land like infectious contaminant. paper flutters in the breeze, waiting for the next intelligence to infect and destroy. maybe this is why earth has undertaken this program of extermination, widespread fire and flood, to wash that ashy fucking slush to the bottom of the sea.   these are the questions that concern me. when humans crowded the earth, we thought for sure we were in control of everything—nature, language, war, money, even water. but who are the real major players who run this planet? i see hundred dollar bills blowing down the street and wonder. i found a gasoline truck. when i opened the cab there was a corpse stuck to the upholstery. i tell how much time has passed by the conditions of the bodies i find. they come in two varieties—infected and liquified—just a skeleton of black glue—or dead of natural causes, like the body in the gasoline truck. he seemed to have died within the past month. suddenly. fright? perhaps he had been living at the radio station.   he was the most recently living person i had seen in a long time. i gave up on the idea of driving the truck back but i siphoned a five gallon can. that should be enough gas to tell the story of how i got here. i'm going to tell it backward, back to the desert, then the sea.   but first i am going to boil water and feast on three ears of wild corn i have been saving for just the proper occasion now that i have your ears i can eat these.   and i know you're listening.

i dreamed of the day of the panic. people
dying, crazed, bleeding from the eyes, ears, and nostrils, running blind, into
walls, walking across one another's squishing bodies, viral fire in their lungs
and nostrils licking from head to head, all of them toppling except me as
the inferno swept through.   i usually don't dream of the
past. before i continue my story, a weather report.

can you hear that wind?

it's trying to
get in.   it's been after me for quite some time.
the weather hates me. i was caught in a tornado last year. i think i was
passing through oklahoma. it started with an ominous rumble on a calm
day. then wind flying back and forth. though it was early afternoon it
got dark. i was passing through a small town. a tattered flag stretched
taut in the wind, rattling, reversing directions inexplicably. grey clouds
poured up from the horizon   billowing, expanding,
moving overhead.   the first rain fell in large cold
drops horizontally, pelting, almost stinging.   the air
filled with leaves turning, rising, floating, suspended, confetti shooting
past.   the sun was an unrecognizable dull splotch wink-
ing briefly between rushing, churning clouds.   rain
got serious, flying in drenching sheets, beneath every eave and awning.
water wings screamed.   the day turned from
green to black.   i forced open the door of a
house.   the pressure evacuated the rank must
of a windless place.   the door slammed behind me. the wind was hammering the windows.   a
pane crashed in and barbs raked my arms.   through
murky light i tried to find a basement, navigating between moving shadows.   there came a sudden violent shaking
gust.   i heard three loud cracks in the timber, and more
breaking glass.   the air in the kitchen began to move and
i almost gagged, the cold sweet thunderstorm air mixing with the stench
of the house.   between shadows a doorknob. i turned
it,   stretched a foot forward.   steps
led   down.   the house
shook.   i stumbled   down into blackness.   lightning screwed through grimy basement windows and there they were.   in that instant of light i took
it all in. i had interrupted a party of some sort.   they
slumped against the walls looking at me.   black and

shriveled, a ragged grimace of white teeth.   they looked
very healthy for dead people.   real corpses, not
liquified.   they had stayed in their basement and
starved,   sealing off their house,   and
avoided infection.   the house screamed and lurched
and something huge crashed.   the door at the
top of the steps blew shut. there was blackness.   just
me and corpses in a basement as the house was wrenched apart up-
stairs.   i crouched on the steps, eyes pinched
tight against the roaring.   somehow the rain
was coming into the basement   or warm wet fingers were poking me.   i stayed out of houses after
that, except for kitchens.   i learned to sleep outdoors.   until winter.   but that's
another story, how i spent the winter. having walked northeast across the
desert from southern california, i wasn't ready for the first winter after
the rains. the first winter without heat gas or electricity, a record winter
without recordkeepers.   when the snow started i was
passing through the plains, trundling through tundra, wading through
wind. it snowed without stopping. i could no longer find roads, nothing
was demarcated. walking across the snow became hazardous. sometimes
a hard crust supported me. other times my boots would punch through
to any depth. sometimes i would fall in over my head. flakes fell endlessly,
coating my face in ice. i thought i was hiking to the top of a tall hill when it
collapsed. there was nothing underneath. i fell into a snowy cavern lit from
above, and landed waist deep in powder drifts.   i climbed
through a windowframe and came out in an underground cathedral of glass
and ice and colored words. ghostlike bluish light seeped in from snowcov-
ered skylights above, a few broken panes dropped occasional clumps of
snow in trails of glittering dust. balconies encircled a central pit. i was on
the top floor of a large indoor mall. to think that i had come so close to falling through the skylight into the abyss of the atrium brought me almost to
my knees with vertigo. clutching the railing i leaned over and saw massive
icicles descending into shadows, and a smooth elliptical snow formation one
floor beneath me like a giant egg. i moved down the row of shops through
patches of darkness where heavier snow covered the skylight. my eyes
became accustomed to the gloom. i tried to ignore the shapes around me.
posters of faces shone with faked joy. mannequins separated from shadow.
a pyramid of wineglasses was dusted with powder from above. a snow-
covered escalator crossed the drop. trying to descend it, i slid all the way to

the level below, a terrifying fall. permeated by an uneven glow, a clothing store was filled with drifts up to the knees of pants hanging in racks. there i saw that the egg was the nose of a crashed jet plane fuselage with sheared-off wings, lodged between crumbling columns. i wondered whether the mall had already been evacuated when that huge plane came in through the wall.   well. there was no way out of the mall, and nothing outside but hazardous glaciers. it continued to snow outside. the mall got darker. drifts accumulated throughout the stores, deterring me from exploring beyond the muted sunlight that fell in the center of the structure. at night i lit candles from a gift store along the railing and used their heat to melt snow for my dinner. i slept in the airplane. the cold made me tired and stupid no matter how many of the little blue blankets i covered myself with. the whole mall just came alive at night. dreaming in the reclined airplane seat, out the porthole i saw shadows of parents and children holding hands, carrying shopping bags, ascending and descending escalators, crisscrossing the gulf, circumnavigating the atrium. i heard soft classical music, smelled caramel and perfume. i remembered how the escalators would lift you over the terrible drop and hold you. they were crowded and you could not move, you had to trust them, looking down over the stores like colorful boxes on a shelf, products with labels. i wondered whether it would keep snowing forever until the mall was dark and i'd finished all the shrinkwrapped meat and cheese samplers, chocolate and bottled juices, with no way to get to the surface of the world. the structure groaned under the weight of snow and winds. i worried about the roof collapsing, releasing an avalanche.   one day i heard someone. a tapping noise sounded as though somebody was trapped nearby, trying to communicate with me. or frighten me.   it had me seeing things in the shadows for a few days. then i discovered it was water dripping from the tips of the massive icicles into a pool at the bottom of the atrium. spring was coming, and bringing its own problems. rivulets wandered out of stores and under the railing. soon water was trickling down everywhere, widening holes in the roof, flowing down walls. the skylight began to fall in bit by bit. pencils of undiluted sun came down. a torso floated through the first floor. from somewhere above the dissolving snow i heard angry thunder.   i hear thunder now. is this violent meteorological instability an attempt to cleanse the world of harmful organisms such as myself? you think about it. i'll be back in a bit. i think i snared a rabbit. those things are vicious. listen for the gunshot.

i'm hearing little green men. are you coming to meet me? you should know that i've become mean. i like to drown kittens. i want to have lots of babies. an army of hairless flesh to chop down all the stinking pine. the second time we're going to get it right. no more environmentalism for me. i want to build a brick wall that covers the entire sky, hang it with buzzing fluorescent lights that keep the woods bright all night and pump rock music into every vista. maybe i should just park a car outside the station and lean on the horn. then this radio show would be the music i miss most. i'll teach my children to pour toxic sludge into every sparkling river and travel the world with elephant guns and crates of ammo picking off every last endangered species.   i want to dropkick a colossal what-the-fuck into space. if there is a god somewhere i want her to hear. she may be the only one listening. i may be the only one praying.   you want me to describe conditions on earth?   it's nasty. i imagine the future is like the past. dense and polluted, diseased and dangerous, poised on the edge. sweet, precious little animals caged in pet stores and zoo museums.   sleeping outdoors at night i watched meteors. there are still satellites up there. could they see me? can they hear me now? i walked hundreds of miles and saw no living person and i always felt i was being followed. no doubt that i have enemies after what i did in the desert. the spring rains brought an endless plain of mud, sometimes covering the highway.   i study marks of human drama. a bridge blocked by two cars mashed together grille to grille. a yacht drifting out in open sea, no sign of a crew. people fled one another.   spring brought new life. disgusting life. cities of roaches, rats, and pigeons. droppings everywhere. dumpsters are cauldrons of rats and maggots. foraging scavengers drag trash everywhere with no one to pick it up.   i used to spend black nights in empty houses, husks that once protected flesh, watching lightning and listening to thunder get so loud and close that it must surely have been searching me out, knowing it needed only strike the right roof to remove my gnat of a human consciousness from the world. it's worse sleeping outdoors when the night is clear, beasts shrieking in the underbrush, the needling of insects in the trees, listening to animals closing in, hoping my fire won't go out.   one night i was sleeping outdoors and woke up to hear someone beside me snoring. i let my heart seize the thought—amethyst is here. i was so happy to have her back i didn't care that i was dreaming. i was afraid to move, afraid of waking up and breaking the spell that had brought her back to me. then came the snap of a twig and i realized the truth. my knife was in my hand when the dog's breathy growl rose and it lunged. as its teeth closed on my fist i buried my knife in its throat. it or i screaming.   the next day i decid-ed to leave the woods and go back to traveling by highway, though the risk of people was greater. it's not easy being afraid of everything. i couldn't find my way out of the woods. i thought that the woods might have already cov-ered everything. above me a jigsaw of serrated leaf fractured the sun. fallen trees spanned a ravine. i followed the rift. it got deeper but i finally spotted a wooden suspension bridge above me. all roads must lead out of the woods, i thought. a wall of wild underbrush rose on either side of the road. "obser-vation tower," a sign still said. the tower was very tall and had no walls. a narrow stairway rose crossing back and forth between beams. vines ended halfway up. at the top was a platform. my feet clanged on the metal steps. already i did not like it.   on the first landing i waited for the shaking to subside. twenty feet in the air the metal steps changed to old wood. it was necessary for me to have at least one of my hands gripping the railing at all times. i kept my eyes on the steps. occasionally my gaze strayed out into leaves until i realized i was looking at the tops of trees and needed to look away. a gigantic bird warbled somewhere nearby. at the top of the tower an observation platform of old wood. i crawled onto it on my hands and knees, too dizzy to stand. a carpet of colored treetops unrolled. i saw an edge of a river. a sliver of red canoe. a woman's blue boot hung from a branch, swinging in a breeze. i thought the dizziness was making my ears buzz. then i thought the buzz was a gigantic insect. but it got louder and be-came the sound of a small airplane approaching. i hadn't heard an engine or seen a person since leaving the desert. i thought it was best not to be seen. going back over the edge was harder than coming up. slowly i managed to crawl backwards down the steps. i saw a biplane banking through flashing thunderheads. a flash and rumble and gust of wind cut through my now sweat soaked clothes and chilled me. my slippery hands slid on the railing as each foot took a turn moving down a step. at the bottom i crouched by the base of a tree. the plane's moan was continuous. it was circling me. i didn't understand the light i was seeing through the trees all around, a rum-bling i thought was approaching trucks. something made a noise inside my backpack. i dumped its contents on the ground. the sky darkened, there was rushing in my ears, a dance of red shadows in the woods. something on the ground lit up blue and chirped. i thought it was a huge insect. a haze drifted across me, i fought cobwebs from my mind. it was the cellphone i had taken from the person i killed in the desert. it shook in my hand. i opened it and held it to my head. my mouth tried to form the word. "hello." i couldn't tell whether i had lost my voice or whether i could not bring myself to utter such an inanity. if the cellphone network were active, it was possible to know the location of every active phone. there were voices in the woods and the one in my ear. hot wind sent me to my knees coughing. and then i understood the forest was burning. they were trying to kill me. i found the river. the water was shining metal, with canoes tied to the opposite shore. behind me trees quivered, black stripes against an inferno of red. i waded into the disturbingly warm water, covered with a layer of smoke and a scum of ash, the bottom soft. burning cinders and leaves rained like a demonic mardi gras. i swam to a canoe. i could feel heat on my neck. the opposite bank also had fire moving deep in the woods. i could hear voices in it. see faces in it. hanging to the side of the tethered canoe, i stared up the river at trees dropping fire in the water. the woods on both sides were burning, but the fire had not yet reached the river, it had surrounded me. a single tree would not catch, uninfected by flame. i untied the canoe, pushed it into the current, and scrambled in. lying in a sludge of water and muddy leaves i tried not to breathe smoke. voices discussed my fate as if a team of doctors. i heard the roaring of angels slicing through the sky, my mouth charred and head hammering. i believed i lay in a casket being carried by pallbearers down a road of filthy water into dusk. when i finally lifted my head and looked upriver a fire stood like a city, clouds flickered crimson. around me in the water floated bits of burnt wood and a trail of soot. a few greasy drops fell and it began to rain.

more gasoline. mindy mix was my name when i did my show on the pirate radio station. the show, and i guess this show, was called parrot radio. i am telling my story backward. i am forty-five years old but i have great hair. red and curly. though now i keep it shaved off, since the day i walked under a tree that dumped a bucket of ticks on me. i kept my body in shape. i was a dancer. i haven't even tried to talk about what happened in the desert. or before.   after i had lost amethyst, people crashing and bleeding in the streets, i walked off to die, past traffic jams of fearful motorists eyeing one another through closed windows, honking and shouting, past tall windmills that continued to spin as the electrical cables they once powered became a highway for squirrels. i walked on into an ocean of red dust from dead stars and bones. i found cars parked miles from roads, where people had gone to escape people. they just drove into the desert until the cars broke down or got stuck.   i remember walking into the desert, but parts are missing. i woke up in the middle of nowhere. i was lying on the sand. a shell, a nautilus, lay beyond my fingers. i dragged it to my ear, but i did not hear the ocean, only a voice saying "you have been disconnected." the earth spoke to me and i understood what she had to say, that the desert, the mountaintops, the poles, and the ocean floor were her strongholds where no man had ever chased her, that in the deepest jungles, she had kept her deadliest weapons hidden, a boobytrap for any species who tried to corner her. there tiny weapons were waiting centuries to strike back.   a ring of paw prints encircled me. i closed my eyes. but i could hear it pacing, padding the sand in a salacious orbit around my body.   the bad idea, she said, had gotten out of hand.   a tremor rattled rocks and a wind came from nowhere, a growl. i shut my eyes tight. a weight, the veil of behavior, lifted. i fell through myself, lying on my side howling silence at the whole fucked up insane violent and insecure lot of my dying species, ripped away like umbilicals. nobody would ever again touch me or hold me or comfort me or nurse me when sick or inoculate me or correct my spelling or blast a whistle at me, not even the tender touch of a rapist or knife murderer would dispel this cold filling my marrow like mercury. circuits dying inside, my mind pushing out to the outside of my skin. draining through these floodgate glands, i thought i would cry so hard i would spew brains through my nose, get to where i didn't care and become another stupid animal wandering, grazing, killing. my chest a keyhole and despair the key that fits it, when turned it rains rust, the pain worse than a gunshot migraine toothache, tinged with sweet anesthesia because it is the pain that says you will never feel again.   clouds exploded overhead, rain poured down in twisting sheets, melting the dunes into sludge. there would be no escape from her. i lay with my mouth open and accepted it.

the day after the rains stop, the desert is filled with wildflowers. i continue east. the sun beats my tongue thick. a distant rock ridge wavers, gets closer and farther away as the eye cannot lock in a perspective, trying to measure the foreshortened and featureless sands between. i set sights on those melting ridges only to discover an impassable canyon invisible from a horizontal perspective, a gorge where a spittle of ancient jagged stones drools into cracks that do not reveal their depths. this desert is a deadly funhouse game in which shapes resolve out of the smoking earth at random. invisible chasms make nearby features inaccessible and distant features lie no closer than a mirage in this telescoping arid inferno. right? left? or backward past a stinking and undrinkable lake lined with the corpses of misled fish, where one taste fills my mouth with burning salt. i can't remember my way out of this place. there is nothing in this mist of rock to fix upon for a mind taught to think with dictionaries, right angles, and money. two black birds wheel, come one for me and one for amethyst. they are vultures, but i follow them. a hum rises above the voices in my head. i haven't heard that sound in weeks, the unmistakable purl of a faroff vehicle, echoing from canyon walls. i see the plume from the exhaust, a ghost of smoke. i fix the position and move in the direction of the sound. i come upon another jagged canyon. on its slopes savage plants occupy territory nothing competes for. i cross a giant sandblasted collarbone, and in the middle of it is a long-dead golf course. a few flags stand atop defoliated plateaus of crumbling sand. a bridge ridiculously spans a bowl of dust, at the bottom of which are shreds of black plastic pond lining and a few corroded tubes. an old putter lies in the dry lake where an outraged loser must have thrown it. but i can't see any road or tire tracks. at dusk i hear it again, and stumble to the top of a nearby dune. i see headlights. i cannot tell how far away. it could be miles or perhaps i could reach out and pick it up in my hand. one taillight sketches a red vector behind distant rifts. i mark the dirt with my toe, unroll my blanket, and sleep. day breaks like a recurring headache. around noon i find a mountain of fresh trash occupied by a few fierce green biting flies, surrounded by baked animal droppings. paper, glass, plastic, empty bottles of shampoo, bits of soap, toilet paper rolls, beer bottles, soiled paper plates, crumpled napkins. i pull the pile apart in search of corners of liquid remaining in discarded water or liquor bottles. stale french fries provide a coagulated salty mush. licking my fingers, i rinse it down with dribbles of flat soda syrup, warm beer, even a trickle of champagne. i line the empties in a long row in the sun like trophies. until i find what feels like a loaf of bread and it's an arm from a

freshly dead person, uninfected hard skin.   perhaps an
hour after i vomit myself to sleep, i sit up knowing the truck will come back.
to see humans again is the most terrifying and nerve-wracking thought. i
don't know if i could bear it. would they kill me? i am an escaped prisoner.
at first light i begin to cover my traces, putting the row of bottles back into
the pile.   i am squatting and peeing when i first hear the
garbage truck. it passes my hiding place showering a wake of dust. i see one
of them through the passenger window. he wears a space suit. they do not
leave the truck. its bed rises and the refuse pours out, raising a cloud. i wade
through the plastic and paper and glass and body parts and climb into the
back. its jaws close partway. i watch the trash get smaller as we pull away.
the truck gets on a paved road. the drive takes a long time and i see nothing
but desert. i conjure up a strategy to steal food and escape. finally the truck
slows and descends a ramp into darkness, and the sound of the engine reverberates in a tunnel. the engine dies, the doors slam. i am braced for
confrontation, but they do not come to the back of the truck. ten minutes
later i emerge beside dumpsters reeking of garbage. there is a sterilization
shower, and the white suits are hung from pegs. i hear nobody
about.   in a service elevator i push the button with the
highest number and rise. and rise. when the door opens, i am face to face
with an old man. his clothes have the look of a uniform. he steps back in
horror when he sees me, but before he can scream i kick him in the throat.
he goes down. it is easier than talking. i have stepped off the elevator onto
a thousand foot high balcony that stretches all the way around a vast enclo-
sure rising seemingly to infinity, walls converging in a point overhead. i very
firmly place my hand on the railing and lean over.   my
eyes water and i blink, and i try to let go of the railing to step away from it.
i am inside a pyramid containing a city. the whole thing must be sealed and
fed filtered air to prevent contamination. the pyramid walls slope outward
below me. and my knees buckle as i realize that beneath the floor is air. the
person is unconscious and wheezing. his head rolls at a funny angle as i
search his clothes and find a keycard with a number that matches a nearby
door. i fit the rectangle in the slot, there is a click and a green light comes
on. i push the door open into a furnished room empty of people. hefting
his legs i drag the sputtering man back inside his room, his head rolling on
the floor as if saying no no no. i put out the do not disturb sign and shut the
door. the room is clean with a turquoise patterned carpet and two large
beds covered with gold bedspreads with drawings of various figures delivering items to a queen. the man's eyes look funny as he spasms for breath. i
pull a pillowcase over his head and with a terrycloth bathrobe belt lash his

wrists to one of the legs of the bed.   i snap on working
lights in a bathroom, turn on a working faucet, and the first sip of tapwater
is a river snaking through dust, ice lightning strikes my stomach. in the
mirror i see why i frightened him so. i shower until the water is no longer
black, and select some new clothes from the wardrobe. i see markings in-
scribed on the cabinets in an unknown pictographic language, a bird and a
hand and various figures mostly in repose. outside the sloping window
mountains stand above the desert floor. the triangular shadow of the pyramid stretches thousands of feet across the brush and stillness. at the base
of the structure is what seems to be the ass of a gigantic stone lion. the
room has wine and i sit and try to make sure i'll be good and drunk when
they come for me. lengthening shadows paint the valley floor. i try to prepare myself for guards breaking into the room. a line of shadow climbs the
mountains.   the person on the floor kicks and is still
again.   i collapse on the bed and am consumed by crazy
dreams.   i jerk awake remembering that under the floor
is a thousand-foot drop. the space yawns beneath me.   i
go out the door. soft cacophony rises from beneath. on a balcony across the
chasm i see two children running, the lights causing their shadows to sweep
hugely across the wall. blood pounds in my head. the balcony pulls me toward the edge. i push my way into a door marked stairs and stand above the
longest staircase i have ever seen, descending diagonally inside the pyramid
wall, crisscrossing back and forth all the way down. the sight is dizzying,
but it is not a vertical drop and i can deal with it. the metal walls are fitted
with pipes and gauges, wheels to shut off steam or water. there are spraypainted markings between ducts. some metal steps pop when i step on them
and the entire staircase rumbles. at the bottom i open a door on a chaos of
light and noise and people. hundreds. they are placid, clean, and have short,
styled hair and loose-fitting colorful clothes. some are talking to others or
seemingly to themselves, but i understand none of the words. as they
stream past me, i fall into step. we march through a poppyfield of light. rows
of colorful computers issue musics. this is an information palace. people
amble from terminal to terminal, the machines chime acknowledgments
and instructions, semantic codes. stone sentries twenty feet high flank a
portal into the city within the building, statues of men with headdresses,
surrounding their heads are glowing fleur-de-lis mounted on brass. a balus-
trade of roughly hewn stone engraved with alien markings overlooks a red
and gold carpeted expanse. at tables set along the railing, diners are being
seated. black statues of strange dogs stand on point. high above me is a
space so vast it makes me nervous to be beneath it. four structural columns

converge in the apex above. a spinning wheel of light projected from an unknown source climbs up and down the columns. i count about sixty balconies. if somebody dropped something from up there it would kill. i flow with drinking and talking people down a curving staircase into an underground ballroom, ornate walls illuminated by electric candelabras, ceiling panels of carved and polished wood. a cluster of old men play cards at a green felt table. an illuminated wall stretches above me with multiple video screens showing sporting matches. on one screen i see a horse race. the camera pans to a crowd of people watching the race. i am incredulous. on another screen a basketball player looks up studiously as he prepares for a freethrow. where in the world are sporting events taking place? below the screens are people sitting in maroon overstuffed chairs watching. i study the wall for an explanation and find the glowing text 2002 april three.   the screens are replaying the day in sports, april third 2002. these sporting events already happened, yet here are people interested in their outcomes.   this is entertainment, i realize dumbly.   i walk up to an unoccupied, flashing computer. will it let me connect to the internet and tell me what is going on in the world?   guess what? video poker. behind it an electronic slot machine. i look around accusingly, beginning to understand why nobody has noticed me. because nobody is really here. the eyes of a man one row over are downturned as he studies his game, mechanically dropping in tokens and pulling the lever. the eyes are human but there is no person behind them.   the hieroglyphs are not a language, they are a design motif. beneath ostentatious chandeliers, sheep stoop over a field of flickering machines, exchanging tokens not for information about the world, but for random combinations of empty symbols, cherries jacks hearts. a man with a suit and headphones eyes me distrustfully. walking back the way i came, i pass a guard watching a row of monitors. glass eyes in the ceiling overlook the tedium. i sit down at a bar. spumes of colored light erupt and neon spirals rotate above a mayhem of musical tones. on the other side of the bar, behind an illuminated row of overturned martini glasses, a stoic faux-egyptian mannequin poles a barge ferrying an aloof waxen priestess to some implied destination. the ferrier is buffed and muscular and sports a golden headdress and loincloth. structurally unnecessary columns seem to support the gilded architecture above the bar. three men in suits and ties drink and smoke nearby.   i give up. i am a stranger. i have found the promised land, the ark where the elite have been rescued to reclaim the earth after the disease dies down, and i will soon be led away by guards. i only hope they don't take me back to dr. white. i am looking into the mirror behind the bar and in shock i cannot find my reflection. seized by unnamable terror, i wonder whether i am really here. then i realize it is not a mirror, the bar wraps around. a uniformed man struts past fondling a portable radio unit. the bartender sizes me up and i order brandy. his eyes look painted on. my only desire is to be as drunk as i can when they catch up to me. behind the bar is a stack of boxes. when the bartender moves away i lean over and help myself. a golden lion with black stripes on its forelegs crouches before the elevator. when i get inside and the doors close i see this elevator is glass. i feel a jolt of panic as it begins to rise above the glittering games, rushing diagonally up one of the vertices of the pyramid. i close my eyes.   when the door dings open i feel my way out. as i carry the heavy box down the balcony to the room i keep my back to the wall, moving sideways, afraid to turn my back on the drop. a red shape on the ceiling is dripping.   i stand there and appraise the stain. i check the plastic key and realize that i am one floor below my room. up the stairs, in my room the person on the floor is motionless. the blood coming from the pillowcase means that i have infected him. after he had died from the broken neck it continued to eat through and liquify his body. it's a unique virus that can feed on a dead host. it works more quickly when the immune system is unable to work against it. if i have brought the virus into this sealed colony, then it will eat all this meat quickly, with no sunlight to kill it or wind to carry it away. the bartender, the guards, all of them will start coughing specks of blood within hours.   i yank out the dresser drawers, trying to figure out where i am. brochures describe the facilities. i pass my finger over the guest directory, the names of many rich and famous people who have been spared. i find my room number. claude reagan, whose room this is, sprawls in his thinning blood.   i try the tv. it is the news, the news from the last day. do they air the last news every day? the gesture seems religious. on other channels are reruns of shows i despised, it brings me despair that they have been saved.   i strip the bed. with my knife i cut open the mattress and stuff all but two of the brandy bottles inside. propping the door to the room open with a chair, i accidentally step on the corpse's stomach in a spray of black blood, as i drag the mattress outside the room and lean it against the balcony. i open one of the last bottles, take a swig, and pour it over the mattress. i open the hotel matchbook and strike a match. an orange flame races to the rectangle's edge. when the flame covers a face of the mattress, i topple it over the edge.   suddenly suspended from my fear of heights, leaning gently on the railing, i watch it turn in midair, it and i floating above

the casino floor. it falls across a row of machines.   tiny
faces look up.   but its fire has gone out. inside the room
i pull the tv set loose from the wall, carry it out to the balcony, balance it on
the edge   and let it fall.   people are
beginning to wake up, and stream out of the way as it tumbles. it explodes
beside the mattress. a rosy halo balloons, a wave of heat hits me. machines
are burning.   back in the room, i lock and chain the door.
i lift a chair and pound the window. the glass is very strong and the chair is
knocked to bits before i inflict anything but a hairline fracture. but the lamp
manages to chip away a hole in the glass. a blast of hot desert wind sucks
the air conditioning from the room, escorting a cloud of viral particles out
to their deaths. i climb outside the window onto the sloping glass side of
the pyramid, holding the last bottle. my feet and hands find purchase on the
panes of glass, and i move crabwise down the long slope of glass to the
desert floor.   i can see into other rooms, but nobody
seems to notice me crawling down their window. i see a man looking lost
staring at the wall. i see a couple having sex without much enthusiasm. a
child bounces from bed to bed, an adult grabs it. a shooting star lights the
outside of the glass. an obese man sits in an easy chair playing a tiny video
game. an old man in an undershirt jerks off to music videos but does not
appear erect. i pass an empty room whose door is open. out in the hall, a
couple leans over the balcony watching the fire.   at the
bottom i walk east, slugging from the bottle, into the cold eye of the now
rising sun, through the baying of strange coyotes snaking into town for the
fresh meat. behind me a thread of smoke rises.

                          since i was in prison when november eleventh hit, the world had already ended for me some time before.   i think my first premonition that the world would end was the month that all my female friends got pregnant. it wasn't joyous. a species that is endangered will make a sudden effort to flower and proliferate, i thought. anybody i shared that thought with would have assumed i was jealous.   i spent my last night in the world in seattle, my home. i went to a mexican restaurant with a guy named blake and ate chicken mole with guacamole.   it was—it was good.   oh.   blake stone was a journalism student i had met at a peace rally, where i was protesting war. he was interviewing some of us for a story in the student paper, looking very sporty with his camera bag, black turtleneck, a tweed jacket, big black eyeglass frames, and just slightly disheveled. mm. i told him his name sounded fake. fake blake. he didn't like that. i tried to back him into taking a position on the war on china. he said that he was not allowed not to be objective while on assignment and had a suspended opinion. he was handy with the double negatives. he agreed to have dinner with me before my radio show and hear me out.   over dinner we had an argument about a book of essays by a—"linguist," is that the word?—who argued against a preemptive first strike against china, and claimed that nuclear weapons were immoral. blake felt he was a holdover from nineteenth century morality. the limited nuclear exchange between india and pakistan had not caused any immediate deleterious global environmental changes. people had once been perhaps rightfully leery of using nuclear weapons, he said, but nuclear weapons had proven to be a practical means of ending conflict, and perhaps even a road to peace in their own right. blake was handsome and affable. he had poise and the ability to make things seem reasonable. he raised his eyebrows and held out his palms as he talked to show he meant it. it seemed to me that we were having two different conversations, but every time i moved to prove it he managed to evade me. i asked him if he was pro-war and he said, "well, i'm not anti-war." as a bisexual (he claimed) he had every reason to be distrustful of our government's policies. he was trying to get the argument on safer ground. you know, claiming minority status by not committing himself to a sexual orientation, and leaving it unclear whether i would have any luck seducing him, to his advantage. when asked if he wanted to live in a peaceful world, he said, "well of course, but—" i found all of this quite charming after awhile. i was getting drunk of course but somehow he managed to remain just slightly less lucid than me. i couldn't tell whether he was stupid and remarkably good at covering it up, or whether he really

had ideas and they were somehow not making the translation to speech. he shyly showed me a poem he wrote that seemed quite serious, mostly because i didn't understand a word of it. i realized he was the perfect man. anybody watching us would assume we were having an intelligent conversation. his square jaw and grey eyes made me drool, and he refused to ruin the effect by saying anything distracting. if he had expressed a clear opinion, it probably would have been one i loathed. he was one of the new generation i called the "nouveau vague." everything on the news those days, was of course fiction, but he called it "national security." i told him i wasn't concerned that the government wasn't telling us the truth, but concerned that through evasive doublespeak they were widely discrediting the very idea of truth. he said, "what is truth?" or "truth is lies," or something clever and paradoxical and arguably true and yet irrelevant, just a perfect way to exemplify my assertion while derailing it. but i didn't mind. i let him confound my conversation about politics and was grateful.   we almost had to shout to be understood in that crowded dining room with the colored fluorescent panels and piñatas. waiters and waitresses took orders on all sides. two televisions above the bar flashed garish music videos. then i started to stop enjoying myself. things got funny. the distance across the table between us stretched. all they had to do, i thought, was keep manufacturing violence until a nonviolent world or even a nonviolent solution to a problem would become inconceivable. once everybody was in some way eligible to be killed, those who had the monopoly on violence would rule on their own terms. then the word "violence" could be used to mean anything. the perfect man was now also the perfect idiot, intelligence was a form of gentle insensibility, and i understood the totality of what had been accomplished. my world was dying. like the water in its rivers and lakes, the words that once irrigated its ideas were rancid. neither food nor language were nourishing anymore.   and it never occurred to me that i was eating my last ever chicken mole with a side of chile relleno.
                                                god i can't
think about mexican food right now—   the things i
have—   i—   have—
lost.   i mean, back then i would have really wanted this to happen. i just thought people were the worst thing that could happen to a planet. because people make war. but, as it turned out, war killed people, so war must live on. the bad idea is out there looking for a new mind to have it. an infected language was the virus that destroyed its human host.   so maybe people, with their inherent capacity to articulate, would have been the world's best hope.   and

to my credit i drank as if it were my last night out, which i generally did anyway, but which this time it actually turned out to be. i put away a number of monstrous margaritas—with real strawberries—i saw the bartender mix them. ah, straw—   a tv across from our table kept capturing our attention. a scientist in a space suit walked through a tent of cots. closed captioning, sound turned down. we watched a news segment. a logo with the words "war on death." "terrorism." an interviewer crosscut with interviewee. a man with white hair, a face i was sure i had seen before. although i hadn't yet. dr. white. this is when i started to realize things were coming apart. when you see a man from your dreams for the first time and he's on television, you feel weird. he was saying something the closed caption was translating as   remember?   SPLITTING AIRS TO SPEAK OF AND FRINGE MINTS OF SIEVE LIVER TEAS IN THIS SIT CHEW A SHUN WE ARE NOW AT WORK DEVELOPING AN ANT TEA WEAPON TO US SURE PEACE   well blake just loved this new word "anti-weapon." he went on and on making me laugh uncontrollably. i don't remember what he said. he pretended to be in favor of anti-weapons, or maybe he wasn't joking, but i couldn't stop laughing. he had repulsed me but won me over. i was hammered. you drink every night and then, all of a sudden, one night it hits.   we watched a mushroom cloud blossom on tv, wondering whether there had been a nuclear explosion or whether it was documentary footage, an interstitial, movie, computer graphic, or commercial. everybody in the restaurant was watching. nobody spoke. nobody turned up the volume. a room of diners and servants watched this monstrous shining radioactive cock rising. it seemed cerebral, sparks of bad ideas flashing within it. cut to staticky footage of a blind woman sitting on the edge of a cot and a man in a space suit giving her an injection. she looked familiar, but i had not yet met her. i thought i was watching this on tv, but maybe it was my mind. i was colliding with my future. things had started to get real strange. disconcerted. i was unable to hear my own thoughts. like standing on a piece of ice that has broken away from reality and is drifting out to sea.   i asked blake to do experimental radio with me, to have sex with me on the air. he refused. he drove me by my apartment. he kissed somewhat like he spoke. it wasn't clear what he meant by it. it seemed shot through with earnestly well-intentioned contradictions, like an emphatic shrug of the lips, but not unpleasant.   my show was on a pirate radio station, like this one, broadcasting illegally from a garage. i always took my parrot ditto in and let it become an on-air personality. parrot radio. some nights i was so drunk i'd let the parrot do all the talking. squawk. i played music they'd never play where i worked as an exotic dancer. that night, when the men broke into the garage to arrest me, i was naked, out of it, doing erotic dancing to mahler. they showed me guns. i asked for badges. they just smiled.   i'll never know what happened to ditto, but i hope somebody at some point opened his cage and let him go. i remember lying on the floor in the back of a van. they were laughing about something. i was pushed and pulled up and down some stairs and shoved into some kind of cell. it was like a hospital room with walls of glass. a woman slumped on the edge of the cot. she did not look at me and i saw she was blind. amethyst. i realized i had been seriously drugged when she told me i was in southern california. i asked her whether i was in an fcc holding tank. except i was so out of it i said fda instead of fcc. which she found very funny in light of what we were being used for.   we slept next to each other on cots, then, later, on the same cot. when i woke up there were three people in white space suits in the cell with us. the one in the middle held a satchel and the other two moved toward me. "hold still," crackled a speaker, and the large ones pinned my arms. the middle spaceman told me i had been volunteered to test an important vaccine, and for my cooperation my sentence would be shortened. i would be set free after the test. but if i did not cooperate, i would receive the harshest sentence for my crime of distributing terrorist leaflets.   one of the men holding me interjected, "broadcasting. this one was broadcasting illegally."   "that's even worse," the doctor said. he had sunglasses perched on his white hair, though he could not reach them through the helmet, an odd accessory.   while i made the toughguy orderlies work for it, amethyst rolled up her own sleeve and did not speak. when i came awake she was lying next to me. i asked what was happening. she said they had shot me up with an experimental vaccine, and sedatives. she said she remembered what happened next. she said "they aren't going to bring us any water. we have about half a gallon left. it's an oversight. lie still. don't panic. breathe as little as possible."   there was a thump as the man in the adjacent room pressed his face against the glass. blood trickled from his eyes. he was panting and unable to take a breath, as if trying to suck air through the window. he coughed black flecks of blood against the glass. when he pulled away he left shreds of flesh clinging to the pane. i shut my eyes.   it makes you thirsty as it liquifies your tissue. you drown slowly as your lungs dissolve. you probably know that. it's not clear whether dementia is a symptom or a healthy reaction to the infection. what would go through your mind as you watched your skin melt away? they tried to get some of the dying to take iq tests, to answer questions over an intercom, but they wouldn't cooperate. neither would i, i just screamed obscenities when they addressed us through the speaker. amethyst made me be quiet, whispered things to me to calm me.   i lay still and prepared to die. in my sleep i wandered a labyrinth of arteries. a river of my blood flowed into a burning forest, forking, changing course, colliding with flames in explosions of red steam, and finding a way through.   we waited for many days and, as we did not die, they began to take an interest in us, even learning our names. the doctor in charge, doctor white, tried to get chummy. he had tried to kill us like lab rats, but now we were his prized pets. "we'll get you some real food soon amethyst, mindy. turns out they didn't plan this experiment well," he laughed, "scientists." it was obvious that nobody had thought we would live, but either our mix of vaccine worked or we were special. amethyst said the fact that we could remember the future helped our immune system fight infection, because it would respond to specific deaths. i thought she was out of her mind and tried to tell her that i could not remember the future. but i was wrong. i remembered the burning pyramid back then more clearly than i do now, after the fact, and my dreams of the man in the lake get stronger every day.   finally the spacemen decided it was safe to bring us water and protein drinks. then, real food. the sight of the victims made them retch even though they had space suits and could not smell what we smelled. they moved us through ultraviolet lamps and showers of stinging disinfectant to a new cell. they said we were safe, but we were both possible carriers and would have to stay in level four until we were safe to be released. they had no idea how long that might take. i demanded liquor. they conceded and we had full room service. they treated us like colleagues and explained the experiments to us. amethyst and i played games. we slept together. we touched each other. they left us alone.   she told me her story. i remember her words.   she thought i might be important, and that i had no choice but to walk in the footprints that were meant for her.   and one day the power went out. i woke up hung over and discovered amethyst had poured out the liquor. she took my hand. "come on," she said.   the electronic lock on our door had failed. she led me down the hallway, her cane tapping a path through the blackness. she opened a sealed door and we moved into a wet shower room stinking of bleach. somewhere an emergency generator kicked in. blue bulbs came on and a crackling announcement over a loudspeaker spoke numbers.   amethyst hissed, "over here." i looked where her cane was pointing and saw only a red biohazard flower on a chute stamped with the words "laundry incinerator." "we can't go that way," i protested. "we have to," she said, "it's the way. follow me." she opened the hatch and put one foot in and then another and lowered herself. her hands disappeared and i heard her exhale as she fell. i stepped in after her, lowered myself down the shaft, hung there, and dropped into a pile of clothes. in the basement, the dust was greenish and had encrusted the elbows of ancient ductwork. blasts of steam permeated the cold dank subterranean air. the walls dripped. the ground was littered with bolts and bricks. in a corner was a mound of shattered glass i realized came from test tubes. apparently someone had dropped a crate of chemicals, toxins, or bioweapons and swept them into a corner. i was horrified at this, the underbelly of the sterile testing facility. she led me through a concrete maze of service tunnels. i pushed open an emergency exit, we went up stairs, and came out a steel door into an alley. the california sky was the color of ash. there was a commotion all around. honking and shouting, car alarms and barking. a sign on the door read monsanto biotech. it wasn't a prison or even a government building where we were being held. just a corporate research facility. a scrap of newspaper blowing down the alley had part of a headline that said "dead." there were throngs of frantic people carrying things. i heard a whistling that with an uncomfortable sensation i came to realize was the sound of release valves on tanks of some supercooled chemicals used in the facility. behind a razor-wire crowned fence i saw the telltale spume of boiling liquid poisons whose refrigeration systems were no longer powered. mists of hazardous compounds, clinging to the ground, would soon flow through the neighborhood, quite possibly killing those who inhaled them. as we moved away, i saw some streets had ad hoc barricades made of parked cars and furniture and duct tape hung with red flags. i kept squeezing amethyst's hand, but she was struggling to get away. "you go now," she said. a stranger with bloodshot eyes ran up to us, and stammered, "the fire is covering four blocks and spreading, the highways are closed. i don't know whether to go back in to work." quite possibly the leaking chemicals were explosive and would ignite. scary thunderheads moved over. it was as dark as night and rained dead birds. flames licked up between metal bars on both sides of us. coming around a corner we saw some kind of rally assembled in a vacant lot. i hung to amethyst's hand, shouting to her, as she dragged me into the crowd. we were packed shoulder to shoulder and cheering singing men moved between us. i looked up to see one of the infected about to give a speech, standing on a balcony with a sound system that kept feeding back. a spark leapt from the microphone and knocked his ear onto the shoulder of his suit jacket.   amethyst pushed a bundle into my hand. I unwrapped it enough to see the handle of a revolver. i did not know who had given it to her. she reached up to stroke my face. "i'm sorry mindy," she said, and jammed her fingers in my eyes. i bent over, eyes watering, seeing stars, feeling the crush of people around. squinting through the pain, across the square, through the crowd of peaceable protesters and panicked citizens, i saw amethyst pinned between two men in white space suits. a third uncapped a syringe and moved to plunge it into her. she doubled over. i turned and waved the gun around, clearing a path away through the crowd.   and then it just disappeared.   recall.   i lost her.   and then i lost it altogether.   there followed a period of which i have no memory.

i think this happened. i accidentally be-
friended a group of surfers. i walked into their house. they were sharing a
hookah and acted as though i had interrupted an intimate moment. they
claimed the cannabis boosted their immune systems. they gave me a rap
about how they would be rebuilding society, experimenting with poly-
amorous relations. you don't know how many guys have used that line
on me. they smoked incessantly. they had amassed a collection of the last
day's news. november eleventh, 2011. newspapers, video recordings, audio
recordings. they went over the stories again and again, building elaborate
theories of what had happened. they were obsessed with a few hours of
the real news network's coverage of the catastrophe, which they said had
keys to understanding the whole thing.   in their favorite
rnn footage, the announcer looked flustered. he stammered mechanically as though on cue. he seemed to be reading a script he did not agree
with. there was a bit of static.   "it was rehearsed—that
whole thing," one of the surfers choked, marijuana smoke curling from
the corners of his lips. "they did it over and over before they shot it. and
this part isn't on location at all, it's really a sound stage somewhere." a
reporter with a protective white biosuit. "okay, that's supposed to be a
tent outdoors, right? but look at the shadows." he hit rewind and the clip
moved backwards jerkily and then forward at his prompt. "they staged this
whole fucking thing. somewhere these guys are sitting around having a
drink, playing poker, laughing. it's all so predictable when i look back on it.
i don't know why i didn't see it coming."   i responded,
"maybe you couldn't see it coming because it was too horrible to look
at."   he snorted derisively. then the generator quit and
the power went out for the last time.   the video screen's
world shrank to a point until it too was black.   the room
suddenly sprang into shaky shadowy life with a matchflare whose lumines-
cence was sucked up the tube of his bong. "they're smoking us out now,"
he laughed.   i said, "dude the only one smoking you
out is you."   "now we have to eat all the food left in the
refrigerator before it goes bad," he said. but there wasn't much food left
to eat.   that evening the first one started to bleed out.
turns out the bloodshot eyes weren't just from the pot. in the morning i was
the first one up. i sat on the couch and tried to figure out what to do. i still
had the gun, and nothing else.   the wall opposite the
couch, behind the dead television, was covered with newspaper clippings,
and someone had notated them with circles and arrows and lines connect-
ing different parts of different articles. i studied it all morning. i learned

nothing.   they lived near an unused wharf on the ocean
between two upscale houses. i went to the beach and did not like the look
of it.   engineers had labored to build right up to the sea
edifices of now dissolving stone, old docks slowly being smashed to bits of
timber flailing rope. the sea danced in malice. tidal waves and monsoons
would leave these mansions in mossy ruins.   the sea was
revealing her true character to me, a living breathing mass, colloidal foam
platelets shifting in the perpetual motion of waves dragging in their wake a
percussive tearing sound, covering rocks with saline scales. the waves were
the breathing of a beast enormous enough to swallow the earth, filled with
submerged tentacles of aquatic monsters. i was unnerved by the constant
low sweeping thunder, the continent coming dislodged under the relentless attack. waves clutched, tendrils of water snaked through cracks in the
rock, fingering the shore.   if nature hated humans, then
the sea is our deepest and darkest and most powerful enemy. yet civilization had grown like mold around bodies of water. now, she turns on us,
floods exploring the streets, drinking the ruins, ingesting waves of refuse,
dissolving everything and scattering the crumbs to the creatures that live
within her deeps, who knows what monsters down there will come up,
streaming bubbles, rolling over and over in the murky abyss. rocks sang
to me in ghostly flute-like harmonies. i tried to walk beneath a dripping
bluff and an unexpected wave blasted me to the abrasive rocks and laced
my cuts with stinging salt.   clouds converged over the
water, a rain squad closing in.   i saw things emerge
from the surf—fingers, red stems, necks—but they disappeared before
they could be fixed.   one rugged duck was combing
the foam offshore, disappearing underwater for minutes at a time, alone
to pursue whatever undersea agenda.   on the wet clay
beach, shrapnel was scattered, shattered shellshards, bits of plastic, styrofoam, strange rocks.   smashing waves sent spumes
up a rock wall, globules of foam dispersing.   out in
the distance the sea itself had spotted land, and was sending troops of in-
vading waves rolling in toward shore, shouting their wash of noise, their
exhalations moving upshore in a misty cloud.   i fired
a bullet into the ocean. thunder rolled across the coast. the sea spat salt-
water in my eye.   i wanted to get as far away from the
water as i could. even though it was already in me.   so
i walked into the desert.   but now my story has been
told. i am almost out of gas again.   i've been dreaming
of a man coming from the sea.   i'm going to chicago.

i'll be waiting by the lake.

For editing, science, police scanners, and juice, the author thanks Dirk Stratton, Jessy Ruddell, Jason Greenly, Travis Alber, Aaron Miller, Natalija Grgorinić & Ognjen Rađen, Chandra Vega, Rosemary Braun, Angela Colmone, Margaret Gillespie, Katie Hays, The Fifth Column, Gary Heidt, & H.P.

Dead Aria was previously published as a chapbook by NeoPepper Press.

Ornaments from Handbook of Pictorial Symbols by Rudolf Modley, 1976, reprinted with permission of Dover Publications, Inc.

An electronic translation of "Biblionaut" is available at morpheus11.com

www.keyholefactory.com

WILLIAM GILLESPIE has published ten books of fiction and poetry under six different names. The recipient of the second MFA in Electronic Writing granted by Brown University, he is co-author of the world's longest literary palindrome (so declared by Paul Braffort of the Oulipo) and an award-winning hypertext novel. His writing and art has appeared in Electronic Literature Collection, Open City, Poets & Writers, The &Now Awards: The Best Innovative Writing, Encyclopedia, Cybertext Yearbook, Ninth Letter, and Word Ways: The Journal of Recreational Linguistics, among others. He works for the School of Molecular and Cellular Biology at the University of Illinois.